Holiday Shorts

Bite-sized stories encompassing humour, war, romance, history, sci-fi, adventure, contemporary issues, and much more. Quick to read in stolen moments – but leaving plenty to think about.

In this busy age it is often difficult to find enough time for a good read. Garfield Collins has produced the perfect answer with his new collection of vignettes: Holiday Shorts. By turns funny, tragic, dramatic and insightful, there is something to please everyone here. Each story is a perfect gem.

(Mary Vernon, book reviewer for The Australian and Colin Roderick Award judge)

Holiday Shorts

Garfield Collins

Matador
9 Priory Business Park,
Wistow Road, Kibworth Beauchamp,
Leicestershire. LE8 0RX
Tel: 0116 279 2299
Email: books@troubador.co.uk
Web: www.troubador.co.uk/matador
Twitter: @matadorbooks

ISBN 978 1838594 039

British Library Cataloguing in Publication Data.
A catalogue record for this book is available from the British Library.

Printed and bound in Great Britain by 4edge Limited
Typeset in 12pt Jenson Pro by Troubador Publishing Ltd, Leicester, UK

Matador is an imprint of Troubador Publishing Ltd

For Gill Collins
... my muse

Best wishes

Gary Collins

Contents

Preface

The pages of a book are given life only as they are opened.
L. J. deVet

So thank you in advance for giving life to my stories through your reading. I hope you will enjoy them. You can dip into them in any small moments of leisure – not just on holiday. Although brief, there is often a wider background to the story, providing something to think about afterwards.

Prior to 2016, my writing had all been for technical books and articles. But in the summer of that year, my friend and neighbour, Alan Reid (author of An Experimental Childhood), arranged a barbecue for colleagues from his creative writing course, and Gill and I were also invited. By chance, I sat next to Roddy Philips, who leads the course. Roddy asked me if I had ever done any creative writing. As an example, he told me that the class homework for the following Wednesday was to write a story about Vermeer's painting, Girl with a Pearl Earring.

I thought about what must have been happening in the Netherlands at the time, the place of the girl in the household and who her observer might have been, and I was hooked. It convinced me that even a very short story could have a rich background. That story is included here.

The spur of having to produce material in accordance with a given subject every week is very stimulating and enjoyable.

It beats the alternative of sitting with a blank page and no creative focus!

For material, I've mined a lifetime of experiences. I worked as a scientist, with information technology and as an entrepreneur helping to develop companies from creation to commercial viability. Other important influences have been voluntary involvement in education and charity work, and in amateur music and sport. I have also been lucky in travelling extensively for work and pleasure. Aside from this, I have a great interest in how we got here – from the Big Bang through to modern history. Consequently, the stories cover many topics.

The great variety of people I have had the good fortune to meet have certainly influenced my ideas, but none of them is directly portrayed in the book!

In producing this book I am indebted to many people. Firstly, my friend Alan for introducing me to Roddy, whose guidance and inspiration have been invaluable. Then my wife Gill, who patiently listened to, and made many helpful suggestions about, every story.

I was privileged that Mary Vernon – a prominent author, reviewer and judge of books – agreed to read my first draft and comment incisively upon it.

Finally, I have to thank the staff of Matador, who have been crucial in creating a professional result, and for advising me on marketing and sales.

I have had a love of Nepal since 1991, when we trekked there as a family. In the past twenty years, I have been involved in a business based in Kathmandu. Happily, this was successful and has created a significant number of jobs there – from animal husbandry through to high-tech biotechnology.

Thus it seemed natural to donate all the revenue from sales of this book to Child Rescue Nepal, which our company has supported for many years. This excellent charity saves children who have been trafficked into effective slavery.

Thank you for supporting the charity by buying this book.

Garfield Collins

Carol

C AROL HURRIED INTO C OFFEE P ACIFICA. *T EN MINUTES early – just time to calm down,* she thought, as she caught sight of her exhilarated expression in the wall mirror.

It had all happened so suddenly. The previous day she had been to an art exhibition where she became aware of someone studying the same pictures she did, and even photographing some of them. Despite her usual reserve, there was something about him that intrigued her. Near the end of the exhibition, as she stood transfixed by a vibrantly coloured abstract, he had asked, "You seem so immersed in this picture; would you mind if I take a shot of you?"

She had posed hesitantly for several different views. Curiosity made her accept his offer to show her the pictures over a cup of tea. He was amusing and drew her out into a lively conversation, so she had gladly accepted his invitation to dinner that evening.

Carol's reverie was interrupted by a sharp hiss of steam from the coffee machine. With a start, she realised that Pierre was twenty minutes late. *I expect that his packing has taken longer than he thought,* she reasoned, as she happily returned to her thoughts of the previous night. At an intimate family-run restaurant, Pierre had again been most entertaining and attentive. It had been so easy to confide in him about her loneliness since her husband had died. As they were leaving, Pierre had said that he would probably be passing her

1

apartment, so they should share a taxi. It then seemed only polite to ask him in for a coffee, despite the late hour.

Gosh. He's now forty minutes late. Poor Pierre must have found he needed to shop for something. Men can be so bad at packing. But he's very good at some things, she thought with a shiver. After the late coffee, as Pierre was leaving, he had said, "We've had such a good time today; would you mind if I kissed you?" She couldn't remember her reply. All she could recall was the way she had clutched him tightly, and wanting him desperately. After they had made love, she lay in his arms, wondering how such intense desire – even lust – had arisen.

Early next morning, Pierre told her that he had to go to Paris that day, and he needed to pack. Her disappointment had turned to delight when he suggested they should meet later in the cafe, and there they would make plans.

Carol surfaced again from her tumultuous memories when the waiter asked if he could get her anything more. As she ordered another coffee, she saw that Pierre was now an hour late. She became quite worried, especially when she remembered that they hadn't exchanged numbers. She sat on, with growing anxiety – her mind racing through increasingly unwelcome scenarios to explain his absence.

Eventually, the waiter approached again. "I'm sorry, madam. The cafe is closing."

"See you at the end, George," said Carol as they entered the *Photography and Expressionism* exhibition. She and George could never agree on how much attention to give each picture, so they had decided it was always better to do their own thing. Fortunately, George, whom Carol had met on the Internet, was in most other ways a good match.

As she approached the end of the exhibition, Carol had a vivid flashback to her meeting with Pierre at a similar exhibition three years previously. He had seemed to have exactly the same tastes as her, and had taken those lovely photos of her against the final colourful abstract. She shuddered as she remembered the passion he had raised in her.

"Nice little exhibition," said George as she emerged. "You look rather preoccupied. What's on your mind?"

Carol shook herself out of her reverie and, attempting a warm smile, took George's arm and said, "Let's go for a coffee."

"Good idea. I know just the place."

"This seems familiar," Carol said as they approached the cafe. "I think it used to be called Coffee Pacifica."

Inside, George sat her down in a quiet corner, saying that he would get their usual drinks. Service was very slow but he waited patiently, as befitted his steady, unemotional character.

The brief affair with Pierre was still in her thoughts, so Carol had ample time to torture herself with speculation. She was by now sure that this had been their intended rendezvous. She relived the pain of waiting fruitlessly for him. Surely their passionate night should have been followed by meeting there to make plans for their future together, as he had suggested?

There must have been a good reason for him not coming, she thought. *Maybe I got the name of the cafe wrong and poor Pierre waited elsewhere until he had to catch his train to Paris. Or he might have had an accident on the way. I can't believe he cynically marked me out as a good prospect in the art gallery – good only for a fling while in London. We made such a connection, and I'm absolutely sure he enjoyed our night together as much as I did.*

When George returned with the coffees, he saw the look of anguish on Carol's face. "Good gracious, love, what's wrong? Have you had bad news?"

"No, George…" Carol paused, and then in a sudden rush she said, "George. I have been very unfair to you. I've been haunted for the past three years by a fleeting affair." Slowly at first, and then with increasing urgency, she told him about her brief relationship with Pierre.

George listened with growing concern, and tenderly took Carol's hand as she paused for breath at the end of her story. "Carol. That must have been very hard for you. I'm not sure how I can compete with such a romantic dream except that I'm here and I'm real and I love you."

As Pierre was driving to Orly Airport for his weekly flight to London City, he reflected bitterly on his latest row with Celine. They had been discussing weekend plans. She wanted to join a friend's impromptu birthday party on the Seine. He had an invitation to a private view of a new exhibition at the Musée d'Orsay.

"It will be the same old people. Why would I want to do that when I have an opportunity to see the new exhibition before the crowds?" he had shouted.

"You're so boring, Pierre. You know I like to be with friends. It's no fun looking at your meaningless splodges of paint," Celine had shouted back as she slammed the door of their spare bedroom.

This isn't what it was supposed to be like, he thought. *We argue more and more.* He thought again about Carol, whom he had met at the exhibition in London three years previously. She had seemed so attuned to his tastes in art. He remembered her being transfixed by the blaze of colour in the final work in that exhibition. He had loved her simple candour when they talked – so different from Celine's air of tired sophistication. He remembered with shame how, after a passionate night together, he hadn't turned up at their rendezvous the next day. He had been confronted by two possible futures. One with Celine, his new girlfriend in Paris, who was vivacious and well established in society there – very beneficial for his business. The other was with Carol. With weekly visits of only a couple of days, it hadn't seemed possible to develop their relationship. Living in separate countries, how could they have managed their life together? At the last moment, he had panicked and abandoned her.

You were an absolute fool, he told himself. *You should have known that you had fallen in love instantly. Carol knew. Instead, you were flattered by the attention of someone like Celine. At first, you enjoyed the whirl of social activity, but it wasn't based on the same essential spark.*

Pierre cursed himself for not having noted Carol's address. In the taxis to and from her flat, he had been too preoccupied to take in his surroundings. Consequently, on many occasions, he had gone back to the cafe where he should have met her – just in case she was there by chance. In desperation, he did so again the day after his arrival in London.

As he entered the cafe, to his delight, he saw Carol sitting there alone. He rushed up to her, but she had turned her head towards an approaching man. Noticing Pierre with a start, Carol said, "George. This is Pierre. The person I was telling you about."

"Oh. So I suppose you'll want to stay for a chat?" George replied.

"No, I'm ready. Let's go." Resolutely, she took George's arm and pulled him towards the exit.

"But, Carol, I wanted to…" Pierre was shocked into silence as she turned at the door and sadly shook her head.

All at Sea

"CAN'T WAIT TO GET BACK TO THE WIFE AND KIDS," said Joe as he waited with his friend Gerry for the helicopter which would take him off the oil rig to Aberdeen Airport.

"I'm not off for another week," replied Gerry, "but the domestic scene's not for me. Tried it a couple of times and it didn't work."

In a house in Bucksburn – a suburb of Aberdeen – Shelley heard the helicopter as it approached the airport. *Another potential client?* she wondered. Shelley paid for the house and her middle-class way of life by being a *poule de luxe*, as she thought of herself. She had regular relationships with a select group of clients, some of whom she had grown to quite like. It was part-time, paid well and enabled Shelley to bring up her daughter Maisie in the way she wanted. She had just taken her to Albyn School – an upmarket private school – where she was to board.

A week later Gerry arrived at the airport, removed the cumbersome safety gear they were obliged to wear in the helicopter and changed into a smart Italian suit. He took a cab to the Jurys Inn in the centre of Aberdeen and collected a key from the concierge. Emerging from the lift on the top floor, he hurried to his suite and unlocked the door. Standing by the window, looking out towards the sea, was an elegant young woman. Hearing him enter, she turned, ran across the room and leapt into his arms.

"Darling Gerry, you're here at last. I couldn't have waited a moment longer."

Gerry felt the warmth of her body wrapped around him. As he lifted her up he smelt her musky perfume and the sharper tang of her long blonde hair as it encircled his face.

"Were you lonely out on that oil rig without me?"

"Sure was, love," replied Gerry as he began to ease her loose-fitting dress down over her shoulders and kiss her fresh-tasting skin.

"Come on, then," she said, in little more than a whisper. "I have a fair idea what you've been missing."

Gerry carried her into the bedroom and shut the door.

Afterwards, they sat opposite each other with champagne and canapés delivered by room service.

"That was fantastic, Shelley," said Gerry, smiling happily.

"I like to please."

"You get better every time," he added as he counted out five hundred pounds in twenty-pound notes and passed them across the table.

Serendipity

"GOOD GOD. IT'S JIM. WHERE ON EARTH HAVE YOU sprung from?" said Giles as he opened the front door. "Hey, Anna, look who's here," he shouted, as he helped Jim in with his massive backpack.

Once they were sitting comfortably with a cup of tea, Jim reached into a pocket of his bulging cargo shorts and produced a well-worn map. He spread this out as he tucked his hair more securely into his colourful bandana.

"This is just the outline of the journey. I started there in Jakarta and made my way through Java by rail and bus. Then I took a ferry across to Bali, where I lived for a few months, before carrying on to the small islands." He paused to pull a photo out of the pocket of his tie-dyed shirt. "While in Bali I met this lovely woman, and for the rest of the time we travelled together."

"That's all very well, Jim," said Anna as she looked dubiously at the photo, "but surely you can't keep on 'going walkabout', as you call it? You'll have to get another job to live. You can't be a hippy forever."

"Not necessarily, Anna. I could easily go back to Bali and live there for the rest of my life, just doing bits of tour organisation here and there. I know Ni Luh would like that. Hello, Felix, give me a hug," he added as his eight-year-old nephew entered the room.

Soon Felix decided the game in his bedroom was much more exciting than listening to grown-ups talking, but as he left he heard his Uncle Jim say, "In any case, the recipe for an interesting life is, from time to time, to create the opportunity for something different to happen. It's what I call a serendipity space."

Serendipity space, thought Felix, *what can that be?* He knew about space – it was one of his favourite things – but he hadn't ever heard of serendipity space. He looked for his science book but couldn't find it anywhere, so he got out his parents' dictionary and read:

> *Serendipity: the finding of valuable*
> *or pleasant things unexpectedly.*

How could you find something like that above the earth's atmosphere? Felix thought with a puzzled frown.

"What's serendipity space, Mum?" he asked the next morning.

"Sorry, I don't have the time to talk about Uncle Jim's daft ideas now," Anna said as she hurried him into the car for the school run.

All that day Felix was puzzled as to the meaning of serendipity space, but came to no good conclusion. When he was back at home in his bedroom, Uncle Jim came in and gave him a spaceship construction toy.

"Thanks, Uncle. That's exactly the one I wanted," Felix said, and he forgot all about his quest for the meaning of serendipity space as he thought happily that he had two whole hours to play before tea.

A Man of No Account

FUTURA GROUP COLLAPSES, SHRIEKED THE HEADLINES.

Next day; *Proctor retains substantial fortune despite losing his company.*

This after an intense period when it seemed Arthur Proctor's troubles were in the news every day. After a brief lull, the headlines began again.

Creditors and shareholders of collapsed Futura sue Proctor for personal redress.

Bitter divorce for Proctor; wife demands £50 million.

Reports about these court battles followed at intervals until; *Proctor declared bankrupt. Lawsuits, alimony settlement and huge legal costs wipe out his fortune.*

A traumatised Arthur, desperate to escape from being the Proctor of popular renown, bought a remote barn with the last of his money and fitted it out as a simple cottage. A village a few miles distant provided for his basic needs and a bus took him to a small town where he picked up his pension – now his only means of support. For heating, he collected wood from the surrounding hills. His clothing was chosen from charity shops to blend in with his rural surroundings.

A year later, as he sat in the sun outside his barn, he realised that, at last, he was happy. He had succeeded in becoming totally uninteresting. Nobody wanted to interview him. No newspapers published articles about him or photos of him being mobbed by journalists and protestors. The occasional walker passing by would nod and say hello, but any curiosity they showed was only out of interest in a simple life.

This is all I need, he thought. *The striving to build a company and to dominate its market, the networking to achieve wider influence, social climbing and, above all, marrying a shallow, fortune-seeking wife all seem just a mirage now. What a way to live! I was just bolstering my own ego.* He shuddered at the thought of the extreme pressure of creating his empire and the even greater stress of its collapse, which had taken such a toll on his health.

A couple of months later, two ramblers took the path which passed Arthur's barn. As they came over the brow of a hill, the woman said to her companion, "Look at that little barn. It looks as if someone might live there. There's a washing line and a battered table and chair."

"Well, it's nice on a day like this," her husband replied, "but I wouldn't fancy it in the winter. Suppose you became ill. There's no help for miles around."

As they neared the barn, the woman sniffed and said, "Can you smell that? It's like an animal has died nearby."

"Certainly can! What a stink."

They knocked on the door and, getting no reply, looked through the small window. Arthur lay as he had fallen six weeks previously after a massive heart attack.

A few days later, the local paper had a headline on an inner page:

Man found dead in remote barn. Police are trying to identify the body.

Nobody was interested.

The Diary

AFTER HE HAD FINISHED HIS BREAKFAST, BERNARD slumped back in his chair. No sound from anywhere in the house. It was this silence he couldn't stand. He reread the notice he had placed in the local paper:

> *Blackwell, Joan Lily, died peacefully at home on the 4th September 1999 at the age of 79. Mourned by her husband Bernard; their children, Derek and Marilyn; five grandchildren and two great-grandchildren. She loved and cherished us all. May she rest in peace.*

Bernard thought how inadequate the obituary was to honour his wife of fifty-five years. Her life was far better represented by the baize-covered pinboard on the wall of the kitchen. Family photos, pictures of great-grandchildren, thank-you cards from friends, a programme for a concert she had played in just two months ago.

After her death, he had been submerged in arrangements, with much help from the family. Left alone in the house for the past two weeks, he hadn't done anything but eat and sleep. To shake off this lethargy he resolved to set about clearing out Joan's belongings. The clothes and knick-knacks could go. He would keep only those things that were precious to him; those that reminded him of their love and friendship.

For many days Bernard sorted through a lifetime's accumulation. Her WAAF uniform from World War II went to a museum. The accumulated books and notes from her subsequent career as a teacher, and the piles of childhood mementos — apart from a selected few — were burned. Her clothes were sent to a charity shop.

After he thought he had finished, he came across a small bag tucked in an alcove in the loft. Inside was a single postcard with faded writing and a small leather-bound diary. The postcard said simply, *I've got Brian's MG Saturday night. I'll take you for a spin. Can't wait to see you. Love, Johnny.* The date stamp was the 2nd September 1940.

Who was Johnny? Bernard wondered as he sat down in the dust of the loft and opened the diary. The writing on the yellowing pages was clearly Joan's neat hand. It started in January 1940. He flicked through, stopping to read selected pages:

22 Jan.: Joined the WAAF today. I'll get my uniform soon and then go for training to West Drayton. Good to be doing my bit. Bernard will be proud of me.

23 Feb.: Not much good at diary. Too busy with training. I'm an Aircraft Woman 2nd Class assigned to Biggin Hill Aerodrome where I'll be assisting scheduling of sorties in the control room. Good to be doing something important. Better than folding parachutes! I'll be billeted in Bromley, which isn't far. Terrible. I only managed to see Bernard once.

5 Mar.: Can't keep up. So much going on. Digs good, with nice lady whose husband is in France. She's lent me her bike so I can get to BH easily. Wish I could do something about my curly mop. Bernard's coming over tonight.

11 Mar.: Said goodbye to Bernard today. He's been sent to Egypt. I don't know when he'll be back. I'll miss him terribly. Meat's to be rationed, like bacon, butter and sugar. What next? Managed to repair my one decent dress, though I don't know when I'll be able to wear it.

12 Mar.: Really getting used to the routine here. Sometimes it's mad, with telephones going and pilots being assigned to sorties and the noise of the Spitfires as they take off! Made a good friend in the control room. Betty's been here since January and seems to know all the pilots in 610 Squadron.

Bernard skipped many pages until he reached:

18 Jun.: Mr Churchill made a big speech today, all about the Battle of Britain starting. That means we'll be in it up to our necks. 610 have already had loads to do. Betty has arranged to go with a pilot called Bill to The Fox tonight. She suggested I go along. Bill's got a nice friend called Johnny. Betty lent me some combs to tame my hair. Those poor soldiers being rescued from Dunkirk. Awful.

19 Jun.: We had a smashing time. I wore my dress! Johnny is a lovely boy. He looks handsome in his uniform, but there's something different about him. I expect I'll find out. We're all meeting again at the dance in the Officers' Mess on Saturday.

23 Jun.: It was a lovely dance. So hot in the Mess, we went outside to cool off. Johnny is so funny when he gets going. We had a good laugh. Then Betty and Bill went off. When he heard a plane, Johnny got very serious and went very quiet. I don't know how it happened but he suddenly kissed me. I stopped him then, I mustn't when Bernard's away, but I wanted him to. He says he likes curly hair!

Bernard read through the pages with increasing concern.

21 Jul.: Went out just with Johnny. We sat outside The Crown and talked for hours. I'm really getting to know him. He seems very confident, and wants to shoot the Messerschmitts out of the sky. But we both know that lots of pilots don't come back. Underneath I think he's frightened. How brave to fly like that! I really wanted to cuddle him. Last night I kissed him. This is getting very confusing. I'm falling in love with Johnny. I should tell Bernard, but I don't even know where he is in Egypt.

22 Jul.: Terrible news. Betty's Bill didn't return yesterday. She's awfully upset. She told me she's pregnant and they were going to get married. They've added tea and marge to the rations now. We'll have nothing to eat or drink soon except the local fruit and veg.

The diary went on, with pages of detail about the aerodrome which normally would have fascinated Bernard, but he was finding more and more mentions of Johnny, and Joan's feelings for him.

12 Aug.: They're attacking aerodromes now, and we are in the front line as we're directly on their way to London. So there are lots of plans being made. We've practised running into the shelter when the bombers come. Johnny's been doing three sorties a day sometimes. I don't know how he can

*stand it. It's hot in the Control Room and I get so sweaty,
but I'm only allowed two baths a week at my digs.*

*1 Sep.: Operations now in a shop in the village. On
Friday, 100 planes attacked us. They've hit the village
and destroyed the radar. Repair shop destroyed and direct
hit on shelter – 40 killed. I was too late to get in, thank
goodness, but it's a disaster. Betty was injured. I must get
time to see her. Here they come again…*

*2 Sep.: It's amazing that the runways have been repaired
and we are flying off planes again. Everybody's saying we
must get revenge. We'll never be beaten. Had a postcard
from Johnny, who's been away for training on the new
Spitfires. He's back tonight, and luckily I can get time off.
Exciting. He's got his friend's MG so we can go to a pub in
Westerham or somewhere for a change.*

*3 Sep.: After the pub, we stopped on the North Downs.
The MG's got a very comfortable bench seat. We lay back
and looked at the stars. Johnny thinks he won't make it.
I kept telling him he's very experienced and that should
keep him alive. Wanted to comfort him. I love him so
much now. It was lovely to be held and kissed by him. I
wanted it to go on forever. It's scary what I want us to do
together. I don't know if I'd be able to stop myself.*

Bernard dreaded seeing the days after this, but they went
unrecorded until:

*7 Sep.: Luftwaffe now concentrating on attacking London.
610 Squad have to fly to intercept them. The boys are
making lots of kills now. We're moving from the shop to*

a proper Operations Centre in Towerfields Manor. That means we can keep control when the aerodrome is being attacked. My bike was damaged in the bombing but I've managed to borrow another one in the village.

18 Sep.: Mr Churchill says 15th was Battle of Britain Day. We have done so much damage to the planes attacking London that they have stopped these daylight raids. Perhaps things will calm down. Lucky I can see Johnny tonight.

19 Sep.: Johnny was in quite a state. He has been on so many sorties and has hardly slept for days. I tried to comfort him, and in the end I think I did. It happened. It was marvellous. We weren't really prepared. I hope it will be all right.

20 Sep.: Johnny's late back from a sortie attacking an enemy port. Surely he'll come? The plane must have gone wrong and he's bailed out on his way back. He'll be picked up, I'm sure. I don't know what I'll do if I lose him.

21 Sep.: Johnny's dead. I can't believe it. My lover, gone. How can someone so alive just disappear? But it must be true. A pilot saw him shot down into the sea. Betty told me and, next thing I knew, I was in the medical room. I must have fainted. It tortures me to think of my poor boy trapped alive as his plane dived into the sea. I hope he thought of how much I love him. I've nothing to live for now. I hope a bomb drops on me. That's the end of this diary. Now there's nothing worth writing about.

Bernard sat for a long time in the attic, just staring at the tear-stained page. He remembered how different Joan had been, back in 1943 when he came home from Egypt. She had seemed so much older and careworn. He had assumed it was all the trauma of being in the front line of the German attacks. But this – how could she when he was away fighting in the desert?

Slowly he climbed down the attic ladder and descended to the kitchen. There sat the small pile of mementos he had chosen to keep. What were they worth now? Wearily, he began to go through them. There were their wedding photos from 1944. Then happy photos of Joan and the children playing on a beach. Pictures of their three houses – each had been the setting for an important part of their lives. Joan's leaving card after she had been the head of the local comprehensive for fifteen years. He remembered the many adults who had come up to them over the years, wanting to thank her for their time at the school. Then some pictures of Joan with her ageing parents, whom she had looked after so well.

As he continued, Bernard began to weep quietly – remembering what a loving person his wife had been. Theirs had been a good marriage full of fun and adventure. Her affair with Johnny was at one with her caring nature, but it had been intensified by the exceptional times they were living through. How could he judge actions taken in the middle of a war, with the constant threat of death? After all, he had given way to his lust on several occasions in Cairo when he was on leave.

As he wiped the tears from his eyes, Bernard pushed the diary into the flames of the old boiler and, with relief, watched it burn to ashes.

Editorial note: Joan and Bernard are fictitious, but the events at Biggin Hill Aerodrome and the background of national events are only too real. Biggin Hill was in the front line and a prime target for elimination by the Germans.

Transformation

"I WANTED TO DISAPPEAR. THAT'S WHY I STARTED wearing it," said Layla.

"That seems like the beginning of your sad story. Why did you do it?" asked Maisha. "It must have been a major change for you."

"Well. I was sixteen and, like many girls, I became sensitive about my body. I felt very self-conscious when boys started to notice me. I had a friend called Ahmed. One day he started to kiss me and hold me. It all frightened me. That's why I wanted to disappear."

"So you suddenly emerged one day wearing the hijab?"

"Yes, I did. I felt secure in my own little space. I could see everybody but they couldn't see me. It did feel as if I had disappeared."

"And how did your parents and other relations feel about it?"

"They thought it must have meant I was very pious. My father had always wanted my mother to wear it. My grandparents, who came to England late in their lives, were very pleased."

"That was several years ago, and now you are here. What made you change?"

"After I graduated, I managed to get a job in a solicitor's office. Unfortunately, I was seen as a representative of Islam, and I dealt almost exclusively with Muslim women. The safe place increasingly seemed like a prison with a very small window to the world outside."

"Is that what made you stop wearing it?"

"No. It seemed that, because I was wearing the hijab, I was getting more and more pressure from the family to adopt other conservative ways. Then they suggested I ought to go to Egypt for a holiday."

"Wouldn't that have given you an opportunity to get a better understanding of them?"

"No. I was scared of the idea. My cousin was taken there on holiday two years before and she was genitally mutilated. The men said it would keep her pure and the women said she would never get married otherwise. The next year she was taken there again and she came back married to an ugly, older second cousin. Her life was ruined. Whenever she visited me she couldn't stop crying."

"So that's why you didn't want to go."

"Yes, Maisha, but one day they woke me up and said that they had tickets for my father to take me to Egypt. I refused again and again, but they took hold of me and tried to force me into the car. I said I would go if only they would let me go back to my bedroom to get my Quran. There I ripped off my hijab, and, dressed as you see me now, escaped out of the window and came here."

"It's a hard path you have taken, Layla, but you are certainly capable of making your own decisions. You are welcome to stay with us, and you'll be safe in the refuge until you've planned your new life."

Enjoying the Magic

NOW IT'S DARK AND THE GARISH ILLUMINATION OF the Disneyland Hotel is an eerie backdrop as I wearily walk away from Disneyland Paris.

How ironic, I tell myself. *All those years ago I thought I had done my Disney duty when we were travelling in western USA.* We had visited many beautiful places. Then we had decided to visit Disneyland. As we descended from the hills we drove towards Los Angeles, wreathed with deadly beauty in a pall of smog.

"There's a Best Western," shouted our youngest as we drove into Anaheim – a suburb of LA. He pointed them out everywhere we went because their familiarity made him feel secure.

In the morning we walked round to Disneyland. My duty was to accompany the children on the bone-crushing rides like Space Mountain, which was not so much scary as painful. Gill went on the gentler ones like the Mad Tea Party. But everywhere there were queues. Just when you thought you had got to the end of one, there was another bend revealing the next togetherness experience. Of course, Mickey Mouse and his friends wanted you to have a photo with them, and then there was the long parade consisting of every character from Disney films to date.

Finally, we had limped away from the magic of Disneyland. We weren't glowing with the joy portrayed in the adverts. We agreed it was quite enjoyable but it didn't match up to the natural beauty we had been experiencing. Bryce Canyon in the moonlight beats Space Mountain any day.

Anyway, I've done my Disney duty, I thought then, *and the boys don't show any signs of wanting to go back.*

A few years later Gill said to me, "Dad wants to celebrate his seventieth birthday by taking all the grandchildren to Disneyland Paris for a long weekend."

"That's very good of him. He must have some stamina for a seventy-year-old. When will he pick up our boys?"

"Don't be silly. We're going too, of course. It will be nice. All the family together."

So now as I arrive back at the Wild West Trailer Park I think wryly of the way in which Walt Disney has ambushed me. Today was just the first day of the long weekend, but it wasn't as bad as I had thought. Certainly, it was tiring. The queues were just as long as I remembered. The food was not fast and the dressed-up actors still assiduously offered their photo opportunities. But I have learnt the secret of survival. It is the It's a Small World ride. There are no queues – it's too tame for most. You sit very comfortably in a boat and gently drift around. When you get to the end you can just start again. Hours of relaxation at your command. The only downside is three hundred traditionally dressed dolls from every continent singing about universal harmony. But you can't have everything!

Salvation?

THE THIN WINTER SUN SHONE DIMLY ON DORIS AS IT crept through the dirty window. Painfully, she raised herself from her favourite chair by the single-bar electric fire, and leant on her stick with a puzzled frown.

An observer would have seen a withered, white-haired old woman amongst the 'kept just in case' clutter of a lonely life. They would have smelt the miasma of cooking, dust, cat litter, and an ageing body. But Doris noticed none of this; nor could her two children, who lived self-absorbed lives thousands of miles away.

She pottered around the kitchen, idly moving objects from place to place. She picked up documents which had come through her letter box, putting them in a pile for later attention. Her bank statement emerged from the junk and she looked at it more closely. Despite it telling her that there was very little money in her account, she nodded with satisfaction.

"I saved my money to leave to the grandchildren, but they are all grown up so no need now," she told herself, as she turned on the ancient television. Warming up, it added the new smell of heated dust to the fetid air. "I used to watch such a nice programme in the afternoon," she muttered plaintively, "but now it just comes up looking like snow." She fiddled with a dial and a different pattern of snow appeared, so, following her usual ritual, she turned the TV off.

Suddenly, realising why she had stood up, she stumbled to the back door and looked out. She gazed unheedingly past the rotting window frames, dripping gutters and moss-encrusted walls towards the overgrown garden.

"Marmie, Marmie, din-dins," she croaked.

The cat made his stately way along the barely recognisable garden path. His original marmalade colour had long since dulled to chime with its drab surroundings. Brushing past her, he hungrily attacked a meagre meal of cheap cat food.

Doris settled herself again by the fire and wrapped her legs in a tattered shawl. Apart from keeping her warmer, the familiar feel of her mother's old garment comforted her. As she held out her hands towards the glowing bar, a smile on her face was illuminated by the pink light.

"We'll be all right now, Marmie," she said softly. "That nice young man helped me invest all my money in a new cats' home and he promised they will pay me a thousand pounds every month."

A Short History of the Short Story

@witsend:	Ho, Nunkie – homework origin of short story. Can u help me? #suicidal
@profeng:	Probably began with Stone Age men telling hunting stories around the fire. Long time – how are you?
@witsend:	OK, thanks. You mean short stories don't have to be written down? Bet a lot of boasting went on!
@profeng:	Longest epoch of short stories was oral. Humans have always elaborated and edited their tales – that's creative.
@profeng:	Good example is *The Canterbury Tales* by Chaucer. He recounts the tales the pilgrims tell along the way. Oral short stories.
@witsend:	Had some of that in class – right laugh, that *Miller's Tale*. #arsehotpoker
@profeng:	Then not much happened until mid 19th century with Poe and Turgenev, who took the form to new heights. #mid19cshortstory
@profeng:	An excellent feminist story by Louisa May Alcott was *Scarlet Stockings*. Belle Morgan does and says what she likes.

@witsend: So it wasn't just the guys who wore the stockings back in the day?

@profeng: Indeed not. That's more 18th C. In the 19th C in UK in 1880s, Robert Louis Stevenson wrote and he inspired H. G. Wells and Kipling.

@witsend: Kipling – he the guy who sent his half-blind son to the WW1 trenches? Diamond geezer.

@profeng: By end 19th C, Chekhov started writing and completely changed short stories. He abandoned the beginning/middle/end structure.

@witsend: I wish he could tell our teacher that. She keeps on at us about "Boys, you must have a structure." No money in it anyway. #hardup

@profeng: Well, there was, at least back then. Scott Fitzgerald made equivalent of $80K for just one story.

@witsend: So what happened after that Chekhov dude did his stuff?

@profeng: Lots of people were inspired by him and wrote similar stories. Like Hemingway and Katherine Mansfield.

@witsend: Yeah, we read some of Hemingway. Couldn't understand it. He goes through lots of stuff then nothing happens.

@profeng: The point is to read below the story and find the hidden meaning, which can be about a much wider issue than the story's subject.

@witsend: Yeah, yeah, but what happened in the 20ᵗʰ C?

@profeng: Some super US writers, e.g. Jack London (*To Build a Fire*)

@profeng: 1st half of 20ᵗʰ C was golden age. Many books & magazines featuring shorts. I loved Somerset Maugham and *Just William*.

@witsend: And now?

@profeng: Grenoble's tourist office has short story machine. *Distributeur d'histoires courtes.* Choose length, get a free story printed.

@witsend: Way to go. What's next?

@profeng: Some TV ads are short stories. Now maybe stories written as tweets. That concentrates the mind.

@witsend: Pull the other one. Give us an example.

@profeng: *For sale. Pair of newborn baby shoes. Never worn.*

@witsend: Right, OK – I suppose that's what they call Chekhovian. Thanks, Nunkie – must write all this up for tomorrow. #bestuncle

The End of the Party

UNIA WAS DISAPPOINTED BY THE WEATHER AND THE fact that Hector wasn't there. She commanded, "TIME", and the Comtact system answered, "20.49, June 25 2153."

"Always too much data. Where can that man be?" she said petulantly as she looked out of the window at clouds of rain being driven across the city. She glanced down at the river, deep within its containing banks. "Thank goodness Terracontrol engineers have managed to stabilise the climate, but I wish they could improve weather."

She commanded, "GET GISELLE", and the face of her friend appeared on the Comtact screen.

"Giselle. Hector – my GenePal – hasn't turned up. I'll never get pregnant at this rate."

"Why don't you just get inseminated like most other women, then?"

"Well. I'm traditional in some things. I like to keep up some of the old ways and I was getting used to him, as this would have been my third attempt."

Unia and Giselle were members of EPOGE (the Elite Party of Greater Europe). They regarded as quaint the feminists like the Suffragettes and the #MeToo movement of the previous two centuries. From the start of the early 2000s girls had begun to outdistance boys educationally, and, as they emerged into adulthood, they had first taken over the professions, such as medicine, accountancy and the law. From there they had gradually taken over governments throughout the world. Machines, bioscience and software had increasingly made engineering, agriculture and many other traditionally male-dominated sectors easy for clever female management. The old haphazard means of procreation had come to be regarded as too random. Now, with detailed and accurate genetic profiling, party members were matched with selected male donors. Their female children were raised to join the elite through a schooling system optimised over many years. Outside the party, there were large numbers of *Unterclasse* – men and women carrying on archaic ways. They were mostly ignored, apart from party members getting them to do the menial and semi-skilled jobs they didn't want to do themselves.

The Comtact system burst into life. It was Hector.

"Where the hell are you? You know you were supposed to be here at 2000 hours."

"Unia, I'm not coming." Hector smiled wryly. "I am on strike. We've formed a male emancipation movement called #WeAlso, inspired by a 21st-century women's campaign. Now it's our turn to object to being taken for granted and having no economic status. We resent having to maintain our bodies and submit to all sorts of biological tests just for the gratification of women in producing babies for the party. So, no sperm from us. Unless our reasonable demands are met, the race will die out. I warn you, the *Unterclasse* is with us."

One evening a year later, Unia was wondering what she was supposed to do with the baby the Childmonita had just handed her when Giselle called.

"Hello, Unia. How's the baby girl? Glad you got Hector's sperm, anyway. We haven't heard anything more about that stupid attempt at revolution he became involved in, have we?"

"No, nothing from that idiot. The baby's OK but I have to keep correcting Corinna – the Childmonita – about the things she says to her. Naturally, the child doesn't understand yet, but it might get to be a problem. I'll have to put up with it, though. It is so difficult these days to find a good Childmonita, despite the fact that they are forbidden to enter into what they quaintly call 'marriage' before they're thirty."

"I know. What on earth are they doing? You'd think they would be glad of the work in good surroundings rather than grubbing around in the Gegends. By the way, I read the other day that we have to watch the *Unterclasse*. The gap in intelligence between them and us is closing. We have to worry about the tendency for our children's intelligence to decline towards the mean, but it also works the other way round. The *Unterclasse* have been breeding offspring who are getting close to our threshold level. Just as bad, apparently a significant number of GenePals are setting up households with *Unterclasse* women. What's that noise at your end?"

"Hang on, I'll see. GET NEWS."

The Comtact screen displayed the streets outside the city.

"I can't quite see, but it's a large mob carrying placards and heading in this direction... Now I can see some of their messages:

We demand rights for the Unterclasse;
Our children should be legally recognised;
Using banked sperm without consent is statutory rape;
Party jobs for men."

"What a load of rubbish. Who do they think they are? Next thing they'll want equal rights with party members. We know what happened last time men were involved in running things. We must resist."

The Comtact screen flashed to a frightened-looking reporter shouting into her microphone amidst rioting *Unterclasse*.

"The situation is very tense here. The rioters are demanding emancipation. By that, they mean equal standing with the party, and the equality of men with women. Oh! Here come the Peaceforcers. I must take shelter before they spray the area with their Happyjuicers… This is serious. A large group of men has turned the Peacers' equipment upon them. Now the whole crowd is heading towards Party City No. 15."

A shot of the main gate appeared, showing men battering it down while shouting for their rights. As they broke through, Unia could see they were heading for her Lifepod. Moments later her door crashed in against the wall and Hector ran in with an *Unterclasse* woman whom she recognised as the Surrogata who had carried her baby. They snatched the infant, and as they ran out Hector shouted, "We are in charge now. Molvina will be a real mother. Your regime is doomed. We are blowing up the sperm banks and taking over. Either you and the party submit to full integration, and what used to be called democracy, or you will be cast out and starve."

Imagining Christmas

"SUSIE, WHY ON EARTH DO WE HAVE TO GO THE Lawsons?" complained Giles as he drove them slowly through the West London traffic.

"I told you before, Giles. Kate is their only grandchild and ours too, so we have to share her. We couldn't agree on having alternate Christmases so we have to meet up somewhere. Jamie and Chloe's place is far too small and we are a bit squashed in our flat, so the Lawsons' place was the only possibility."

"Yes, I get that, but he's so patronising, and she has some strange ideas about bringing up children. We're bound to end up arguing."

"Well, you'll just have to bite your tongue, for Jamie's sake. He and Chloe will want to give Katie a good time. She's just three, so this year she'll really be into Christmas. Whatever you say about them, Chloe is a lovely girl and a very good mother."

The frustrating journey continued until they finally arrived at the Lawsons' imposing house in White Waltham. The door was opened by Eustace Lawson in a merry demeanour. "Good evening, old chap," he said, shaking hands with Giles and then kissing Susie enthusiastically.

They were ushered into the capacious kitchen, and there were greeted by Ophelia. "So sorry I can't be more welcoming. As you can see, I'm up to my elbows in flour. Just making some last-minute mince pies. It was manic at the bank this week. No time for anything. How's it been for you?"

"Oh, not bad at all. Nobody wants yoga lessons just before Christmas and Giles's school broke up last week."

"Granny," shouted little Katie as she ran into the kitchen, "Father Christmas is coming. We've just given him a mince pie and some carrots for the reindeers."

"Well, he's going to have some difficulty in a fully centrally heated house," whispered Giles to Jamie and Chloe as they followed their daughter in.

"It's easy, Dad," said Jamie. "The answer to any question is 'It's magic' – no need to explain."

Katie was eventually persuaded to go to bed. Assuming she would be up before dawn, the adults agreed, after a light supper, that it would be a good idea to go to bed early too.

As expected, there were cries of delight at 5am and Katie informed them that Santa had been. She was overjoyed to find that he had deposited several presents under the Christmas tree.

"Can I open them?" she asked, jumping up and down with excitement.

"Not yet," replied Chloe. "Grandma and Grandpa want us to have breakfast first."

"I've finished my breakfast," said Katie after a few minutes.

"Katie, be patient. We are still eating."

She squirmed in her seat, checking intently on the progress of breakfast until the grown-ups took their coffee into the Lawsons' drawing room, as they termed it, and gave Katie her presents first.

"Here is our present to you, Katie," said Ophelia as she handed her a slim parcel.

With eager anticipation, Katie ripped off the wrapping paper to find a leather wallet. "What's this?" she asked as she opened the wallet and drew out an iPad.

"It's something to help you with your words and numbers, and it can tell you stories, Katie." Eustace turned to Giles. "I got one of the IT chaps at our chambers to set it up, so it's very simple to use." He demonstrated how it could tell a story.

After looking at it for a few moments, Katie put it down and said, "Can I have my other presents, please?"

"Here's ours, Katie," said Susie as she handed her a much larger parcel. Again there was much frantic tearing of paper until Katie arrived at a large box which declared, *Carpet skittles – fun for all the family*, in large letters on the side. Turning to the Lawsons, Susie explained, "Giles, forever the PE teacher, thought it would help Katie with developing good hand-eye coordination."

The skittles were immediately set up in the dining room and they started playing. Katie seemed a bit overwhelmed by it all, but the adults enjoyed it. After some time, Jamie said, "Where on earth has Katie gone?"

They searched the house until they found her in Eustace's study. She had found a large cardboard box. The end flaps had been set open as doors. On top was a book with a cup for a chimney, and on the sides, with a childish hand, she had drawn some windows. Inside were her teddy and her androgynous doll. Just outside the doors were a mince pie and a carrot.

"Santa forgot Teddy and Frankie's presents, so I hope he'll come back and give them some. I've got to make them some breakfast now," Katie said as she disappeared into the box.

Redemption Deferred

"FORGIVE ME FOR POINTING THIS OUT, BUT YOU WON'T die of thirst if you are deprived of water for an hour," James said to the girl seated next to him during a performance of a Prokofiev piano concerto. He thought he would never hear a better performance, but his pleasure was marred by his neighbour's need to sip from a bottle of water every five minutes. She also constantly referred to the phone in her lap.

As she haughtily passed him at the interval, he noticed her expensive outfit and hairstyle.

During the Tchaikovsky symphony that followed, she continued her perpetual lubrication. It suddenly occurred to James what a rich-world situation this was. He was privileged; she was spoilt and self-obsessed. Either status would be a rare problem in the Third World.

That night, James lay in bed, thinking about the contrasts across the world. As he drifted into sleep, he seemed to fly effortlessly across continents until he landed on the edge of a rubbish dump.

"Where am I?" he asked a girl of about eleven, who was standing barefoot upon the stinking heap.

"You are in Lal Bagh," she replied. "Papa says it is near a place called New Delhi."

"Who are you and what are you doing here?"

"I'm Amisha and I'm collecting plastic. I do it with my brothers. We sell it to a man who makes it into plastic pellets."

She took his hand and they flew high above a slum. He could see many tiny shacks with narrow alleys running with filth between them.

"Forgive me," he said.

"What for?"

"For being so concerned with my comfortable life. I don't ever think about you. In my country, we sometimes worry about what we call the 'left behind'. We never think of you and your family, who have hardly even started. Forgive me."

"I must go back to work, otherwise we won't get enough money to eat," Amisha said, and whisked him back to the dump. She scrambled up the foul mound, calling for her brothers. At the top, James saw the girl from the concert. She was looking about her with distaste, sipping water from a bottle and shaking her phone in irritation at the lack of signal.

As he glided upwards again, the dump became a mere dot in a landscape of deprivation as he flew towards London. A brutal crash brought him back to reality – lying on the floor of his bedroom.

Over breakfast, he was very thoughtful. The dream had really upset him. He realised what an easy life he had led – untroubled by world poverty. By chance amongst the post was an appeal from Asha – a charity working in the Delhi slums to provide a better life for children like Amisha, the mentor from his dream.

Later that day James phoned the charity and pledged to them the money he would receive from selling his Porsche and downsizing from his Docklands penthouse.

Two weeks later, Charlotte hurried into the concert hall. *Lucky my company sponsors the orchestra*, she thought, as she made her way to the corporate bar. *It'll be a much nicer evening* than my last visit. *That was terrible. Sipping water all the time to prevent myself coughing, and trying to get some news of Jenny in hospital.*

James appeared in the bar soon afterwards and noticed Charlotte immediately. *I must get to talk to her,* he thought as he picked up a glass of wine. *Strange, though. I could swear I've seen her before.*

"What's your connection with the orchestra?" he asked as he came up to her. He often found this to be a good way of opening a conversation there.

"Oh! It's you. You're that very rude man who sat next to me last time I came."

Realising where he had seen her before, James knew that their conversation wasn't going to be easy. He couldn't deny, either, that he found her attractive. "I'm terribly sorry. I was a bit brusque, but you must admit you were rather a fidget."

"But you didn't know the reasons. You only thought of your own needs." She went on to explain the stress she had been under that evening.

"I'm most terribly sorry. I had no idea. Now I know what pressure you were under, I admire the way you managed to survive the concert at all. Listen, I have to look after a client we've invited tonight. Could we meet for a drink after the performance, so I can apologise properly? I'm James, by the way."

"Charlotte." She paused a moment as she considered his offer. He had upset her, but was seemingly very sorry and there was something about him she quite liked. So she continued, "OK. See you afterwards."

The post-concert drink was a success. James repeated his apologies and she quickly forgave him. So it was easy for her to accept his offer of dinner the following night.

As James drove to pick Charlotte up he thought how lucky it was he still had his Porsche, and that maybe he had been a bit rash in pledging the money from its sale. Perhaps it would be good to delay that until he had impressed Charlotte.

The dinner confirmed their mutual attraction, and many others followed. James found that his luxury flat was much to Charlotte's taste, so he decided to delay his pledge to give that up also. As an interim gesture, he made out a standing order to the Asha charity and explained to them that he had some legal issues to work out before he could fulfil his pledge.

One evening, a year later, they were sitting in James's flat overlooking the sunset on the Thames when Charlotte suddenly said, "James. We're mad. You're a senior company broker and I'm at a similar level on the legal side for company acquisitions. We do very well, but why don't we set up on our own, then we won't have to share fees with the senior partners?"

"That's a fabulous idea, Charlotte. I had been thinking along similar lines myself. OK. Suggest you get a handle on the legal aspects and any constraints on us, and I'll set up a company ready for when we can launch. Obviously, we need to make sure we have details of all our contacts."

The following months were a fury of preparation and James had no time at all to think about his commitment to the Asha charity. As well as setting up their company, he and Charlotte had to find a larger flat which suited them both and was appropriate for entertaining high-end clients.

Five years passed. JC Partners became the premier boutique corporate advisers in the UK. Charlotte and James married amidst great splendour in the Kensington Palace Orangery. They purchased a ski chalet in Chamonix. The frantic pace of their lives, further fuelled by Charlotte's increasing love of luxury, caused James to forget completely his concern for poverty in the Third World. They were intent on securing and extending their wealth and position in society.

Some time later, on one of his increasingly rare visits, James slipped into his seat in the concert hall just before the orchestra started playing. He was almost exhausted with the pressures of the day and annoyed that Charlotte had abandoned him to go to their ski chalet with some friends she described as "perfectly lovely people". He had been on the phone all day trying to tie up a very large merger. As a result, he had almost lost his voice. During the performance, he regularly sipped water to ease his throat and surreptitiously looked at his phone to follow the progress of the deal. At the interval, he rushed out and flagged down a taxi to return to his office.

As he travelled, he remembered how he had been so indignant at Charlotte's disruptive behaviour when she had sat next to him by chance during a concert. He realised he had been acting in exactly the same way during the performance he had just abandoned. It was as if, in retaliation for his condemnation, she had cast a spell on him. A spell which had caused him to lose his sensitivity and philanthropic instincts in the pursuit of money and power, until he was brought down to the state he had so despised.

Feat of Clay

"Shh, Jonesie," Taffy said, as he applied the listening device to the ceiling of the candlelit chamber they had torn out of the clay soil.

He heard the faint sound of boots high above them.

"We're there. The Hun's right above us," he breathed. "Time we buggered off."

They slid almost effortlessly over the slick clay as they went back down the tunnel they had so painfully dug over many weeks.

Taffy and Jonesie were members of the group nicknamed the Bantam Brigade. They had answered a call from the Royal Engineers in their home village:

Wanted: miners for important war work.
No man over 5'4" need apply.

Their task was to build tunnels under the German positions so that they could be blown up from underneath. It was dangerous work, with the risk of their excavations collapsing onto them, and also from discovery by the enemy. At times, tunnellers from opposite sides fought underground when they accidentally met.

As they slipped and crawled back to their lines, they passed an occasional caged canary in dim candlelight. Then a chamber piled with containers of high explosive, waiting to be placed at the end of the tunnel.

Their colleagues in the Bantam Brigade had been very busy too. "This must be a huge operation, Jonesie," Taffy said. "We've never had to dig so many tunnels in one place."

"'Course, they never tell us what the plan is. We just have to dig away like two moles, but we'll certainly know when it happens."

A few days later, Taffy and Jonesie were standing on a box in the reserve trench behind the front line. They knew by then that fresh troops were concealed there, ready for a massed attack on Messines Ridge.

Suddenly, a huge flash of white light burst into the sky – followed by a blast which tore towards them, flattening the few trees still left standing. A massive cloud leapt upwards – a mixture of earth, rock, fragments of concrete, parts of artillery and bits of shattered bodies. More cataclysmic explosions followed. The whole ridge, which until then had seemed solidly impregnable, was now suspended as airborne fragments.

A lump of metal landed just ahead of their observation post. "Get down, Taff!" Jonesie shrieked above the roar. They fell down, bent double on their platform box, clutching their hands to their ears. Further explosions completed the destruction of the ridge.

Taffy, his outlook now refocused from Armageddon to his mate's clod-encrusted boots, shouted, "Jonesie, you better get those boots cleaned before the sergeant major sees them."

Battered by the brain-numbing noise, Jonesie giggled manically, and, as if possessed, they clutched each other in hysterical laughter.

Accidents Will Happen

"ACCIDENTS WILL HAPPEN," SAID GEOFFREY'S AUNT AS she applied a plaster to the finger she had carelessly cut whilst chopping vegetables.

"You make it sound as if you believe they are fated by some higher power," replied Geoffrey. "An accident is always caused by human action or inaction."

Geoffrey was an expert on accidents. He was a zealous health-and-safety officer at his company; relentless in his search for strategies to avoid 'slips and trips', as the jargon of his trade had it. Machines in the factory had so many guards and fail-safe operating procedures that productivity had declined ten per cent since his appointment. Geoffrey had the ISO standards as his holy script. If anybody stood in his way he would threaten failure at their next audit. Continuing certification was demanded by their most important customers.

It was thus with considerable authority that he continued, "I have sympathy for you, Aunt Ethel, but you brought it on yourself by the way you were using that knife. Accidents almost always happen because of shortcuts, overconfidence, not starting with enough information, mental distraction—"

"Geoffrey! For goodness' sake," his aunt interrupted, "there you go again. What about the article I read the other day? This woman had her house wrecked by hurricanes *five times*. That's just bad luck." She put the offending knife back in its drawer and banged it shut.

"No, Aunt. You are wrong. She was not acting on good information. After the first, she knew that she was living in a hurricane-prone area. The next house should have been built with hurricane-proof techniques."

"Geoffrey. I've had more than enough of you. It's time you went off on your weekend trip and left this ignorant old woman to her self-inflicted pain," Aunt Ethel shouted as she pushed her insufferable nephew towards the door.

You can't convince some people, even though it is for their own good, thought Geoffrey as he walked along a narrow path in the Lake District. There was a high wind and the outlook was for early snow. But he was not worried. He had informed the hotel of his exact route. His rucksack bulged with safety equipment. Even if the wind got too strong, he had a long rope to belay himself along the path from secure point to point.

Geoffrey was happy. He had won a substantial battle at work over the necessity of having an emergency clinic in the factory. Feeling a little like a prophet in his own time, he strode along with a sense of great self-satisfaction.

High above him, a random swirl of the strong wind dislodged a piece of the slaty rock. A huge gust picked up this fragment and whirled it earthward. It fell on Geoffrey's head, its sharp edge killing him almost instantly. Adamant to the last, he gasped, "That was completely preventable. I should have been wearing a helmet."

The Arrow of Time

THAT'S ABSOLUTELY FASCINATING, HENRY THOUGHT, frowning in concentration at an article in the *New Scientist. I thought that it was impossible to reverse the arrow of time.*

"I'll be back later," Elsa said as she shrugged into her duffel coat and opened the door. "There's a pie in the fridge if you feel like taking your nose out of that magazine."

"OK. See you later," muttered Henry, not really hearing his wife's instruction. Their marriage, which had started so well, had gradually cooled and they were now two people on parallel tracks.

He read on: *Scientists have shown that time can run backwards in a system of two coordinated particles...*

Hang on, what did she say? Something about eating, was it? Distracted from his reading, Henry started thinking about their relationship.

What a good thing it would be if we could go back fifteen years. We used to have such fun together. If only we could travel backwards in time. Henry liked to philosophise, so he developed the theme further. *We are migrants through time,* he thought, *always moving to a new landscape – destined never to immigrate to the sunny uplands of the past. But what if we could?*

He returned to his reading: *This cannot be taken as a total reversal. It only shows that the normal idea of the forward arrow of time doesn't work at a quantum level. Neither does the effect last.*

Well. That's the end of that idea. Anyway, better find something to eat.

To his surprise, Henry found a pie in the fridge, which he heated up. As he sat eating it, he thought again about his and Elsa's relationship and his wish to go backwards in time. By chance, he noticed an advert in a magazine which his wife had left open.

Give a gift of grooming to the one you love, it urged. *Super weekend package. A complete makeover is achieved in just three short days. We advise on the best outfits and help you buy them. We style your hair and advise on make-up.*

The next day, Henry organised this for Elsa. At first, she protested, but was secretly tempted so she agreed to go.

While Elsa was away, Henry took a good look at himself. He saw a middle-aged man. Corduroy trousers, a patterned sweater, and a greasy ponytail above aviator glasses. Shocked by this, he embarked upon a crash self-improvement course. After two frantic days, he looked again in the mirror and saw a smartly dressed forty-year-old with cool glasses and a neat hairstyle. Reassured, he unpacked his shopping and spent hours following a recipe for dinner for when Elsa returned. He was ready just in time.

As she came through the door, Henry was stunned by her transformation.

"Why, Henry, what's all this?" she said. "It's just like old times."

"Maybe we really are immigrants in time."

"What's that?"

"Oh. Nothing to worry about," he said as he poured their champagne.

Above and Beyond

AIRY AND LIGHT. THAT'S HOW IT FEELS. PAIN ALL gone. So simple to slip out of my body and float above my own funeral. I was completely wrong about the afterlife. I thought it didn't exist, but here am I, memory intact, floating invisibly with no bodily constraints.

Lucky those dead acquaintances who've been wafting around can't tell anybody what they've seen. No point in worrying now, though. Look at them all, trying to appear mournful.

There's a vicar they have dredged up from somewhere. Strange thing to do for an atheist.

"Today we gather together to mark the passing of Herbert Foster, known to you all as Herby. Husband, father, grandfather, friend, business colleague. We are joined in sorrow at the loss of such a wonderful man..."

Sanctimonious twaddle. Didn't know me from Adam.

There's my wife. Heavy black gear – looking as if she's lost a winning lottery ticket. She's probably dead worried she'll have to make a decision about marrying my cousin she's been having an affair with for years. Not a bit on the side any more, Joan! There's Fred wondering if she's going to come over all wifey and then he'll have to choose between her and Gladys.

Now they're taking turns in talking about me. My son's speaking on behalf of himself and my daughter. Enough to make my heart bleed (if I had one, that is). Apparently, they are distraught to lose such a wonderful father. All they were interested in was how much money I would leave them. Glad I decided on not much.

This afterlife is great fun. I can even hear what's in people's minds. If my mother-in-law Edie knew that, she wouldn't be thinking, *Best he's gone. She should never have married him in the first place. She turned down that nice Charlie with a good accountancy job for him – a builder.*

Hang on, Edie. You forgot Charlie was done for embezzlement and I built a significant building company. She never liked me, though, and turned Joan against me too.

Short and sweet. Now they're filing out of the crematorium to the tune of 'My Way'. Hypocrites. Most of the time I had to do it their way.

I follow them to what they've called a wake. Obviously, they don't know a wake involves staying up all night with the coffin. Imagine them doing that for me. I can hear them thinking, *Thank goodness that's over.* Now they're all getting stuck into the booze.

Wow, old Wally's got up to make a speech. Don't know how he's got the nerve after he nearly ruined my company by leaving it and taking my biggest customer.

"Can't end without saying what a wonderful man he was. Always fair and straight. My best ever business partner. Missed by all his family and friends. Let's drink to a fantastic guy – so successful in life and loved by all who knew him. Herby!"

What a wonderful life I had. I only wish I'd realised it sooner!

Can You Hear Me?

"CAN YOU HEAR ME, BERT? CAN YOU HEAR ME?" WALTER shouted as he lay behind a wall in Colenso. The scream of shells and the huge 'crump' and explosion as they landed shook the ground beneath them and threw up a cloud of debris which threatened them again as it fell to earth. He was relieved to see Bert sliding from behind a pile of rubble.

"Yeah, I'm still with you, Walt. Dunno what we're supposed to do here. Only a few of us got through, and look down there. What do they think they are doing, forcing the poor sods to try to cross the river right under the Boers' noses? With those Mauser rifles, they're cutting our men down like they're scything corn."

"The idiot general's pushed our big guns up ahead of us, right into the range of the Boers. I don't know how we managed to take the village without their help. Looks like they ran out of shells, so they've left the guns and taken shelter. What a bloody mess. The generals have no idea how to deal with the Boers. They're too good with those rifles and they can reload in seconds. I tell you, Bert, they make us look like a load of amateurs."

"Dead right, Walt. I don't think we can last out. The shells keep coming in. They're far too bloody accurate for my liking. Wish we'd never volunteered for this game. I'd much rather be back at the mill."

"Only two weeks to Christmas. Not that there's much chance we'll be back home for that. That was a near one,"

Walter shouted as a sniper's bullet ricocheted off the building behind them. There was an anguished cry close by. Walter saw that yet another of their company had been hit. He lay back against a wall, clutching his shoulder, with blood oozing through his khaki uniform.

An officer covered in dust crawled up to them. "General Hildyard's ordered us to retreat. The reinforcements are not going to get here. A few of you need to stay in Colenso and fight while the rest retreat. Also, we need volunteers to help rescue the guns. We need to haul them out with teams of horses."

"I'll go," Walter shouted back. "Anything's better than hanging around here. You, Bert?"

"Not me. I'm no good with horses. I'll stay and hold out as long as we can, but what about him?"

"If he can't walk out he'll have to take his chance when they take the village. There's no way I can get stretcher-bearers up here. Let's get going!"

Joseph arrived at the Queen Street Mill on the 8th January at 7am. He went straight to the loom which had broken down. Already there was a cacophony from the hundreds of other machines in the factory. It was almost a relief to him that his hearing was nearly gone after years in that din. He hardly heard the regular thump and sigh of the steam engine turning the rattling overhead shafts, the slap of the forest of leather belts coming down from the shafts as they drove the looms or the crashing of thousands of shuttles hurling the cotton thread backwards and forwards across the weft of the cloth. He looked down the rows of machines being tended by the young girls who had just started their twelve-hour shifts. "It's no life for those poor girls," he murmured. "If we have granddaughters I'll never let them come here. They'll be old before they're thirty. They can't even talk in this terrible noise, except by lip-reading."

He thought about his son Walter, and William's son Bert, who had gone out to South Africa to fight in the Second Boer War. Perhaps the hell their boys had chosen was better than this home-grown version. *At least it's in the open air, and if they dodge the bullets they'll be better off. I'm not surprised that they gave up stoking the boilers for twelve hours a day,* Joseph thought. But he was puzzled as to why the might of the British Army, with volunteers from around the Empire, was having so much trouble with a bunch of farmers.

Returning to his task, he started to disassemble the loom so he could replace the broken beam. Suddenly there was a scream which pieced even Joseph's dulled hearing, and, looking round, he saw a girl writhing on the wooden floor, clutching her face. One of the shuttles had flown off a machine and struck her. Its pointed end had buried itself deep into her cheek. Joseph shouted to another girl to call for help and knelt beside the victim, trying his best to comfort her until she could be taken to the local hospital.

Someone tapped him on the shoulder and shouted, "The governor wants to see you. He says it's urgent."

"Right, I'll have to go. Would you stay by this poor girl until help arrives?"

Joseph walked through long lines of machines, trying to think what could be up. As he walked into the office, he was alarmed to see by the governor's face that something was badly wrong. Raising his voice above the noise of the mill, the manager told Joseph, "Your wife came just now with a letter she had received from a Sergeant Black in your son's platoon. I'm very sorry to tell you that your Walter was killed while trying to rescue some heavy guns. The party succeeded in getting two out, but he was killed as they went back for a third.

Apparently, he conducted himself heroically. Black also said to tell William that his son Bert was taken prisoner fighting a rearguard action on the retreat from the village they had been occupying."

Emerging from the office in a daze, Joseph sat down on the chair by the door, covering his head with his hands. Sometime later, William came past and, stooping by Joseph, shouted, "Can you hear me, Joseph? Can you hear me?"

But Joseph gave no sign of recognition as the tears ran through his fingers onto his soiled overalls.

Editorial note: This story is based on the action in and around Colenso in the Second Boer War. The British, who originally expected an easy victory over the Boers (the original farming settlers from the Netherlands), had to amass an army of four hundred thousand before they could win the war.

The Pencil Box

A children's story

ONCE UPON A TIME, A LADY HAD A PENCIL BOX. I expect you know what that is, even though you might use a computer more these days. This pencil box was a magic one, because the things in it could talk.

One was called Ruler. She said this was because she always knew where to start and where to finish. There was another one called Compass, because he claimed to be wise. These were the aristocrats, since it was an old-fashioned society. The next layer consisted of the pens. One was Biro. He came from Hungary and thought himself very modern compared with the ink pen. Although the ink pen wasn't used very often, the lady wrote on pieces of paper called cheques, which turned into a lot of money. So Fountain, as she was known, was well respected.

None of them understood Propelling Pencil. Compass said that he ought to be like a rocket, able to escape from the pencil box in a puff of smoke. But PP never went anywhere and was treated as a failed experiment.

The lowest class in the box comprised the ordinary pencils, the sharpener and the rubber. They quarrelled a lot because they didn't have much to do. Sharpener said that the pencils were lazy and never needed him, so what was the point? Rubber said that she was superior to them because she was able to put right their mistakes. As a result of their bickering and idleness, they were looked down on by the rest, who thought them useless troublemakers.

The least likeable of the pencils had *HB* written on his side. He said this was short for Herbie, and he thought himself better than all other pencils, most of all the one with *2B* written on her side. Herbie said this stood for 'not to be'. Notabe, as she became known, was very sad, and cried because she was sure she would never be able to do anything. Protractor, who liked a long argument, tried to convince Herbie that he was wrong, but he wouldn't listen.

Then one day the lady opened the pencil box and took out Notabe. At first Notabe wondered what was going to happen, but she soon realised that she was going to help the lady draw a beautiful picture. When she returned to the box three days later, they all wanted to know about her adventures. From that day on, Notabe was happy because she knew that there was something special that only she could do.

Lying Back?

THEY LOOKED AT EACH OTHER ACROSS THE TABLE IN THE ridiculously expensive restaurant. He a successful director of a City firm which sold financial derivatives that nobody understood but everybody was convinced they needed. She an attractive girl who had swept in wearing shoes which had cost a normal month's salary and clothes from exclusive boutiques. It was an arrangement. He had the not-unusual urges of an alpha male who spent too much time away from his wife and family. She had university fees to pay. He thought a measure of his status was how large a wine bill he could create alongside the preciously served cuisine. She had her figure to preserve, so limited herself mainly to the wine – picking at her food as he ate, boasted, and imbibed.

A couple of hours later, he suggested they go back to his flat to have some fun.

"Oh! I thought you were never going to get round to it," she said. "I can't wait."

In his bedroom, they rapidly undressed. He complimented her on her expensive lingerie, thinking that was money well spent. Rather sheepishly, he apologised for his capacious waistline. She said that she liked a man with a bit of a body. Not like some of those overly toned young men you saw in the magazines all the time.

The next-door neighbour was in. The hot night meant that the windows of both flats were open. She was surprised by the cacophony of noise emerging from the next flat. Slaps and grunts. Yells of pleasure. It reminded her of that famous scene from the Meg Ryan film.

Wow! She must be enjoying it, she thought.

As he lay back smoking a cigarette, the man said to his companion, "That was fantastic. How was it for you?"

"Marvellous," she replied, with less conviction.

Wanting more flattery, he pressed on. "Come on. Tell me what you were thinking as we were making love."

"OK," she said, having had too much of him by then. "I was thinking that your ceiling needs decorating."

Room 101

JAKE'S DAD STOPPED HIS CAR AROUND THE CORNER from the school gate, saying, "Sorry, Jakie, I'm late for work. Can you get out quickly here?"

Jake stood by the kerbside, feeling frustrated. He normally stepped out of the car backwards, left foot first, and was handed his satchel by his dad. Right arm through the strap, then the left. Then he would put his cap on. To reimpose order on his day, he counted the steps to the gate: "1, 10, 11, 100…" Jake's mathematical mind always worked in binary. He derived great satisfaction from being able to convert other numbers into his favourite system instantly.

Inside the school, he looked up his first lesson on his iPad. Mrs Wardle – Room 5. "Right, that's Room 101," he said to himself. As he walked along the corridor, he converted the room numbers: "1, 10, 11, 100, Room 101, this is it," he said in a loud voice.

Inside sat Mrs Wardle – a special needs teacher who was an expert in helping gifted children. Her pupils, like Jake, often suffered from (she would say 'were blessed with') Asperger's syndrome.

"Good morning, Jake. I'm very pleased to see you."

Mystified as to why she should be pleased by a mundane act like entering a room, Jake sat at his usual desk and positioned his iPad carefully. Then he took nine pencils from his bag and carefully laid them out. Despite not understanding her fully,

Jake liked Mrs Wardle. She gave him interesting things to do and was also a perfect binary match. He had asked many of the teachers how old they were. Knowing that this was an obsession typical of his syndrome, they had mostly complied with an answer. Jake was fifteen, or 1111 in his system, and he had discovered that Mrs Wardle was thirty-one, or 11111 as he thought of it. That was a nice correlation that he had represented by the layout of his pencils. Next year they would be 10000 and 100000 – so they would stay aligned.

"Today, Jake, we are going to do some programming with this software which lets you draw complex patterns using something called recursive programming—"

"I know what that is," Jake interrupted, "and I know how the program works. I read about it on the Internet. So if you keep quiet, I'll get on with it."

Mrs Wardle sat silently, marvelling at his rapid grasp of the software and what he achieved with it. At the end of the hour, she congratulated Jake on a beautiful folded helix pattern and added, "Jake, I've something to tell you. Mrs Thompson takes these classes for older pupils. So in September, you'll be with her."

Jake sat completely still for a few seconds. He knew that Mrs Thompson was twenty-nine, which in his terms was 11101 while he was 1111. Next year she would be 11110 when he was 10000. Neither was compatible. With silent intensity, he deleted his complex program and one by one, broke his pencils in two.

The Missing Page

"WHERE IS THAT BOY?" SHOUTED HUMPHREY, AS HE lay painfully amongst the wreckage of the baggage train. He was waiting for young Percy, the son of a local squire who had been sent to serve him the year before. Humphrey, Duke of Gloucester, had become very fond of his faithful young assistant.

It had been a long campaign. Harfleur had been much harder than they had expected and the army had suffered grievously. In the long march across France, many more had been afflicted with disease, but Percy had been a constant presence. He always seemed to find good victuals and to make the tent comfortable for the night.

"I must find him. I need him to bring honey and lard to soothe my wounds."

The battle was fresh in Humphrey's mind. Early that morning they had formed up at the head of a valley near Agincourt. The French were assembling a formidable host of mounted knights and men-at-arms in what looked like impenetrable armour.

They had no plan, though, Humphrey thought. *Not like King Henry, who knew well how he wanted the battle to go.*

He clutched his roughly bandaged head. *Gadzooks, this hurts. I hope Percy comes soon.*

The duke had fought alongside the King himself and owed his life to Henry's swift action as a French knight was about to deliver the final thrust. He dimly recalled the scene. The sky dark with English arrows. French dead piled six feet high in a pool of mud and blood. Retreating knights and panicked horses creating a confused mass of men in their heavy armour at England's mercy.

"Will, go and find Percy. I must have the remedy he is seeking. Our supplies were looted from the apothecaries' wagon."

Humphrey's mind returned to the battle, which he only hazily remembered after he was struck down. But plenty of men had told him of the scenes of devastation after the French had fled. They had retained a few high-ranking prisoners for ransom, but most were helpless in their armour against the halberds or daggers thrust through their visors or slashed across their throats.

With tired eyes, he gazed across the battlefield in the fading light. A horrific scene of thousands of slaughtered and dying men and horses.

Thank goodness for Henry, he thought. *His use of the archers with their massive longbows crushed the French nobility, and most of our brave men still live. He will regain his feudal rights to Normandy and maybe he will even win the throne of France.*

As Humphrey slipped into a fevered sleep, he grew ever more anxious about the fate of his faithful young page.

The Bitter Ending

IT WAS THEIR FINAL QUARREL; THAT MUCH WAS CLEAR. Jane could see that this time she had gone too far. Brian's face expressed extreme pain, but it also hinted at a new resistance.

In her twenties and thirties, she had been too busy with building her career for romantic entanglements, as she called them. But the approach of forty had made her think again. After a flurry of dates organised via a website, she had selected Brian. He was several years younger, intelligent and good-looking, but had rather drifted through life. Although happy with him at first, Jane increasingly criticised him for his lack of ambition. She was desperate to have children and wanted him to support her while they were young. Their quarrels became frequent – building up to this final clash. They faced each other across the expensive dining-room table, exchanging increasingly bitter accusations.

Finally, Jane hadn't been able to stop herself, although she knew she risked everything as she shouted, "You are useless. I make all the money while you live the life of Riley. I've asked you, again and again, to get a proper job and stop wasting your time at that art gallery. You never worry about what I want. You're clearly not interested in having children. You are selfish in the extreme."

"But I'm the same person you met two years ago. Ever since you've tried to change me into someone else. I like working at the art gallery, and to be honest I don't give a damn about your super house and expensive tastes," he replied fiercely – very differently to his usual conciliatory manner.

"Well, that's not the person I respect or want. You can't even make me pregnant, let alone support a family. You're doubly useless," she shrieked, hammering her fists on the table. With each sentence, she saw him recoil as if physically attacked, but she could not contain her fury and frustration built up over many months.

"OK, Jane. I give in. You have dedicated your life to getting on. Now you've decided to become the earth mother and it's not working out as your neat career has. It's obvious I can't fulfil your fantasy, so I'm leaving tonight."

After packing a few belongings, Brian left with a curt goodbye. Jane slumped down on her designer couch and cried pathetic tears.

Two years passed and Jane continued her ascent, but her life seemed increasingly hollow. She had lost all confidence in seeking a partner, and her dream of motherhood drifted away.

One day she had to visit a client in what she regarded as a rather downmarket part of town. After her appointment, she walked briskly through the shabby streets, telling herself how much better off she was where she lived.

Then, with a shock, she noticed a familiar figure passing across her path. It was Brian with a young companion. They were chatting happily as he pushed a baby in a buggy.

Misplaced Love

SALLY LOOKED DESPONDENTLY DOWN AT HER MEAGRE breakfast – stale bread with a scraping of jam. It didn't seem fair. Len, her mum's new boyfriend, was enjoying bacon and eggs.

Eleven-year-old Sally and her mother Cynthia had recently been moved into a 1960s estate due for demolition. Its drab grey walls seemed in keeping with their fraught lives.

The arrival of Len had added to poor Sally's unhappiness. He had no job and didn't look like getting one. Sally's few remaining toys had been sold to fund just one night's drinking. After this, she had lain crying in her bed as she cuddled the small stray kitten which she had adopted as her own. "He can take away everything else but I won't let him take you away from me," she had whispered into the kitten's soft fur.

"Eat your breakfast, love," Cynthia urged. "Nearly time to go to school. You look really pretty in that nice dress I got you."

Sally was already overawed by the school, which she had joined in the middle of the first term. There were a few children like her, but many from the nearby private estate. The dress now made it impossible for her to go. One of the well-meaning liberal mums had taken pity on Cynthia at the school gate and offered her the dress, saying, "This dress would look very nice on Sally. It's a bit small for Samantha now. She's growing so quickly."

Cynthia had gladly accepted. The school's lack of a uniform created peer pressure which she knew she couldn't match for her daughter.

With the eye of a sensitive child, Sally had recognised the dress and dreaded the thought of meeting Samantha.

With an anxious look, Sally pleaded, "I don't feel well, Mum. I've got a headache."

Len scowled at her and shouted, "Get yourself off to school, you miserable whinger."

"But, Len, maybe she could stay here with you while I'm at work. Perhaps she'll feel better tomorrow."

"You keep out of it, Cyn," growled Len as he hit her with a backhanded blow, sending her staggering into a corner with blood streaming from her nose. Tugging Sally by her hair to the door, he thrust her out. The kitten yelped as he trod on her tail. Further enraged, he propelled the kitten after Sally with a vicious kick.

Hours afterwards, a late commuter on her way to the station came across a little girl clad in a smart dress with tear-stained cheeks. She was sobbing bitterly as she tightly clutched a small, lifeless kitten.

Stooping down, the woman tried to get her to explain why she was there and what had upset her, although she suspected that the dead kitten was the likely explanation for her distress.

"Your poor kitten. Did it get hit by a car? How terrible. I'm Sarah. If you tell me where you live, I'll take you home. You can't stay here by the road on your own. What's your name?"

"Sally," the girl replied between sobs, "and I never want to go back home. Len will just hit me again."

Although she had been hurrying to catch her train, Sarah forgot about her normal routine as she thought about how she could help Sally. She could see that there was no prospect of her going home immediately, or even being prepared to say where home was. Fortunately, Sarah was a social worker in the borough so she decided to take Sally with her to the office.

Later, when they had managed to get Sally to talk about her circumstances, they knew that she couldn't be taken home without further inquiries, so she was temporarily taken into the care of the borough and her mother was contacted.

That afternoon, Sally's mum arrived at the office with Len striding belligerently beside her.

"Where's my daughter? Is she all right? We must take her home."

"Bloody load of interfering do-gooders, you lot are," Len shouted as he pounded the desk with his fist.

"Len, I'm sure they are doing their best for Sally. Thank you for looking after her," Cynthia added as she turned to the social worker who had taken up Sally's case. When can I see her and take her home?"

"I'm afraid that won't be possible just yet. You see, there are some circumstances we need to investigate first. She was extremely distressed when she was found and had evidence of bruising in several places."

"Stupid kid ran into a concrete post. She does it all the time. Can't see straight. Now let's get going. I've had enough of you bossing us around. Who do you think you are?"

With some difficulty, Cynthia managed to persuade Len that they should leave, which he did while still swearing at the staff.

The social worker turned to the colleague who had helped get them out of the office and said, "What a shame. She's such a lovely little girl and her mother seems very nice too, but we will have to investigate their home life. It seems evident that the man is the problem. Did you notice the cut on the poor woman's face?"

"Yes, I did. We see too many cases, I suspect like this one, where the woman wants a man in her life and makes a hasty decision. What a tragedy that nice people don't necessarily form relationships with nice people."

Jealousy

As they gazed at Munch's print *Jealousy*, Michelle was wondering what it portrayed. Was it the infidelity of a lover, or just the loss of an object of romantic desire?

"What a pathetic loser he looks," Matt observed in his normal confident fashion. "I'm not surprised she is open to other offers."

They had come to the Munch exhibition at the Albertina Museum in Vienna on the only afternoon Matt had off from the international conference he was attending. Michelle was relieved to be away from the patronising 'partner events' the organisers had arranged. Shopping and prancing horses.

She regarded Matt coolly, dressed to impress in expensive smart-casual wear, half-turning to see if he was making an impression on the attractive woman beside them.

Michelle looked again at the haunted expression of the disappointed lover in the picture. She saw his abject horror as he watched the woman he loved being seduced by a more attractive rival.

"I am sure there are two ways of looking at that," she replied, not expecting that he would take any notice. Touching his sleeve to attract his attention, she went on, "Matt, I feel I need a bit of fresh air. I'll meet you in the entrance hall at four o'clock."

Sitting outside in the crisp autumn air, Michelle thought again about the picture. She recalled her own feelings when she discovered Matt's affair with a younger work colleague. She had been everything that Michelle was not. Self-assured, overtly sexy and adventurously single. She recalled the sense of betrayal; the deep, iron grip of jealousy which seemed to take over her whole being. She remembered how this had gradually softened to a dull ache in her soul.

Eventually, the fire had gone out of the affair and Matt's amour had moved on. Michelle had tried very hard to rekindle their relationship but a succession of further affairs had worn her down to a meek imitation of her former self. As far as Matt was concerned, she existed merely as a partner to be wheeled out at important business events. She thought wryly of how she was about to cast him in the role of the 'pathetic loser' – to use his words.

Her phone rang and she answered it eagerly.

"Hello, Michelle here." The frown brought on by unhappy memories disappeared as she listened to the familiar voice.

"Yes, I am sure," she said with great conviction. "I am leaving here tomorrow – the day before Matt does. I'll join you in London as soon as I've had time to pack a few things. Then I'll come to you."

She looked up at the bright sky as she listened again.

"No, I am not at all concerned about Matt. He is even now flirting with a woman in the art gallery we are visiting. I have more than done my duty by him over all these years. I know life with you will be so different. I can't wait until we are together completely."

The Library Book

MARK LEANED AGAINST THE EMBANKMENT WALL, looking idly at the Thames rushing downstream. As a dealer in rare books, he had been searching through the stalls below Waterloo Bridge. He hadn't had much luck so far, but thought he would have one last try.

He found nothing which would benefit his business, but he noticed a book which seemed out of place amongst a rack of paperbacks. It had a leatherette cover and the gold-embossed title on the spine was *The Tribes of Borneo*. Intrigued, he opened it and found that it had been a library book. The cardboard receptacle for the control tag and columns of stamped dates were there, just as he remembered from his childhood. He noticed that the last date had been in March 1985. A further red stamp across the date page declared, *Withdrawn from circulation: Tunbridge Wells Library.*

Mark flicked through the pages of text interspersed by smudgy photos of primitive tribes. A handwritten note on a yellowing sheet of paper fell out. It said, *Deborah. See you at the flat 2pm Sat. If that's OK, remove THIS note. Paul.*

Mark purchased the book and took it to a nearby cafe where he looked again at the note and wondered how it had come to be there. Gradually, he constructed a plausible story, and with it a feeling for Deborah and Paul. Tunbridge Wells was a small town, and, in the '80s, house phones could be answered by anyone. The pair must have been lovers who had devised a clever method of communication. They had chosen an obscure book in a rarely visited part of the library and used it to deliver their messages. They must have thought it very secure as they used their real names. Or, were they names made up for the purpose? Obviously, they had to foster identities as book lovers to excuse frequent visits to the library.

After all this speculation, Mark found that he was getting quite fond of Deborah and Paul. He imagined them in a passionate relationship enhanced by the thrill of secrecy. But sometime in 1984, maybe, Paul had posted his note and it hadn't been removed. Perhaps this was the second time that had happened, because he had written, *If that's OK, remove THIS note*. He would have been desperate for news of Deborah because she clearly hadn't taken the previous note from the book. Perhaps she had a husband who had guessed about their affair, and she had confessed and promised to end it. Maybe she had suffered a terrible accident. Or, could the lovers have quarrelled at their last meeting, with Deborah demanding a deeper commitment which Paul was unable to give?

The more he thought about it, the more Mark wanted to know the end of this romantic adventure. He so wanted there to be an answer to the mystery that he resolved immediately to write a story about it.

Once installed in a quiet corner of the cafe, Mark ordered a coffee and set up his laptop. He knew little about Tunbridge Wells, so started by Googling some information about it. He decided Deborah had been an unmarried young woman in love with an older man. Soon Mark was lost in his writing. After four hours and countless cups of coffee, he read over his completed story...

Paul hurried into the library. Thoughts of Deborah dominated his mind. He was still under the spell of the passionate weekend they had managed to arrange in an oast house well away from Tunbridge Wells. Desperate to see her again, he went immediately to the anthropology section, where he took out an obscure book and hurriedly leafed through its pages. Her father had forbidden their relationship, so they had devised a clever messaging system. He had left a note: *Debbie, see you at the flat 2pm Saturday. If that's OK, remove this note.* Paul turned to the agreed page and found no note. He had to suppress a shout of joy in the quiet of the library.

The freedom to abandon themselves to each other on the previous weekend had been a welcome change from their usual meetings in her friend's flat. These were somewhat inhibiting but it was all they had, since, anywhere else in Tunbridge Wells, they were liable to meet people who knew her family. Her father – Sir Archibald Moresby – was a well-known businessman in the City and a local magistrate.

When they met on the appointed date, Deborah told Paul she wouldn't be able to meet the following weekend. Her father had said, "Make sure you are free next weekend. No traipsing off to that friend of yours you are always going to see. We've been invited to stay the weekend with the Falkonburys. They're a respected county family, good Catholics, and young Lawrence is a fine lad. You're eighteen now and it's about time you had a nice boyfriend."

"Don't worry about him, Paul," Deborah said. "I can't stand Lawrence. He's a stuck-up prig."

The lovers continued their affair without detection for many weeks after that. Sometimes they varied their regime by meeting in Dunorlan Park. Deborah loved walking by the lake there. Then, one sunny day in March, she arrived at the flat and joyfully announced that she was pregnant.

"That's fantastic, love," said Paul. "We ought to get married, but what will your father say to that?" His expression of delight turned to anxiety.

"Well, he won't like the fact that you are divorced and that I continued to see you after I was forbidden to, but surely when he knows he will have a grandchild that will change?"

Paul worried about Deborah and her family's reaction to the news for days afterwards. He left one of their notes in the book, hoping that she could meet after her art class on the following Wednesday. The note was not removed.

That whole week, Deborah had been in furious arguments with her father, who, on hearing the news, had stated, "I'm very disappointed in you, Deborah, for disobeying my explicit instructions. That man Paul is never going to be my son-in-law, I can tell you. He's divorced, to start with, and he's only a teacher. You can do much better than that."

"But, Daddy, surely you would like a grandchild? I expect you'll change your mind when you see him. I'm sure it's a boy."

"There's no way you are going to keep that baby. Abortion is out of the question. It's against everything we believe in, but you will go down to Cousin Bronwyn in Aberystwyth. There you'll have his brat and then the Catholic Adoption Agency will take care of it. No arguments about this. I knew we shouldn't have let you join that theatre club."

Whenever Deborah ventured out to the library, her mother went with her. She had no means of communicating with Paul. He left another note – Deborah. *See you at the flat 2pm Sat. If that's OK – remove THIS note.* But it was not removed. He was distraught, but couldn't think what to do. Realising that the note could apply to any Saturday, Paul kept going back to the library, hoping for some response. After three weeks he resolved to visit the Moresbys' house and brave the wrath of

Deborah's father. But as he was leaving the library, he caught sight of the headline on the local paper left casually on a table.

Girl in lake identified

With a feeling of dread, Paul picked up the paper and read:

> *The body of the young girl found drowned in the lake in Dunorlan Park on Thursday 29th March has been identified as Deborah Moresby (18), daughter of Sir Archibald Moresby, the prominent businessman and local magistrate. The police are not looking for anyone else in connection with her death. In a post-mortem, she was found to be three months pregnant. Moresby said he had no idea she was expecting a child, and that they would have welcomed the baby into their family rather than lose a lovely daughter.*

In a daze, Paul left the library and walked through the town, grieving for the family he would now never have. He felt totally alone.

Although Mark was pleased with the story, he left the cafe feeling a little guilty at having explained the note to himself with such drastic consequences for the lovers. *But it's better than it remaining an unsolved mystery in my mind,* he reasoned. *I can forget about it now.*

Back in his bookshop in Totnes, Mark put *The Tribes of Borneo* on his shelves, but couldn't imagine ever selling it.

He often had browsers in his shop. He didn't bother them, but looked at them surreptitiously. He liked to guess their lifestyle and occupation. He often found out in a later conversation whether he was right. So one day he was mildly intrigued by a well-set-up man in his mid sixties who was rather flamboyantly dressed. His interest sharpened when the man took out *The Tribes of Borneo* and, after flipping through the pages, asked to purchase it.

"Do you have a particular interest in that book?" Mark asked. "I picked it up in London and there was a mysterious note in it. I guessed it was a method of communicating between two lovers. For some unknown reason, I decided he was a divorced teacher in his mid twenties and she a teenager of eighteen. In my imagined version of events, it all ended tragically."

"Well, you may be interested to know you were entirely wrong. It was I who left the note you found. Susie, code name Deborah, and I had played opposite each other in *She Stoops to Conquer*, and this started our affair. As we were both married at the time, we arranged meetings, as you have guessed. After she didn't respond the second time, I was a bit cut up, but I soon found out she had fallen in love with her new leading man in *Separate Tables*. It happened all the time."

Visiting Another Country

KARIN SAT UP IN BED, SCREAMING WITH FRIGHT.

Her husband Karl gripped her tightly. "It's all right, love. You're with me. Was it that nightmare again?"

She relaxed a little as she realised where she was and, still shivering, told Karl about it. "Yes, it was the same dream, but I've just realised that it was caused by the final conversation I had with my father in 2006. He said that he met my mother in Munich in the late '50s. Because she was English, they were able to move to the UK just before I was born. He said that he didn't want me to know about the terrible times he had lived through, so they made a fresh start and he never talked about them.

"But he changed his mind, so just before he died, he said to me, 'Karin. I want you to have this photo of your grandfather – Albert Munter – taken in Munich in 1942 with some of his medical students. I'm sorry I didn't tell you about him before.'

"In the photo, I saw a handsome man, only thirty-five according to my father, but he looked much older – gaunt and frowning with worry.

"Dad went on. 'I was only six in 1942 so I didn't know what was happening. One day, my mum (Grannie Elizabeth to you) came into our house in a panic, saying that the Gestapo had taken my father, Albert. She didn't know what for, or where he was, but she rushed away, saying she was going to find out. That was the last I saw of her, as she was killed by the Americans' bombing. My Aunt Gertrude took me in and brought me up.'"

"So that was what you were dreaming about," Karl said.

"No. Not all of that, just the bit about my grandmother getting killed. The nightmare is always the same. I see her running through the rubble and dust of the ruins of Munich, saying that she knows why the Gestapo have taken my grandfather. She is carrying a wilting white rose with a broken stem – then another bomb tears her apart. That's the ghastly scene which makes me wake up in such a state."

"Well, I think you will never be at peace until you find out about your grandfather. It sounds as if he may have been involved in some action against the Nazis. So you ought to go to Munich and see what you can uncover."

A retired teacher of sixty-three, Karin was able to travel to Germany almost immediately. She went to see the old Nazi headquarters; still a bombed ruin, just as it had been in the 1940s. She was just turning away when she noticed a plain-fronted building with words above the entrance: *The City Without Jews, Foreigners, Muslims, Refugees.* Karin went inside and found a museum dedicated to documenting the phenomenon of Hitler's National Socialism. A 1920s silent film, made in Austria, depicted a fictitious city attempting to banish all Jews. This gave rise to the quotation on the outside of the museum, which reflects what actually happened in the Nazi regime.

Karin had little detailed knowledge of the events in Munich leading up to World War II, so, with mounting horror, she followed the rise of the National Socialist Party under Hitler. She was amazed that, after failing in an attempt to overthrow the government in 1923, he was sentenced to five years and allowed to write *Mein Kampf*, which sold millions of copies and spread his racial hatred everywhere. He was let out early and President Hindenberg thought they could control Hitler when they appointed him Chancellor, but he quickly seized power and removed all opposition. Munich was the centre of this revolution.

After a few hours, she took a break and rang Karl.

"Hello, love, I've found a very good museum full of facts about the time my grandfather was alive. It was terrible, but at first the Nazis were extremely popular. I couldn't understand why there was no opposition when news of the slaughter of the soldiers on the Eastern Front started coming through. But then I came across the story of the White Rose movement. They were a group of professors and their students who printed anti-Nazi leaflets and distributed them, hoping that the terrible facts of the war and the deportation of hundreds of thousands of Jews would bring people to their senses. I wonder if my grandfather was involved with them. I'll go back and find out more."

Feeling happy that she might be close to discovering the facts about her grandfather, Karin hurried back into the museum. She found that the White Rose movement existed for only a short time. She read about the founders – Hans and Sophie Scholl, Heinrich Bauer – and there on the list of active members was Albert Munter. With great excitement, Karin read on:

The movement lasted from about June 1942 to February 1943. Their information came first-hand from medical students who were made to act as medical orderlies on the battlefields. They came back with tales of the pitiless sacrifice of men in appalling conditions without even proper winter clothing. They had witnessed savagery on both sides and millions of civilians being left to starve, with the SS urging the troops on to massacre the Slavic 'Untermenschen'. The Gestapo infiltrated the White Rose group and they were eliminated one by one. They were tortured to try to make them disclose their collaborators' names, and many were executed by guillotine or hanging.

Trembling with dread for what she might see, Karin turned to a display of photographs. There was a picture of the public hanging of a White Rose member. *Surely it's not him*, she thought as she took out the photograph given to her by her dying father and compared it with the one in the display. "Oh, God! It is my poor grandfather," she whispered as she clutched at the display case in despair.

Karin left Munich on the first available flight home. She couldn't bear to remain in the place that had bred this animal regime which had thrown itself upon its enemies at home and abroad with such ferocity.

Back home, she finally gave way to her sorrow and cried bitterly on Karl's shoulder as she told him of her discovery.

"At least you now know what happened to your grandfather, and you can be proud that he was such a brave man."

That night, in bed, Karl watched over Karin as she fell into an exhausted slumber. Suddenly she started in her sleep and appeared to be trying to walk backwards, but then she relaxed and smiled.

The next morning, Karl asked her about her dream, hoping that her trip had made a difference.

"It was marvellous, Karl," she replied. "It started the same, with my grandmother appearing through the ruins of Munich, but as she approached I could see that the rose in her hand was a full bloom on a strong stem. 'Come with me,' she said as she took my hand and led me to a circular flower bed that had been created amongst the rubble. There stood a rose bush with many white blooms on it, which grew rapidly until it towered over the whole of Munich."

Editorial note: The museum in this story is the Munich Documentation Centre for the History of National Socialism. Albert Munter is a fictitious character, but the historical context is correct.

A Lot Too Late

The reading of the will of Joseph Miller will take place on the 5th October 2018 at the offices of Strut, Sutter and Roberts at the above address. As a beneficiary, you are invited to attend.

WHAT A THEATRICAL PROCESS, MARCUS THOUGHT. *I'll never forgive the old bastard for what he did to me.*

His mind went back to the traumatic event of 1998. The finance director in Joseph's oil-broking business had resigned suddenly. Marcus had been promoted to take over. He was inexperienced, but welcomed the opportunity. At the time a complex negotiation with various Middle Eastern countries and Russia was coming to a conclusion. A huge pile of contracts, side agreements and commission agreements had been created. The day before completion, Joseph had announced he would have to attend an important negotiation in Nigeria. So he arranged for Marcus to be the firm's signatory to complete the deal.

Late into the night, Marcus had tried to understand the morass of documents, but found them impossible to comprehend fully. In the end, believing that Joseph knew what he was doing, he signed them anyway.

The firm went on to prosper, with deal after profitable deal. But then disturbing rumours started to surface about the one Marcus had signed off. A campaigning journalist had uncovered the reality. The entire structure of documents was a ruse to avoid sanctions on Iran. Marcus was extradited to the US to face charges. He was convicted and jailed for seven years. Joseph had escaped by claiming he had instructed Marcus not to sign until the documents were checked for any irregularity by their lawyer.

So he's going to mock me from the grave by leaving me some trinket. Surely it's enough that I've been banned for life from acting as a qualified accountant and my wife ran off with someone else while I was inside? But I will go. I'll tell them all what an unprincipled scoundrel their Joseph was.

A week later at the solicitors' office, Marcus sat amongst Joseph's immediate family. The reading began: "I, *Joseph Miller, being of sound mind…*"

Marcus's attention wandered as he watched the participants. He could tell who was being mentioned by their facial expressions. Joseph's trophy wife looked incredulous as she heard of an allowance of a mere one hundred thousand pounds per year and ownership of the house she was living in. His middle-aged offspring were told that they had benefited enough and would receive nothing further. A number of charities were given substantial legacies.

Finally, the solicitor read, "*Now to Marcus Williams. I have to finally set the record straight. I now declare I was to blame for the illegal contract which put him in jail and left me to continue to make my fortune. Hence, much of what I possess, I owe to him. He was duped into signing that disastrous deal, and to make amends I hereby leave the rest of my fortune to him.*"

The Hobbyist

THE OLD CLOCK'S SLOW *TICK-TOCK* SEEMED TO MOCK their inaction as Brenda and George looked glumly at each other across the dinner table. They had sat like this for many an evening. Out of frustration with years of ennui, Brenda suddenly burst out, "We must change this boring existence. We need to find something we can do together."

Awoken from his stolid silence, George looked online for inspiration. Google suggested an article titled *Save your marriage by playing together*, so they looked at the list of ideas.

Have more sex together. Guerrilla gardening. Share a sport. Adopt a stray cat. None of that appealed, so Brenda took up embroidery while George was inspired by the suggestion to *Make a bunker to survive the Apocalypse.* Unfortunately they were individual hobbies, but they thought at least they would have something to talk about.

He was no great intellectual, and found the Apocalypse a confusing concept. Nonetheless, he thought it was more likely to be survivable in the shelter of an underground chamber. So he started digging in the back garden and soon had a decent-sized bolthole. He didn't like the sound of the Four Horses of the Apocalypse, so he laid in a stock of 'Treats for a Frisky Horse' he found in a local pet shop. Then there was famine to deal with. This necessitated the construction of a side chamber for the storage of emergency supplies.

It can't go on longer than about a year, he reasoned, as he stowed away boxes of food and fuel for the stove. He had found a recipe for roasted locusts, but generally plagues sounded nasty so he built a double entrance with a pesticide spray.

All this preparation was physically and mentally demanding, but for the first time in his life, George felt fulfilled. He found friends in an exclusive club of Apocalypse bunker enthusiasts with whom he swapped information.

One of them gave him the idea of creating a fresh produce room. He planned to have beds of vegetables growing under LED lights powered by a pedalled generator connected to large batteries. George had run out of space under the garden, so for this he had to dig under the house, and within months had nearly finished his horticultural project.

While all this was taking place, Brenda and George grew even further apart. She sometimes didn't see him for days as he slept down below in his construction site. In his frequent absences, however, she made good progress with her own hobbies. Embroidery had been an absorbing pastime, but later she progressed to etching. It was just another way of making patterns, but it had a novelty which appealed to her.

One day, returning from the shops, she saw to her horror that the house had collapsed into George's underground garden and its massive weight had filled in his Apocalypse bunker.

Brenda's grief was not great. She had long ago lost her husband to his subterranean project. Although not previously renowned for her wit, she etched a plaque which she placed above the rubble. It said:

In memory of George Herbert, the hobbyist.
Apocalypse Now.

Zoryx

ONE MORNING MY NORMAL TRAIN ARRIVED IN THE guise of a fiery asteroid with flames streaking along the sides of the first carriage. As it drew alongside I could see that there were some details sketched in but still to be painted. A signature – *Zoryx* – appeared modestly within the artwork. Some of my fellow commuters gasped in admiration, but many complained loudly about vandalism and called down retribution on poor Zoryx.

Weeks later, as I walked to Waterloo Station, I made a detour under one of the many long arches it created. It is one of the places in London where wall art and graffiti are tacitly allowed. Every surface is covered. It is understood that any work is temporary, and often a lone painter can be seen blacking out an extensive canvas for his masterwork. The vaulted roof is fifteen feet high, and yet paintings in perfect perspective appear there.

Perhaps as a result of my artistic diversion, a small item caught my eye in the evening paper:

Railway vandal caught

The painter who vandalised several train carriages has finally been caught. Daren Davies (18) was apprehended at the railway sidings at Grove Park. He had failed to complete his work in one night and had returned to finish it. The railway police anticipated this and set watch. He has been charged with criminal damage and will appear at Southwark Crown Court in four weeks.

That must have been Zoryx, I reasoned. The painted train I had seen operated on that line and its art had been incomplete. I was quite pleased with my detective-like conclusion, but soon forgot all about it.

Two years later, as I was leaving a concert at the Royal Festival Hall with my wife Gill, we came upon an exhibition of art created by inmates of British prisons. Many of the pieces were impressive. There were huge, brooding self-portraits in oil; delicately embroidered tapestries; a model of St Paul's Cathedral made entirely of matchsticks.

But the piece which most caught our eyes was a splendid graffiti-like painting with its message in jagged multicoloured letters set against a background of London landmarks in silhouette. After we had told the young man on exhibition duty that we wanted to buy the painting, he related how he had been in prison for a year and a half, having been convicted of criminal damage by graffiti. He was a very pleasant young man, who then proudly revealed we had chosen his painting. He assured us that, since his sentence, he painted only on board and never on public property.

As I was hanging the painting, I was thinking how glad I was that its artist would never again be jailed for his art. I read once more the title blazoned on the picture – *THE ART OF CRIMINAL DAMAGE*. It was only then that I noticed it was signed, *Zoryx*.

Her Winter of Discontent

AWAKENED BY THE WIND HOWLING ABOUT THE teahouse at Gosainkunda Lake, Katie pulled her sleeping bag more tightly about her. She had been told to expect it to be very cold, but little snow was forecast. Despite that, the sound of the wind tearing at the roof heralded some very bad weather. Katie couldn't get back to sleep, as she once again went over the unlikely chain of events which had brought her there.

The previous year, she had been invited to a large ski party in Les Deux Alpes. It was an annual get-together of a group of friends from university, one of whom had become ill at the last minute. Katie had been invited to make up the numbers. When she arrived she was almost overwhelmed by the long-practised bonhomie in the chalet. One of the crowd who seemed particularly popular was Oliver. He was tall and handsome and very self-assured. His physique had obviously been carefully honed in the gym, and he seemed able to converse on any subject. Naturally, he was very popular with the women in the party. Thus Katie had found it very odd that he went out of his way to befriend her. She had never thought of herself as being superficially attractive. She was rather quiet on first acquaintance – preferring to develop relationships over time rather than with immediate familiar banter. But Oliver persisted, and had continued to pursue her after the holiday. Katie had never experienced such attention before, and had quickly become deeply involved.

She thought it part infatuation, certainly sexual attraction, and perhaps love. She wasn't entirely sure as she had nothing to compare it with.

They kept their own flats in London, but spent most of their time in his penthouse in Docklands, where he was a director of a fast-growing financial services company. With great self-assurance, he was the instigator of much of their activities together. So it was no surprise to Katie when he burst in one day with the news that he had booked them flights to Kathmandu so they could go on a trek in Nepal. As had become normal, she had been swept along by his boundless confidence.

Still unable to sleep, Katie thought of the events of the past few days. A plane to Kathmandu, a bus to Dhunche and four hard and increasingly breathless days' trekking to Gosainkunda at 4,500 metres. Finally, she drifted into a fitful sleep, only to be woken by Oliver shaking her shoulder.

"Come on, Katie; they say the weather is worsening. If we don't start soon we'll never make the pass."

For the first time, Katie had second thoughts about one of Oliver's schemes. "I'm not going higher from here. It would be madness. We must go down. Descending is much quicker. We can be right back at Dhunche by this evening."

Reluctantly, Oliver agreed and, after a breakfast of tea and bread and cheese, they set off. As soon as they left the teahouse the severity of the weather was apparent. They were battered by a fierce wind, and huge black clouds were mounting above them. After they had gone only a few kilometres, it started to snow. The flakes tearing into their faces soon became a blizzard. The path, the scenery and the sky merged into one white searing cloud. They only knew they were upright by the pressure of their feet on the frozen ground.

Katie knew Oliver was panicking as he shouted, "We've lost the path. You can't see a thing in this. We must turn round and go back."

"No point in that. We don't even know which way we are facing. We must walk in any direction which is downwards, and when we find a stream, follow that further down. It's our only chance," Katie shouted back.

So they blundered on, almost doubled over against the storm. After a short while, they came across a small stream and stumbled down its stony path. As they descended there was some shelter from the wind, but it was still snowing heavily. After many kilometres, they were beginning to think that they had survived the worst, but they were halted by a cliff which was pierced by narrow gullies, down one of which their pilot stream escaped. To double their misfortune, that stream suddenly became a gushing torrent. The storm must have dislodged a barrier higher up.

"We're done for now. There's no way we can climb back up," Oliver cried, with panic now clearly marked on his face.

"There's a cave in the rock ahead. We'll set up camp there and work out a plan," shouted Katie as she forced her way through the snow towards it.

The cave was dry and sheltered from the blizzard. They sat and faced each other wordlessly as they came to terms with their predicament. Katie was the first to speak.

"The teahouse knew we were trying to go down to Dhunche, so when we don't turn up they'll initiate a search for us. We'll just have to cope until we're found."

"But they'll never find us down here. We're miles off track. We should never have followed that damn stream," Oliver replied plaintively.

"Well, I'm not going to give up. Let's do a check of what we have to keep us alive until they come." So she laid out all that was in their rucksacks and made a mental inventory. "We've got a selection of nut bars and the packed lunch we were given today. We could make that last nearly a week. After all, we don't have to use much energy here."

The first night passed with neither of them sleeping. They had sleeping bags designed for very cold conditions, but nonetheless, they were shivering the entire night. In the morning Katie insisted that they do whatever exercises the limited space in the cave allowed. She then allocated them their ration of food and water according to her plan. She had ready her red bandana so that she could go into the open and wave if (or, as she said, when) she heard a helicopter. The storm had blown itself out overnight and the sunlit peaks of the steep valley rose above a frozen waste of snow still faintly etched with Katie's path to the cave. She was relieved that at least winter had not really come.

Thus their daily pattern was set, but by the fifth day they had used all the food they had.

Oliver became wilder in his comments, often raging against their misfortune and blaming it on Katie. "We're doomed," he shouted as that day commenced. "We'll never get out of here. My whole life is ruined. The company will fail. All my contacts will be lost. It will be as if I've never existed."

"Well, I'm not ready to give up," retorted Katie as she scooped snow into her cupped hands. "We can exist without food for at least another ten days, and I'll continue to melt snow like this for us to drink. It's easier than struggling across to that cascade."

More days passed. Katie was glad of her medical training, and optimistic about returning to take up her first post in a hospital. She insisted on them continuing with exercises despite their increasing lethargy from lack of food. She knew that a good blood flow helped the body make use of stored fat and eventually muscle tissue.

"I wish you would stop nagging me all the time," complained Oliver on the morning of the eleventh day as Katie again urged him to stir from his sleeping bag.

"It's only for your own good," she patiently replied. "I have a feeling they will come for us soon. Remember we saved an energy bar to celebrate when we are spotted. Focus your thoughts on that."

Another night passed with both of them in a state which wasn't quite sleep – more of a listless coma. As the dawn light penetrated the cave, Katie suddenly came alert. She was certain she had heard a distant helicopter. Frantically pulling her sleeping bag off her legs, she rushed out into the open, waving her red bandana wildly. The helicopter passed over the narrow valley and seemed to pause above her before flying off.

Katie returned to the cave, exhausted by that supreme effort, and whispered, "I am sure they saw me. It won't be long now. I'll get that energy bar out and we'll celebrate." She searched both their rucksacks, but found nothing. She was too disappointed to say anything and sank back in disgust. Knowing she could do no more, she relaxed at last and fell into a deep sleep.

She slept for many hours, dreaming of flying off the mountain and swooping towards the ground with wings which helped her land safely. She became aware of a hand shaking her. Slowly, she emerged from her dream and saw a Sherpa was standing above her.

A week later, Oliver and Katie stood side by side in Kathmandu Airport, waiting for a flight out. They had been rescued by helicopter and spent a few days recuperating in hospital. Oliver, thinner, but in a way which still left him with haggard good looks, was talking to a small crowd around them. They had become minor local celebrities, having survived for nearly two weeks lost in the Himalayas. With regained composure, he was holding forth in his self-confident style. Katie caught snippets of his posturing.

"Yes, we were unlucky that we got trapped, but we made a plan which would maximise our chances of survival. It was necessary for us to conserve what little food we had and keep as fit as…"

Katie stopped listening and stood quietly beside him, conscious that in his 'we' and 'us' there was an implied 'I' and 'me', with her role cast as that of a meek follower.

Looking with pity at Oliver, she was already planning her life without him.

Lying

"SHE BROKE IT," SHOUTED GEORGE.

"No. He's lying. It was him."

"Your sister's right. I saw you do it," their mother said.

At this, George was seized by his father, and shaken violently.

"You must not lie. The Bible says, *Thou shalt not bear false witness against thy neighbour.* Exodus 20:16." Like all fundamentalists, he used chapter and verse like rivets to fasten the message irrefutably.

"What's false witness?"

"It means lying, and if you do that, you will end up in the fires of hell."

Six-year-old George had been shown a furnace when the family visited a power station and was desperate to avoid such an end, so he resolved he would never again tell a lie.

By the time he was seven he was not very popular at his school as he always told on his classmates. To no avail, he told them that it was for their own good since it kept them out of the hands of Saturn. His mum came to have far fewer friends, and severe reservations about his veracity, after she heard him answering the phone to her acquaintances.

"No. I don't think Mummy can come to your house because she says that your dog makes the whole place stink and she gets covered with hairs," was a typically frank interaction she overheard as she rushed to grab the phone.

One evening, his father went off as usual to his Bible study class. George's mother took little Suzie up to the back bedroom to try on some clothes she had made. George sat in the kitchen, playing with his model farmyard.

Suddenly the door burst open. A masked man lunged through and seized George.

"Don't say a word or I'll kill you," he said, holding a knife against George's throat.

The man had carefully watched the father leave the house, but was alarmed to find only a small boy there. He had planned to force the woman to call her husband and say that she would be killed unless he opened the safe at the building society where he was deputy manager. The boy couldn't be relied upon. He seemed scared speechless.

"Where's your mother?" demanded the man, pricking George's throat with the knife.

George was petrified. He could smell the rank odour of an unkempt body and a sweet pungent smell on the man's breath. The mask had slipped, and a rough beard in which bits of pizza were embedded rasped at his cheek. The poor boy was in a state of terror, but not just because of the immediate threat. He was being asked a question, and if he didn't answer it truthfully he would go to hell and burn for all eternity. If he did speak the truth, this man would get his sister and mother.

George eventually found his voice and sobbed as he said, "She... she w-went to visit the policeman's wife down the road."

Who Was I?

"What's your first memory?" one of them would ask. I don't know why they kept asking me. My answer was always the same. They told me I had fallen off a ladder onto my head and it had affected my memory. Apparently, I am Peter Simpson and I live in London. They haven't told me much else and I have no idea how I came to be here.

I can easily recall my first memory. I heard a pulsing sound which got progressively louder. Gradually a small window of light opened out and became brighter – like emerging from a thick fog. As I woke fully, I heard a steady *beep-beep-beep*. Something around my arm squeezed and then relaxed. A voice said, "Welcome back, Peter. I'm Dionne, your nurse. You are in St Thomas' Hospital. Press this button if you need anything. Now rest until the doctor comes."

Sometime later, a woman in a white coat appeared and said, "Good afternoon, Peter. Pleased to see you are awake. You've had an accident. Can you remember what happened?"

That was the first time I had heard that question, so I answered readily. "No. All I can remember is waking up and seeing Dionne." I felt relieved to have a present, if no past.

"Someone's here to see you," the doctor said, and a nice-looking lady rushed up to me, buried her head in my chest and said, "Thank goodness you have recovered, Peter. We'll be able to get you home in no time."

Get me home? Do I live with this woman? I thought with inner panic at my loss of a past life.

"Peter, Peter. Don't you recognise me? I'm Emma – your wife."

"Mrs Simpson, it is evident that Peter has lost his memory. May I suggest we leave him to rest now and we will do some more tests?"

That was two days ago. Since then I seem to have become a circus act, with endless examinations and probing about my first memory. As prime exhibit, at least I am in a private room. Emma came again yesterday and cried over me once more as I struggled to respond as her husband. When she left she said that she would return today with something which will wake me up properly.

A knock on the door, and her face appears in the partly opened doorway.

"Peter. Here is my surprise," she says excitedly as she pulls a lovely little girl of about five into the room.

She seems vaguely familiar, although I can't remember seeing her before. She runs over to my bed and, says eagerly, "Daddy. I've started school and Mummy says I can go to the ballet class. I love you, Daddy. Come home soon."

She clambers up on the bed and I hold her. Feeling very bewildered, I look over at Emma. With tears trickling down pallid cheeks, her face is a picture of desolation.

Absence

JULIETTE SAT HUNCHED OVER HER PHONE. ITS GARISH light illuminated her face, etched with lines of worry as she distractedly thumbed the screen. Her partner Miles had been away now for three months.

They had met at Bath University on the psychology course. Afterwards, she had qualified as a psychiatrist, while Miles had made a name for himself as an expert on the psychology of the workplace. Now he was on an extended tour of Australia, delivering his trademark course, *Mindfulness for the Executive*. Although his absences were never welcome, they managed. But this time Juliette was very worried.

Miles had been keeping in regular contact by email, and she was now rereading a number of his messages with close attention.

13/03/2006

> *Hi, Jules. Arrived safely in Perth and travelled down to Fremantle where the course is being held. It's a pleasant little town from which you can look out across the ocean, all the way to India. The course is in a nice centre overlooking the harbour. Wish you were here with me. Love, Miles xxxxx*

05/04/2006

> *Hi, Jules. Now in the middle of the course in Adelaide. It's*

getting very hectic. The rednecks from the mining industry in Darwin were quite a handful last week, and I am getting asked to fill in between courses with a lot of private client consultancy. I am going to get the office to send out some support. It would have been good if you could have come, but I know you think that this is all smoke and mirrors. Love, Miles xxxxx

17/04/2006

Had a break at last. Sydney is an amazing place. On Sunday I took the ferry to Manly. A fabulous ocean beach, and a great view of the town when you climb up on the heights. You would enjoy it here. The course starts today. They have sent Jessica Hollace to back me up. She's on the young side, with limited experience. I hope it works out. Miss you. Love, Miles xxxxx

28/04/2006

Wow. It's full-on. Now nearly at the end of the second Sydney course. It is great to have Jessica here. She has worked out very well and has the delegates eating out of her hand. Yesterday she took the whole afternoon so I was able to go to Bondi Beach for a swim. One more course here and then it's on to Canberra. Love, Miles. xxxx

05/05/2006

The end of the last Sydney course. What a demanding schedule, with all the one-to-ones in the evening. It has been great to have Jess with me; she has turned out to be a star. We both need to relax for a few days before going on. Hope all is well with you. Miles xxx

Juliette started as her phone rang.

"Hello, Juliette here," she said. "Oh! Jonathan. Thanks for ringing. It was good of you to listen to all my troubles last night." She listened attentively. "Yes. Despite everything, I enjoyed it too. I'll be OK. See you at the clinic tomorrow."

Her smile disappeared as she returned to trawling through Miles's messages.

22/05/2006

The Melbourne course starts today. Sorry not to have been in touch last week. Canberra is a strange place, but Melbourne is much more civilised. Lots of ethnic restaurants. Not that we will have much time for those. It is going to be easier for me this week. I am going to get Jessie to take a third of the sessions. She really has stepped up to it. By the way, we need to go to Hobart next week. Miles xx

09/06/2006

Well. Goodbye, Melbourne. That's the last of the Australian courses. What a trip. I'm exhausted and so is Jessie. We have to go to Singapore next week. A late booking. See you soon. Miles

That was the last message – now over a week old. Juliette paced up and down. She was sure there was something terribly wrong. Was the Singapore trip really a business opportunity?

Her reverie was interrupted by the ping of her phone. She grabbed it. At last, a new message.

21/06/2006

Jules. I am sorry to tell you this. I wouldn't have wished it this way. The truth is, Jessie and I have fallen in love, and when I return I'll be joining her at her place. I'll call you as soon as I'm back. We'll have a lot of arrangements to discuss. Very, very sorry. Miles

Juliette sat very still for a long time. Then, with an air of decision, she took up her phone and dialled a number.

"Hello, Jonathan. I desperately need to talk to you. Can you come round tonight?"

An Evening Butterfly

"My mother sang all the time. A constant background of beautiful sound. It was lovely. I had no notion then that she was to become a famous opera singer." Emerging from her reverie, Ann turned in her wheelchair to face me and continued, "So, Neil, what brought you here? We heard nothing from your part of the family until now. I didn't even know you were born." She spoke with a slight trace of an accent which was difficult to place.

"Finding out about your mother, my Great-Aunt Eileen, became an obsession of mine. All my father knew was that she became an opera singer. When she married De Luca and went to Italy in 1938, he lost all contact. While researching family history I came across an Ann De Luca, and that led me to you. I don't suppose your mother is still alive?"

"Amazingly, at ninety-seven, she is. After Papa died in 1990 we came to England and lived here in Islington. Although her singing career was a distant memory, she never got over the loss of the fame which went with acclaimed performances at venues such as La Scala and La Fenice."

As she spoke, I noticed fading opera posters around the room proclaiming the name Eileen De Luca. The worn Persian carpet and brocade tablecloth, together with Ann's gypsy-like clothes, added to the dated, artistic style. There was no sign of Great-Aunt Eileen.

"Ann. Where is she now?"

"She's in a residential home in South London. I haven't seen her since I was confined to this damned wheelchair."

"Well, we must go together and visit her, then."

A week later I picked Ann up. We parked in a private square. Three of the houses were joined together and a board outside stated, with macabre humour, *The Last Movement: Residential Home for Retired Musicians*.

As we entered we heard '*Un bel dì vedremo*' ('One Fine Day') being sung poignantly with ghostly command.

"We are here to see Eileen De Luca," Ann said to the receptionist.

"I'll show you to her room, but I am afraid Eileen might not recognise you," she replied, leading us to a large room overlooking a pond at the back of the house.

Eileen was seated at the window. Her emaciated frame was clad in a silk dressing gown. The remains of her hair were fastened on top of her head with two wooden sticks, and she was cuddling a life-sized baby doll. She was still singing the aria, while looking out of the window intently.

"She thinks she is Madame Butterfly," whispered our guide. "It is as much as we can do to get her to eat and rest." With a firm tone, she continued, "Eileen. You have some visitors."

The old lady turned and, with surprising resolution, said, "I'll talk to them after my husband Pinkerton arrives."

Life Can Be a Lottery

THE SERPENT'S MALEVOLENT EYE SLOWLY EMERGED from the dense coloured foliage.

"Nearly done," said the tattooist.

Greg lay in the constricted and garishly lit parlour and, despite the discomfort of the needles, thought over the events which had led to this moment.

His mother had exaggerated ideas of his abilities. This made him wary of failure, so he drifted in a fog of indecision. His father was very sure of his own opinion and often told Greg he was useless. Poor Greg went through life hoping not to be noticed in his indecisive mediocrity. After leaving school, he worked at a junior level in a rather boring job in an unexciting business.

One day, rummaging in the garage, Greg came across a hidden book called *The Dice Man*. After he had read all the dirty bits on pages with turned-down corners, the book inspired him to make a dice with just three numbers, and each time he had a decision to make he would write down three possibilities. A typically bland, Greg type of action; a nice action; and an adventurous choice. A toss of the dice would make the choice for him.

He started slowly by deciding which breakfast cereal he would eat. He asked the dice about outfits. It gave him trendy gear which marked him out from his colleagues in the office. He then gave the dice the opportunity to invest a small inheritance:

1. Under the mattress.
2. As a building society deposit.
3. By putting it on the horses.

When it chose the latter, he asked which horses to back in all that day's races. At the betting shop, the man asked if he was doing an accumulator. Not wanting to expose his ignorance, Greg said he was. Later that afternoon, he was amazed to find that a succession of outsiders coming in had netted him 115,300 pounds and a ban from the bookie.

Over time, Greg's image changed. He became known as a bit of a maverick, but an often surprising one, adding greatly to the gaiety of office life. Emboldened by this new-found prominence, Greg set out his options for approaching Sheryl, the best-looking girl in the office:

1. Ask her to have lunch one day.
2. Invite her to go to see a film.
3. Offer to take her away for the weekend.

The dice told him Number 3. To his amazement, Sheryl acquiesced to this idea. When he told her about the dice, she was enthusiastic. They had an adventurous time together, and became an item. Sheryl encouraged Greg to join the trend for body decoration. So he put the decision to his dice:

1. A nose ring.
2. Stretched earlobes.
3. A tattoo.

"There – all done," said the tattooist.

Greg looked with admiration at his multicoloured sleeve. The evil serpent snaked through wild foliage from wrist to shoulder, and down the whole length of his arm ran the words: *Insecurity? No Dice.*

Disillusion

"I'm desperately worried about Abdullah," Jabala said to her friend Azra, as tears dropped gently into her coffee. "Even when he was a little boy he would wander off and we would look for him for ages. It was almost as if he did it to show us he was separate from us. But he changed last year and kept telling us we were bad Muslims. Then he just disappeared... But I'm sorry, Azra. You didn't come to listen to my worries, I'm sure."

Azra hesitated before she spoke. She had put off telling her friend the real reason she was visiting. She had a dreadful feeling that the tattered package in her bag contained terrible news.

"Jabala, I came with this. It was delivered to the mosque. They recognised Abdullah's writing and asked me to give it to you. I'll leave you to read it in peace."

After her friend had hurried off, Jabala eagerly opened the package and gasped when she saw her son's handwriting.

The first page of the letter was missing. The rest was dusty and crumpled, but Jabala could just about make out the words. She wept tears of joy at eventually hearing from her beloved son Abdullah, as she read:

Massad and I agreed that Western civilisation had to be made to change. The Deobandi imam at the mosque was so persuasive. He taught us how the West was trying to pervert devout Muslims. The true path, he said, was jihad against them. When the worldwide caliphate was created, we would all live according to the law of Allah and the decadent Western ways would be no more. We decided that the best way we could help this happen was to join the Islamic State.

Jabala had heard nothing of her son since he had disappeared a year previously, just after he had qualified as a doctor. Her tears formed rivers in the dust on the page as she thought of him in such terrible danger.

Sorry for the awful scribble; they are bombing northern Fallujah where I am sheltering.

We crossed from Turkey into Raqqa, where we had basic training as foot soldiers, not medical staff. That was the start of our disillusion with IS, and, Mama, you won't believe how they treat women. There were girls in the town from various European countries who were given to fighters as if they were trophies. I refused and had a difficult time persuading them I wasn't homosexual. Massad couldn't resist the temptation and he was allocated Rebecca, an innocent 16-year-old. She hadn't a clue how to be the subservient housewife they told her she ought to be. She'd never cooked a ready meal, let alone the random stuff we get here.

Jabala turned the page.

Then we were transferred to Fallujah. The city has been pounded by the Iraqis for nearly five weeks and they are now very close. Our squad is tasked with driving suicide bombs into the advancing troops. Last week Massad was forced to go. He blew himself and about 50 troops up with him. The zealots who run this place immediately gave poor Rebecca to another jihadi. My turn as a suicide bomber was yesterday, but I am sickened by the bloodshed and hypocrisy, so I escaped from the car bomb to this hell in the centre of the battle.

The bombs are falling very near and I can now hear shouts. I think there is an attack coming. I have written your address on every page so I hope that at least some of this will get to you. I love you, Mama. Kiss Maala for me. I intend to give myself up when they arrive and hope that I can have a use in persuading others to…

For a few moments, Jabala searched the page for the lost words; then, with a terrible cry, she saw, across the bottom of the page, a deep red stain.

A Mother's Day

"EVERY BLOODY DAY IS MOTHER'S DAY, MORE'S THE pity," said Becky as she pushed two-year-old Evie through the shopping mall with Ollie dragging along beside the buggy. She was reacting to a string of adverts suggesting she made the following Sunday 'a special Mother's Day'.

"Want a lolly," Evie shouted as they passed a sweet shop.

"You two think I'm made of money. Here's a biscuit."

"Don't want biscuit," wailed Evie.

"I can't get my trainers from Sports Direct," said Ollie; "they don't have the new Nikes. They'll laugh if I turn up at school with old stuff."

"Ollie. You're eight years old. I don't know where you get all this nonsense about designer shoes. You'll get what I give you and I can't afford even that."

Becky emerged from the mall feeling stressed as usual. On the bus, she looked at the children. In Ollie's face, she saw the husband who had abandoned them when Ollie was a baby. Evie's features reminded Becky of the boyfriend who had left after only a year.

I'm stuck with the results, she reflected ruefully, *and not a penny from their dads. I hope Jack will be better. It'll be nice to have a man around again.*

Becky thought about Jack. *Not bad-looking. Got a regular job. Seems to be able to put up with the kids. But he's not often around. I wonder what he does all the time?*

Back at the flat, she served the children their tea. When they were finally in bed, she quickly showered and changed, put some make-up on and blow-dried her hair. She wanted to look good for Jack's visit. She nervously watched TV until eventually, he arrived with a bottle of wine and a takeaway Chinese.

"Sorry; got held up at work. Then I bumped into Fred. Hadn't seen him in ages, so I had to have a drink with him."

He poured them both some wine and served the meal. After bolting down his food, he moved behind her chair, nuzzling her neck. "What about it, love? Fancy a bit of fun?"

Afterwards, Becky lay, disappointed, next to Jack, who still had his shirt on. He was sound asleep and snoring gently. A heavily tattooed arm lay across her body. She hadn't looked at his tattoos properly before. There was an elaborate pattern, in the midst of which she saw *Jack and Molly Forever* against a red heart.

Can't see much future with him. Why do I punish myself like this?

She moved his arm away and slid a hand gently between her thighs, trying to imagine the last time she had been satisfied by a man.

Suddenly there was a loud cry from Evie and a shout from Ollie: "Mum! She woke me up again. I don't want to share a bedroom with her. It's not fair."

Wearily, Becky slipped out of bed and went into the children's bedroom…

Revenge

NORMAN WAS GETTING VERY EXCITED ABOUT HIS onions. As always in September, he was preparing for the 'Biggest Onion' category in the Much Mulching Horticultural Show.

"Only three days to go, my beauties," he whispered, but as he lovingly stroked his favourite bulbs, his mood darkened. He remembered how Jeremy had won the prize for the previous three years. *It isn't fair*, he thought. *They are supposed to be organic. I bet he's using commercial fertiliser.*

The more Norman thought about it, the greater his frustration became. He resolved to visit Jeremy's allotment the next day and look in his greenhouse to see if there was any evidence of sharp practice.

As he arrived, he saw Jeremy cycling away. "Smug-looking bastard," he muttered as he peered into the greenhouse. Alongside some magnificent onions was a box which declared on its label, *Fast growth supplement for all vegetables*. Norman slipped inside. His reading of the ingredients verified his suspicions. His envy turned to rage.

The next morning, Norman took with him a syringe filled with a poison for killing weeds. He selected the best three onions and injected them close to their roots. He knew the poison would take a couple of days to take effect, which suited his plan well.

They delivered their onions to the showground the following day, so they would be ready in good time.

"Good luck, Jeremy," Norman said as they placed their prize onions alongside each other, "but I've a feeling it's my turn this year."

On the day of the show, there was the usual crowd oohing and aahing at the various vegetables and flowers, but it was the announcement of the winners which was to be the high point of the afternoon. Jeremy's onions were looking very poorly. They had begun to wrinkle and had lost much of their healthy shine. Norman was quietly confident.

After many prize announcements, the happy moment arrived. The chair of the judges said, "Now to the onions. We were particularly impressed by the huge onion from Norman Busby, which is the clear winner."

Norman accepted his plaque and walked proudly away, showered with congratulations.

"I'll have the soup ready in an hour," Mary called to him. She ran a refreshments stall, with many local dishes and snacks with a rural theme. It was a tradition that a soup was made out of the prizewinning onion.

Later, Norman returned after being photographed for the local paper with his plaque. He took the ritual bowl of soup. Since by now he was quite hungry, he started to spoon it up enthusiastically. But something was wrong. It tasted terrible. He clutched his throat and felt a searing sensation as the liquid trickled into his stomach.

Mary, busy with her customers, shouted over her shoulder. "I didn't like to chop up your onion, Norman. It looked so good. So I used Jeremy's, which needed to be used before it went right off."

The Golden Ticket

"I'M BACK, GLADYS. THEY CERTAINLY DID ME PROUD," Terence said as he stumbled into their small bungalow.

"No need to shout, dear. You've obviously had a few drinks – unusual for you."

"Well, it was quite a do. They hired a room in The Kings Arms and lots of people came. The old man gave a speech and thanked me for my forty years' service – and guess what? He handed me a cheque for one thousand pounds from the company. Then Joe, you know, my boss, gave me a present from our department. A bit mysterious. It's in this gold envelope. He called it the Golden Ticket, and said not to open it until I got home."

"Come on. Let's see what it is. Might be a voucher for a nice trip to Majorca for us," Gladys said as she tore open the envelope. "Crikey. It's a ticket for a trial gliding lesson. That's not quite you, is it?"

"No, I was looking forward to a bit of time for hobbies, but not that. Bit of pottering in the garden. Regular walks. Maybe an occasional cruise with you, love. But gliding? I don't think so. I've never liked flying anyway."

Terence had been an effective middle manager in his company but had never wanted to "take chances with my career", as he put it. His uneventful working life was paralleled by the cosy domesticity of his marriage to Gladys. Consequently, he put the ticket aside, meaning to talk to Joe about replacing it with something safer.

Two weeks later, Joe phoned. "Terence, I'm going to my gliding club on Sunday. I could pick you up and take you for that taster session."

"Oh... Er... OK, what time?" Terence hadn't yet shaken off his habit of following Joe's instructions, and felt bound to agree to the arrangement.

On Sunday, Terence awoke to bright sunshine and blue sky with little wind – dashing his hope that the weather would give him an excuse not to go.

"Great day for your first flight," Joe said as they set off for the club.

After a briefing, Terence was seated ahead of Tom, the instructor who was taking him up. He saw that the glider was attached to a small plane ahead of them. His hands trembled as he clipped himself into the safety harness. Flight Control gave the signal to go and the plane's engine roared to a crescendo. Terence felt the glider being dragged along the grass at ever-increasing speed until it was lifted off by the climbing plane. He was surprised to feel rising excitement as the field dropped away below them. When they were at the right altitude, Tom released the towline and the plane peeled away with the cable trailing behind it.

As Tom manoeuvred the glider, Terence gasped at the sweep of the countryside below them. He was amazed by the almost total silence. There was just the faint whisper of the wind through the stays of the wings. He had never felt such exhilaration. His few flights in cluttered, noisy jets on his and Gladys's occasional package holidays had been mere irritations, but this was freedom. He felt like an eagle. Below, he caught sight of a bungalow just like his. It seemed incredibly small and insignificant. *Surely that can't be the limit of my experience for the rest of my life?* he thought.

"Your turn," Tom said through the intercom. "Put your hands on the controls and feel what I do."

After a short time, Terence sensed how easy it was to control the craft and he was allowed to take over.

"There's a good thermal on our left. Steer counterclockwise."

Terence did as suggested, and was thrilled to feel the glider float higher as he spiralled within the updraught. He began to feel at one with the craft. It was as if the wings were his.

He was very disappointed when Tom said, "Time's up. But you can feel the controls as I take her down."

As the glider approached the landing field, Terence was already a convert to gliding. It had taken his mind into another dimension, along with his body. He had sensed how limited his life had been, and was determined to change. He would soar above it by becoming a qualified pilot. The thousand-pound cheque would enable him to take the course he'd seen described in the clubhouse. Then he could fly solo regularly to build up his expertise. Maybe he could even become an instructor. These thoughts raced through his mind while the glider slid gracefully to a stop. Terence was almost overcome with emotion. He had never experienced ambition before.

The Story of an Hour

SALLY SAT FORLORNLY IN THE WAITING ROOM. *I MISSED the train by just a few seconds. There's not another one for an hour,* she fretted as she reached for her phone. "The damn battery's flat," she shouted in frustration. *I bet he won't wait.*

It had taken her two years to get over splitting from her husband. Finally, she had decided that, at thirty, she was far too young to remain single, so she had started looking for a partner online. After exchanging many emails, she had agreed to meet Rob. He seemed very much her type.

I wonder if he'll still be sitting in that cafe wondering what's happened to me? she thought. *But I'll take the chance and go.*

In the appointed cafe, Rob Wescot was waiting nervously. He had a copy of the *Financial Times* on the table. He had suggested this as a signal because, without admitting it, his online profile had used a photo taken ten years previously. After forty minutes he was about to depart, when he heard, "Good gracious, is that you, Rob? I haven't seen you since the reunion two years ago. What are you doing here?"

"Oh. Hello, Tim. I was meeting a friend but she doesn't seem to be coming. How are you?"

"Good, thanks. Is she your new girl? Last time we met, you and Suzy had just parted."

"Not exactly. Well, I might as well tell you. She was an online date, but obviously she has taken fright."

They chatted on for another ten minutes, and then, with sudden decisiveness, Rob stood up and shook hands with Tim, saying, "That's it. I won't wait any longer. She's obviously not coming. I'll leave you the *FT*. I've read the damn thing from start to finish."

With that, he left. Tim ordered his snack and settled down to read.

Shortly afterwards, he was interrupted by a young woman who rushed up to him and said breathlessly, "Thank goodness you are still here. I was sure you would have gone. You're not a lot like your picture but I don't think that matters."

"But I'm not..." began Tim. Then he thought that she was rather nice and maybe it would be unkind to disappoint her immediately, so he went on, "...bothered about waiting. The main thing is, you are here now."

Tim ordered her coffee and something to eat and they started chatting. After two hours, Sally suddenly noticed the time and said apologetically, "I'm terribly sorry; I've got to go. My last train."

"I'll walk to the station with you," he said as he helped her on with her coat.

Outside the station, there was a moment of uncertainty until Sally said, "That was very pleasant. Do you think perhaps we should meet again, Rob?"

"I would like to very much," he said as he gently kissed her on the cheek. "But would you mind if my name was Tim?"

the Birling Gap

THE SEA WAS POUNDING THE CLIFFS AS I SAT IN THE BIRLING Gap Cafe, having a well-deserved coffee after walking over the Seven Sisters cliffs. The cafe had been taken over by the National Trust and the refreshments were now much better. I thought of the rock cakes and the weak tea provided by the former proprietors. The teeth-challenging rock cakes could have been used to buttress the cliffs and save the coastguard cottages opposite.

"Mum, what happened to that bit outside where we used to sit with our drinks?" asked a little boy.

"It fell over the cliff," said his mum as she scrolled through the latest trivia on her mobile phone.

"Why did it do that?"

"I expect it was global warming or the ozone layer or something," she muttered, as she read the trending celebrity news.

A man in prepared-for-anything clothes turned to the boy. "Actually, it was caused by cliff erosion," he said. "The softer soil underpinning the chalk gets washed away by the sea, and so the cliff face falls down. One by one, the coastguard cottages are falling into the sea."

"Oh my God!" said the mother. "Beyoncé's done it again."

The warm conservatory made me drowsy, so I couldn't stop myself drifting off to sleep…

"What's that you say?" said Cottage Number 2, as she winked her shutters at me. "Shame about the erosion? I should say so.

We've been here for one hundred years but they do nothing to help us.

"Now you're asking how we got here. Well, we were built to look after some coastguards. They've long gone but we have had some famous friends living in us. That Barbara Castle's mother. John Bratby's wife – didn't see a lot of him – and Lord Howie of Troon. They tried to get us protected from the sea but a lot of us have been knocked down because the cliff edge still keeps getting washed away. The National Trust says that this place is special because they can watch erosion as it happens. How would they like it if we wanted to watch their stately homes being washed away? Eh?"

The house shifted sideways, arm in arm with its remaining companions, but, trembling with rage, it slipped and fell over the cliff.

Crash! I woke up with a start and looked around. Part of the outer wall of the cafe garden had fallen down. The boy shouted in alarm, while his mum took a picture with her phone. The depleted terrace of cottages opposite looked much the same, except that now I noticed the one I had dreamed about was separated from its neighbour by a vertical gap. Was that a cry of chronic pain I could hear, or just the wind blowing through the new stairway to the beach?

Betrayal

As he prepared to brief his latest PhD student, Professor Robert Tyler picked up a paper titled *Agnostic remedies for cancers*. He was startled to see the author's name – Dr Nicola Evans.

He was immediately back nearly twenty years to when she was his research assistant. He took her on as a recently qualified PhD. Her experience in immunology had been impressive. As they worked together, he found his normal quiet absorption responding to her vivacity and enthusiasm. He increasingly came to depend on her dedication and ability. They developed a productive relationship – far closer than any he could remember.

He recalled the critical night of their project. They had come to the laboratory to assess whether the drug they had added to a cancer cell culture had worked. Looking down the high-powered microscope, Robert shouted, "Nicola – it's working! The cancer cells are being destroyed! I'll project the image."

"It's wonderful. We've done it," she shouted as she looked at the screen. Then, in the elation which accompanies such rare peaks of achievement, they hugged each other. The hug turned into an embrace, and as they drew back, they kissed gently. They kissed again – hungrily this time – and he felt her whole body against his as he pressed against her; the lines of the cell image making camouflage on the back of his lab coat. They took their coats off and she leaned back against the bench, pulling him towards her. It felt as if they were one as they moved together. He slid his hands under her top and began to caress her breasts. More breathless kissing and fumbling with buttons; then suddenly she pushed him away. "Stop. I want this as much as you do, but Security will be here soon. We mustn't be caught out. The conference in Berlin is only a month away. We'll have to wait until then."

He remembered only the frustration of the wait. Any feelings of guilt regarding his wife or Nicola's partner were suppressed by his longing for her.

At the conference, they became passionate lovers, and, in the succeeding months, they managed to find opportunities to continue their relationship. With a feeling almost of pain, he remembered their last rendezvous. She seemed distracted as they made love. Afterwards, Nicola spoke of a friend who wanted her lover to divorce his wife and live with her. He was married with two young children. She asked Robert for his opinion.

They both knew that this was a coded plea. His answer was, "She should think carefully about it. Divorce can be very messy and leaves nobody any better off."

Soon after this, Nicola had moved to Canada to pursue her research. Robert was glad in one way. It had removed a major decision from him. But it was as if the temperature in the lab had fallen. Work was much less fun, and he ached from the loss of their intimacy.

Back in the present, he thought of his wife, Mary, and how he had never confessed his affair. Their marriage had been quietly successful and their children had grown up well. He was very grateful to her. But his guilt was less for her than for Nicola. She had left thinking he had been just an opportunistic lover.

He had often worried he had disrupted her life, but now he knew where she was, he could perhaps make up for that.

Back home, he chose a card with a medical theme and wrote anonymously, *I always loved you.*

She will know who sent it, he thought. *I'll address the card at the lab tomorrow.* Now he felt less remorseful about his relationship with Nicola, but guilty at being unfaithful to his wife once more.

"May I use your printer to print out my bridge results?" Mary shouted to Robert as she climbed the stairs to his study.

"Of course. Help yourself."

As she sat down at Robert's desk, she noticed, lying on top of it, a card with a picture of Madame Curie. She opened it and read the words, *I always loved you.* No signature.

How strange, she thought. *It can't be for me. He would have put 'Love from Robert' or something like that.*

Unsettled by this random find, her mind teemed with half-forgotten memories of conversations and events. Finally, she came to the conclusion that he must have been planning to send it to another woman. A woman with whom he had a relationship in the past. Mary's dejection at this conclusion quickly turned to rage. *I'll go down right now and have it out with him,* she thought. But her experience as a psychologist made her pause.

So, when she left the study, she shouted down, "I'm feeling a bit achy from my tennis this afternoon; I'm going to have a nice relaxing bath."

As she lay back amongst the foam, Mary started to organise the chaos of her thoughts.

Her mind focused on the time, nearly seventeen years previously, when Robert's work on the cancer drug had been at its triumphant peak. He had often been absent at the lab, and had been in great demand at conferences all over the world. She had put down their lack of lovemaking to the exhaustion that he was clearly suffering. He had returned exhilarated from that conference in Berlin. She supposed that the acclaim he had received there was responsible, but now she thought of it, didn't his assistant Nicola go too? Then there was the time in June of that year when he was supposed to be staying with a colleague in London. She had tried to contact Robert. She remembered the unsatisfactory telephone conversation:

"Hi, John. Sorry to ring so late, but Gemma is quite ill and I need to speak to Robert."

"Oh! Um... Hi, Mary. Sorry to hear that. Robert's not here at the moment. I think he must have gone down to the off-licence. I'll get him to ring you when he comes back."

She had been thinking, *Robert's not much of a drinker. That's a strange thing for him to do,* when he phoned back. It was odd. It sounded like a different phone – more echoey. Not that she thought much about that at the time. After she explained about Gemma's illness, he said, "I'll come back first thing. The trains are almost non-existent at this time of night." Hardly the concerned parent.

Finally, she remembered how glum he had been when Nicola announced she was going to Canada. It had taken him months to get back to his old self. Shortly before her departure, Nicola had visited their house. She was pale and hesitant and asked to speak to Robert. When Mary told her that he was out, Nicola had looked defeated and said, "What a shame. I had wanted to say goodbye – to both of you, of course." Then, after a polite exchange about plans, she had hurriedly departed.

Obviously, it was Nicola, Mary thought as she ran more hot water into the bath. *Fancy me not putting two and two together before. So the card is for her.*

Now Mary had to decide what to do. She tried to assess their marriage objectively. She now knew she had a husband who was feeling guilty enough about disappointing a past lover that he was seeking to reassure her. Good luck with that. But, apart from that brief period around 2002, their marriage had been successful. He was a little too serious at times, but his enthusiasm for sport and 'fresh air', as he termed it, had created enormous fun for them over the years and had been excellent for the children. Now the grandchildren were arriving, it had all started again and they were having a great time together.

As she dried herself and dressed, Mary made up her mind. She wouldn't make a big thing of Robert's folly, but she couldn't resist a minor revenge, so, when she joined him for a cup of tea, she said, "Thanks for the card, love. There was no need. I knew you loved me when you didn't leave us all those years ago."

Survival

FROM THE VERY BEGINNING, IT WENT WRONG, I thought gloomily as I waited for the train.

I had been due at a business meeting in Leeds at 10am, but to start with I slept through the alarm. Then I had to scrape thick ice off the car in the dark. However, after I had left a message to delay the meeting until twelve, I thought my problems were over.

With clear skies, it had been a very cold night, but it turned into a brilliant sunlit morning for early January. Although the M1 was still covered with a mixture of heavy frost and salt, it seemed to pose no problem, and I felt happy to be travelling on such a day.

But in an instant, disaster struck. As I overtook a lorry it threw slush right across my windscreen. I pressed the screen washer button. The washer fluid was frozen solid. The wipers just smeared the mush across the windscreen. The horror of what followed flashes once more through my mind.

All I can see are the white lines at the edge of the windscreen. I move into the centre lane slowly and carefully. Still not enough. Must get to the inner lane, but no chance – cars advancing there. The windscreen gets even more opaque as the following lorry flashes angrily. More pressure on the brake. *Smash*. The lorry hits. Seat back breaks. I am only supported by the steering wheel. Everything seems to happen so slowly. A graceful spin, and then *smash* as the car hits the central reservation. The pirouette continues. I come to rest, looking up at the roof of the car. Silence. Is this what heaven is like? No, it's hell. I can hear that, by sheer chance, there is a gap in the traffic, and I am lying in a stationary car on the motorway. Doubly lucky, I manage to get to the hard shoulder and every part of my body seems to be working. I walk back down the motorway, waving my scarf in warning. Then, out of the corner of my eye, I see a weird scene. My Rover headed north, exactly in the centre lane, but now the length of a Mini. A foolish young man has stopped his car immediately behind the wreck and is advancing towards the traffic, holding up his warning triangle like a medieval priest trying to keep Satan at bay.

This horrific accident must have taken only a few minutes, but it played out like a slow-motion film. Then time reverted to its normal pace as the police arrived. They quickly heaved the car to the side and interviewed me, with gentle regard for my shocked state. Eventually, the car and I were taken to a nearby garage. Now, standing on Leicester Station, clutching a cardboard box holding the residue from the car and my briefcase, I hope, when I arrive home, my wife doesn't think I've been made redundant.

A Travelogue: El Calafate Argentina

1st December 2000

The new disco was vast and had been fitted out very well. We were the first people to arrive, other than the people running it. So, with free drinks and smoked salmon sandwiches, we sat by a window with an impressive view of the town and the sun setting behind the hills. Reflected in the glass were the whirling lights and a great illuminated ball like they used to have at the Palais de Dance. This looked like a huge new planet in the sky. Then the moon came up and stars started to shine. The whole scene was like an interplanetary version of *Apocalypse Now*.

That morning we had been on a tour to the Moreno Glacier. We started out along steppe which was a little greener than the grass yesterday around the estancias – the former sheep farms – which are set amongst poplar and willow trees. We saw condors, ibises, eagles, geese with young goslings, and flamingos. The most notable was an eagle which was posing right by the road on the most picturesque tree stump it could find.

After we stopped for a break the guide made some maté (matez), which is made from an infusion of herbs in a special communal cup with a spout. It was passed around. I imagined tea made with mixed cooking herbs would taste similar!

The glacier was quite magnificent. Seventy-five metres high above the water and deep below. It is five kilometres across and thirty kilometres long. It reached the land on which we stood. The surface of the glacier was heavily folded, so that, as it came to its terminus, there were magnificent pillars of ice towering above the water. The ice groaned and cracked, and every fifteen minutes or so a chunk would fall with the sound of thunder into the lake. Sometimes these were minor falls down internal fissures, but on two occasions we saw a huge piece of the face crash into the water. The sun came out and the blue of the fissures became intense, in places coloured a deep azure. We spent two hours just gazing at the mighty edifice.

Haiku to the glacier:
With stealth and huge force
The glacier goes forward
To a noisy death

We had been persuaded by our guide to go for free to the opening of the disco on the promise that there would be a tango floor show about 10.30pm. That evening, after a very pleasant Italian meal, I had persuaded Gill that we should skip it and go to bed early because I had a headache.

Back at the hotel, the smartly dressed manager of the disco was waiting. Before I could go through the dying act, we were whisked into a swish car. All the guides turned up, and only eight other unconnected people like ourselves. No disco-dancing happened. Several times the manager came up to explain that they were waiting for more people before beginning the tango show, which eventually started at 12.30am. It was good – but was it worth waiting for?

When we left at 1pm he got us a car. As we passed the police and armed soldiers who had been assembled to contain the masses, I couldn't help thinking that I was a strange person to select as the 'face' to launch a disco. Did they imagine me telling all my hip friends about it as we drank our maté?

Nostalgia

"But, Grandad, that's just rose-tinted nostalgia," said Thomas after listening to old Joe's reminiscences.

"You can say that, Thomas, but things were a lot better in the '40s and '50s. There wasn't all this mad consumerism and teenagers suffering all sorts of syndromes. In our day we just got on with it." Old Joe poked his wood fire hard to add emphasis to his remarks.

Thomas was studying economics and history, and was particularly interested in the post-World War II years. "To start with, from the '40s right up to 1954, you had rationing. The government debt was two hundred per cent of GDP."

"That may be so, but we had a lot more freedom and we created our own amusement. Not like today, where young people can't concentrate on anything for more than five minutes."

"You might have had a lot of freedom, but I don't think your parents did. Your mum must have spent hours on Mondays scrubbing clothes with a washing board and soap. Your dad would have worked at least a forty-eight-hour week."

"I suppose you're right about that, but it was a healthy life. We didn't stick indoors. We were always out on the street playing with our mates."

"Very nice, but I wouldn't call it healthy. Most people in London heated their homes with coal fires. That meant that everywhere was black with soot and you had terrible fogs. I read that fogs shut down London and drove tens of thousands to an early death. Anyway, I've got to go home to do my homework. Thanks for the cake and the chat. I love talking to you, Grandad, but I think your nostalgia is very selective."

After Thomas left him, old Joe sat looking into the fire. "Nostalgia. Nostalgia." The more he said it, the more it sounded to him like something unpleasant, like neuralgia. He picked up his Chromebook – something Thomas had set up for him.

"At least there are some advantages to the modern age," he muttered as he searched for 'nostalgia'. On the first page, he was intrigued to see a piece titled *When nostalgia was a disease.*

Joe read that the term was coined by a Swiss physician in 1688. He described it as a disease like paranoia, but the sufferer was manic with longing, not perceived persecution. Soldiers were said to be particularly susceptible to nostalgia. Some were even sent home. It became an easy excuse, so the military decided to stamp it out. For example, in 1733 a Russian general told his troops that the first one to exhibit symptoms of nostalgia would be buried alive.

Joe thought about all this for a while and then sent an email to Thomas:

Dear Thomas,

> *Maybe you're right. See the article I've attached. Perhaps I'm a sufferer. I'll try it without the rose-tinted specs. In the words of the old joke, it's obvious that nostalgia isn't what it used to be! Come and visit me soon.*

Love, Grandad.

Saint Nicholas

Early one grey morning in April, Ron and Eric were peering out of the cabin of the small yacht that Eric had just bought.

"We have got to get off now. I promised I would pick my son up at Cowes this afternoon. It's a super high tide. We'll easily get out of the harbour."

Ron wasn't so sure. Neither had much experience of the sea, but he had agreed to help his mate collect his new boat.

"Look at that windsock almost blowing off its pole," he said doubtfully.

Eric was insistent, though, so they blundered out of Poole Harbour. They managed, with difficulty, to reef the sails and soon were well clear of the port.

Ron's conviction of their folly increased as he saw they were alone. Streaks of foam were blasted off the waves as they heaped up behind the twenty-eight-foot yacht carrying it forward in sickening surges. "We must go back," he shouted over the screaming wind.

"No. We'll stay close to the shore. This will blow itself out before long, I'm sure," insisted his friend.

With the south-west wind mostly behind them, they approached Hurst Point and turned into the entrance to the Solent. The peak tide which was surging through the narrow channel against the furious wind was creating massive waves. One heaved the boat right over. The sails, now flat to the sea, were driven down by the furious wind. The two friends were thrown into the cold sea, still harnessed to the boat overturned by a huge wave. Ron's harness strap was caught up, so he was dragged underwater each time a wave surged past the boat. Despite this, he managed to help Eric onto the upturned hull.

As he rose above the water once more, Ron gasped for air and, to his horror, saw the radio drifting off. He knew he couldn't survive much more of this water torture, but with a surge of relief, he remembered the Swiss penknife in his pocket. This enabled him to cut himself free and join his companion on the hull. There they could see they were the only idiots on the water and, as a punishment for their stupidity, they were drifting towards the Needles.

"You had better start praying to St Nicholas, the patron saint of sailors. We're going to be smashed to pieces," Ron informed Eric bleakly.

After hours alone on the sea, they were almost as cold as death. Their tenuous hold on the hull was becoming harder and harder to sustain. Then, miraculously, they saw a boat heading towards them. The crew shouted that they couldn't pick them up in such conditions, but they had already radioed a Mayday.

A mercifully short time later, a helicopter rescued them from the doomed boat. As Ron looked down on the hull, approaching its destruction, he made a promise to himself.

Since then he has become an expert seaman, but he has kept his promise. He has never sailed with Eric again.

The Sixth Impossibility

"The Truth Cafe is fabulous. It's the best around here. It's healthier than the Half Moon, although that's good if you're really hungry."

"OK. We'll go to your fab place," I replied. After an early morning visit to the gym, we needed some breakfast.

"I see what you mean by fabulous," I said as I looked at the choices on the Truth Cafe's menu.

"I'll get a Benny & Joon with bacon and hollandaise sauce," Geoff said to the waiter.

"A Weekend in Paris, please," I added. "And we'll both have a double espresso and a glass of water. I suppose because it's French toast they associated it with Paris. Wouldn't mind an actual weekend there, though."

As we waited for our order, we sorted out the football news first.

"Pity about Fulham. They lost to Reading in the play-offs. Could have got into the Premiership again."

"Well, what about Newcastle being promoted and Middlesbrough and Sunderland going back down? Mixed reactions in the North-East, I expect."

"I pity the clubs that go up. They're against the top teams with owners with bottomless pockets."

After that, the talk turned domestic. I told Geoff I might follow up the Paris idea and take my wife for a weekend. He said that sort of thing costs too much money. He has enough trouble keeping a lid on domestic expenditure. Geoff doesn't like spending money on anything when he can avoid it.

"Hey. Look at that," Geoff said as he looked around the cafe. "See what it says on that noticeboard?"

I read, *Sometimes I've believed as many as six impossible things before breakfast.*

"OK. Let's think of six impossible things that people have believed before *our* breakfast," I suggested.

"Right, for a start, I believed we might get our breakfast served quickly. I'm starving, but it's not going to happen," Geoff complained.

"The earth is at the centre of the universe. Your turn," I said.

"One day you think you'll be able to lift sixty kilos," Geoff said; rather cruelly, I thought.

"If you entangle two particles and take one to Australia, what you do to one will be instantaneously replicated on the other, despite Einstein's rule that you can't travel faster than the speed of light."

"Blimey. We're into quantum physics now, are we?" Geoff commented, before adding, "Elvis Presley is alive and well."

Our breakfasts finally arrived and we stopped our discussion to give our full attention to the much-anticipated food. After we had finished, we told the waiter we didn't want anything else and he produced the bill.

I was just thinking that we hadn't got the remaining impossible thing yet, when Geoff picked up the bill and said, "That's OK, I'll get this."

Geoff was always very careful with his money, so, astounded, I replied, "There you go – that's certainly the sixth impossible thing, but I have to admit I didn't believe it before breakfast."

Editorial note: The Truth Cafe does exist. It is on Fulham Palace Road near the Hammersmith flyover. Two of the menu choices are as described above, and the message about impossible things was recently chalked up on a board there.

A Father's Grief

LILA, LILA. HOW SOFT HER NAME SOUNDS," SAID
Stephan wistfully. It was the 30th October and he always
thought of Lila on the day he lost her. He imagined his
daughter as she would have been by now – a lively blonde-
haired five-year-old playing in her bedroom in a pretty dress.
He and Sophie would be downstairs getting her favourite tea
ready for her birthday. They would be chatting about the party
they had organised for her at the weekend.

Every year Stephan thought of her on that date, as well
as at many times in between. There was something about the
fantasy of her at five which was especially poignant. Lila's loss
had been a blow to Stephan from which he had never properly
recovered. Once more overcome by grief, he rested his head on
his arms and wept.

There was no birthday tea and Sophie wasn't downstairs. She
was no longer part of his life. Thinking of what had led to their
parting changed Stephan's sorrow to bitterness. A long-festering
resentment overcame him and he rang Sophie on an angry impulse.

"Soph. You know what today is, don't you?"

"Oh. Stephan, it's you. No, as a matter of fact, I don't."

"That really surprises me. It's the date we lost our child."

"We didn't *lose* our child, as you put it. We chose not to
have a child."

"*You* chose not to have our child. She would have been five
today."

135

"Stephan. How many times do I have to remind you? We didn't even know what sex it would have been, and anyway, you've got a very strange idea of a birthdate."

"I'm sure she would have been a little girl. I just felt she would have been. You killed her."

"OK, Stephan, this is the last time I'll answer your stupid romanticism about my abortion. At the time we were hardly more than teenagers. You were still at university. I had just started my career and couldn't manage a baby as well as the demands of the job which sent me all over the place. We discussed it many times. You said that it was my body. I would have to bear almost all the consequences, and so it was my decision. So I decided to terminate my pregnancy. That was what happened. I've moved on with my life. I suggest you do the same. Goodbye."

His anger spent, Stephan said plaintively into the silent phone, "But I didn't mean it, Sophie. She was my child too. I didn't mean it."

An Injection of Hope

"WHAT, ONLY FOUR JELLY BABIES?" I HEARD GILL SAY as she answered a call from Emily.

"That's all Alex had during the first part of the race," Gill told me, as we returned to watching the live finish of the Courmayear-Champex-Chamonix ultra marathon. "Apparently Emily met him at the refreshment point at forty-three kilometres and he had a couple of sandwiches there. Since then he's had to run another fifty-eight kilometres, but he should be through by now."

The top twenty-five elite runners had finished many minutes previously. After a pause, there was a burst of activity and we saw Alex come through in thirty-second place out of about two thousand entrants. The delay had been caused by a downpour which had turned the downward path into a torrent.

Alex knew the terrain well. He had spent five days running and exploring the area a month before the race – often sleeping under the stars.

He had always been a keen runner and was mad about the mountains around Chamonix. He was also in *The Guinness Book of Records* as the fastest fully clothed animal in a marathon (tiger: two hours, forty-eight minutes). So he might have been expected to do well, but the outstanding feature of the Mont Blanc achievement was that he has Type 1 diabetes.

I remember the year he was diagnosed. In just a few weeks he had degenerated into a gaunt shadow of himself. He was worried that he might have cancer. After much wasted Googling, he consulted his doctor.

Many tests later, he called us: "I've had some good news."

"Fantastic. What is it?"

"I've got Type 1 diabetes."

"You call that good news?"

"I certainly do. I can deal with that. I thought I had cancer."

The consultant tried to reassure him. "With care, you'll be able to live a fairly full life, but you'll have to give up serious running. Particularly in the mountains, as the insulin mustn't get too cold. And you'll have trouble keeping track of your blood sugar levels, so you could pass out with a hypo in a remote place with no help available." He then looked at Alex's expression and, with a sigh, added, "But you're not going to take a blind bit of notice of me. Are you?"

After this, Alex made his body a subject of detailed study. Frequent blood samples were taken; the carbohydrates in all his meals were weighed and the appropriate amounts of insulin injected. He also discovered that vigorous physical exercise was a great way of keeping blood sugar down, and it was easy to keep an insulin supply warm by body heat alone.

The first real test of his new regime was an ultramarathon in the Brecon Beacons. The course was seventy-six kilometres with many hills. He tested his blood sugar regularly to verify that his calculations were correct, but, of course, he had an emergency supply of jelly babies to compensate quickly for any sugar deficit. As he ran, he was once more enjoying the freedom of the hills. He thought of his wife, Emily, waiting for him at the end of the race. Running felt good and his energy level was high. He knew he was going to finish well up the field. Alex suddenly realised he had overcome the apparent constraints of Type 1 diabetes, and tears of joy flooded down his cheeks as he sped onwards.

Escape

By six that evening we were back home in our kitchen and everything looked the same. For a few moments, we looked around. There was comfort in the familiar scene. We live in a traditional cottage rather than the ultra-functional buildings which are normal these days. We liked the high mantelshelf with the wood-burning stove below. The lino floor with the traditional Victorian pattern and the old curios were all reminiscent of a loss which was more than fashion. A faded woven cloth covered the table.

"That wasn't too bad, was it?" said Lihwa with a look of relief. "I bet… What on earth are you doing?" she continued as I suddenly embraced her.

"I just wanted to give you a cuddle. You seemed so nervous for no reason," I said in a loud voice, and, as I pulled her tighter, I whispered in her ear, "I had to stop you mentioning names. That tea caddy has been moved and I can see a tiny camera set in the wall.

"Let's have a nice cup of tea," I said, as I placed a kettle on the stove, put some leaf tea in the old china teapot and replaced the caddy on the mantelshelf. Lowering my voice again, I whispered to Lihwa, "I've covered their camera as if by accident, but they can still hear us. Just follow my lead."

Speaking again in my public voice, as I now thought of it, I said, "We need to worry about money. We haven't worked for two weeks. Let's look at our accounts." I put our computer on the table, feigning not to notice that I had pulled the Unilink connector out.

They are definitely on to us, I typed, *otherwise they wouldn't have pretended that they were just asking routine questions. They banked on our coming back and giving the names of our resistance colleagues away as we chatted. While we talk as if we are dealing with our finances, I'll type instructions.*

"Wow, we'll have to stop spending on that," I said loudly.

I continued typing, deleting each paragraph as soon as Lihwa had read it. *As soon as they see I've covered the camera they'll be suspicious. This is what we must do.*

"We can't afford those. We'll have to find some work soon," she said with mock horror.

Pretend to call your mother and tell her you are worried about her heart and we're driving over to check up on her. We'll go to a safe house, I typed.

After Lihwa's call, we put the computer back, picked up our coats, and as we left, I said, "We'll leave the fire on. We'll be back in an hour or so."

Two hours later, there was a loud banging at the door. After a pause, it was kicked in and two Guardians of Right Thinking entered. In the kitchen everything looked the same, but for the kettle slowly cooling on the back of the stove.

The Little Red Book

ALBERT HALL WANDERED ACROSS THE LITTLE GARDEN which surrounded his block of flats, reading the morning paper. Ever since his parents had named him with a misguided sense of humour, he had lived the life of a downtrodden outsider. He felt at home in the garden, which, he thought, like him, lacked any human care and few people used it. As usual, the garden was deserted – except for a red book which lay sunning itself upon the gravel path. As Albert noticed this he thought it was completely out of keeping with its dowdy surroundings. He was about to kick it into some scrubby grass when an idea occurred to him, and he picked it up for a closer look. It had many pages, all of which were clean. "Just what I needed," he said to himself. "Now I'll be able to really get the buggers."

The block consisted of thirty-two flats and Albert occupied the ground-floor flat nearest the main entrance. He noted every coming and going of his neighbours, of whom he thoroughly disapproved. He made mental notes about their behaviour in the belief that, with enough evidence, he could get the landlord to get rid of them. Because he had difficulty remembering all his observations, the idea of writing a detailed dossier in his new notebook appealed to him.

As soon as he arrived home, he divided the pages up, giving each flat its own section.

Over the next few months, he accumulated observations, with a summary for each flat which was enhanced from time to time.

> *Flat 9. Miss Elthwaite. Several men every night and occasionally women. She has some stamina, that woman, but this is no place for a hussy like that to run a brothel.*
>
> *Flat 22. Mr Morrison. Not here very often but keeps a woman in his flat. Not his wife, but he says it's his sister. I think it's his floozy.*
>
> *Flat 15. Johnny Lake. Always having pizza delivered. No one likes pizza that much. Bet he is getting drugs from a fake delivery boy.*

Albert had copious detail on all his neighbours but hardly spoke to them. Their ways of life repelled him. Then one day, a single mother with a five-year-old daughter moved into the flat next to him. His notes on her were uncompromising:

> *Flat 4. A single woman with a child. Expect that she'll attract all sorts of undesirables as so-called boyfriends. Dreadful hair – multicoloured plaits – and a dress like some Middle European peasant.*

The red book allowed a greater focus for Albert's antipathy towards his neighbours, and his notes, based purely on observation, cemented his poor view of those around him. Then one day there was a knock on his door. When he opened it, he saw the child from the next flat standing there meekly.

"Hello, Mr Hall. Mummy said could you come to a meeting in our flat on Thursday about improving the neighbourhood?"

"No, thank you very much," Albert said brusquely as he

shut the door firmly. But afterwards, he felt a rare moment of compassion. After all, the girl was only the messenger.

In the weeks that followed, Albert noticed many changes. The woman next door had organised a band of volunteers who were transforming the garden – trimming bushes, planting flowers and collecting rubbish. It actually began to look rather nice. Other projects followed, such as repainting the corridors between the flats. It made the place much more welcoming, Albert had to concede. Following all this activity, the little girl knocked on his door again.

"Mummy said would you like to come to the party for the flats on Saturday? It will be in the garden."

Albert didn't want to be as rude to the girl as he was on her last visit, so he said, "What's your name?"

"Millie, and Mummy's name is Emelia Most people call her Emmy."

"OK, Millie. Tell your mum that I'll come if I can," he replied, with no intention of attending.

Early on the day of the party, the garden was transformed. Bunting was hung between the few trees. The bushes were given coloured baubles and a barbecue was set up with a few small tables and chairs around it. Albert was so busy spying on these preparations that he forgot to go for his newspaper until the event had started. Nervously, he tried to edge around the garden to get to the newsagents, but before he got very far his neighbour blocked his path.

"I'm so glad you decided to come, Mr Hall. Let me get you a drink."

Unable to think of an excuse, he allowed himself to be settled in a chair near the centre of the event. One by one the neighbours sat with him and chatted. He was astonished at what he found out. Far from being a woman of ill repute,

Miss Elthwaite was a sports masseur. Her clients came in the evening after their work or training. Mr Morrison's sister really was staying in his flat because she had lost her own and had nowhere to go. He had to work far away so wasn't there every day. Johnny Lake was a computer geek who was trying to create some obscure financial system that Albert couldn't understand. He didn't have any imagination left over for eating anything other than pizza. Albert's neighbour of the flaming plaits worked in the costume department at the National Theatre. Her husband had died of cancer three years before.

As he heard these stories, Albert had to admit to himself that he had been completely mistaken and, despite accurately recording many innocent activities, had come to the wrong conclusions entirely.

After the party, he became good friends with Emmy and Millie. He volunteered to help in the garden, where he often chatted to his neighbours. He began to see in their reaction to him a respect which until then he hadn't even given himself. The little red book went out with the rubbish.

The Seeds of Doubt

MRS FINCH WAS BUSY DECORATING FOR CHRISTMAS.

"Come and help me with the nativity set, Josh," she called over her shoulder to her son – a smart little boy of eight.

Reluctantly, he put down an Agatha Christie novel – his current reading obsession – and joined his mother. Josh hadn't thought about the scene before. It was just there every year.

"Are Mary and Joseph Jesus's mum and dad?"

"Well, yes. That is to say – sort of," replied his mum. "Jesus is really the son of God."

"So he's got God's DNA, then," said Josh, pleased he had remembered a book he had read called *Where We Come From*. He wasn't clear on all the details, though, so he went on, "Does that mean God kissed Mary? Didn't that annoy Joseph?"

Mrs Finch's forte was certainly not theology, so she said, "You'll understand when you are older."

By now Josh knew that this sort of response meant a grown-up didn't know or was avoiding answering. Father Christmas and the Tooth Fairy hadn't stood up to his extreme curiosity either.

"What have those old men got in their hands?" he went on, to humour his mother.

"Gold, frankincense and myrrh. They're gifts for the baby Jesus."

"What's frankincense and myrrh?"

"Myrrh is a sort of oil and frankincense is a perfume."

"Was the perfume because the stable smelt bad with all the animals, and what was the oil for?"

His mum sighed and said, "Get your dad to take you to football training. I'm too busy to keep answering all your questions."

In the car, thinking his father might be more forthcoming, Josh asked him, "Is baby Jesus the same Jesus the vicar said gave his life for our sins?"

"Yes. That's right."

"What are sins?"

"A sin is doing something that's not right."

Josh sat in silent awe at the thought of such drastic punishment. He only got his pocket money stopped when he was naughty.

At the park, Josh waited with his friend Ahmed for their turn at dribbling practice. "Do you have a nativity set in your window for Christmas?" he asked.

"No. We're Muslims. We have our big celebration at Eid, not Christmas. Jesus isn't the son of Allah. Mary had Jesus under a palm tree in the desert. Mohammed is the greatest prophet anyway. Peace be upon him."

On the way back home, Josh told his dad about his chat with Ahmed and asked, "How do we know that what we say is right and Muslims are wrong? S'pose they are right, or the Buddhists we learnt about at school are?"

"Well, there are different levels of truth, but God has given Christians the best knowledge."

At home, Josh sat quietly for a long time and then, with a puzzled frown, said to his dad, "I thought about what you and Mum said but I still can't figure out what it all means."

The Benefit of Euthanasia?

I FLOAT AS IF UNBOUNDED BY TIME AND SPACE. I SUPPOSE I have a body, but cannot feel it. No clues reach me about time. In the City, a flash of blinding pain hit me. Then nothing until I was in a swirling mist – a fog of colours – through which I emerged as if down a tunnel to this strange aerial existence. I was at a loss as to who, where or even what I was at first. Was I a brain being manipulated by some superior power? Was I human – but if so, where was my body? Then I remembered what that French guy said: I think, therefore I am.

Good enough for me. Slowly, I realised. I am Mark Sinclair, the successful banker.

After an uncountable time, I began to hear sounds. At first, just beeps, and then muffled voices. I could tell I was in a hospital. All I need now is to get out of this bind. Then I can pay some expert to fix me up.

I hear voices again, clearly this time. Perhaps I can find a way to tell them I am here. I wish I had read that book about the Butterfly Bell.

"Thank you for coming, Mrs Sinclair. This is a difficult time, I know, but we have to deal with your request for a clinical review of your husband Mark's condition."

Must be a consultant at the hospital.

"There are three possibilities. A coma, what is popularly called locked-in syndrome, or a persistent vegetative state. In our opinion, the last is the most likely. He cannot even move his eyes or any facial feature."

"Don't kill Daddy." *I hear the voice of my lovely Lucy.* "I am sure he is in there somewhere. We must find a way to get him out."

As her voice gets louder, I imagine her touching my face and stroking my hair. My wife speaks.

"I have talked this over with Tarquin, who is a very good friend of us both."

What is she doing talking about me with that touchy-feely toad who has wheedled his way into our family?

"We have both been assured by Mark that if he were completely immobilised in any way, he would not want to be kept alive artificially. So, with great sorrow, I have to ask you to remove life support. How long will it take to… to end?"

The miserable, conniving bitch. She just wants all our money and that unctuous, fawning bastard in bed with her.

They've opened the door. They are going away, but I still hear the consultant.

"Just a day or so. We will give him something to ease his passage in case there is any residual distress."

I'm sacrificed to convenience and lust. Come back. Come back. Don't abandon me. There must be a way of getting me out. I am alive – come back!

Harmony

WE FIRST MET WHEN WE WERE TRYING TO FIND THE *same book*, said the headline in the regular romantic feature in the Saturday paper.

"I don't know why they do it," Jonathan muttered. "Suppose it makes them feel like celebrities. Five minutes of fame. Come to think of it, though, that's almost the way I met Sally."

A year earlier he had been feeling very sorry for himself. His long-term girlfriend had recently announced that she didn't find him exciting enough and departed. The people in the neighbouring flat complained again about his piano playing, so he couldn't even console himself with music. Then his car had broken down and he couldn't afford to get it fixed. The reality was too much, so he fell back on fantasy. He had always wanted a caravan. The sense of freedom attracted him. He decided to go and have a browse in the central library. Without a car, it was an unlikely ambition, but at least he could dream.

After a quick search of the index, he found just what he was looking for. *Caravans and Caravanning: The Best Vans and Where to Park Them*. But when he located the book he found that someone was already in that section. Jonathan hovered politely nearby, pretending to read another book until she moved. He couldn't help observing the girl, though. She wasn't dressed very fashionably. Rather dowdy, he thought, but despite this, she had an unconscious grace. She replaced a book and selected another. This seemed of more interest, so she took it to a nearby table and started to read, with an earnest frown behind her heavy glasses.

By now Jonathan was very interested to know what had caught her eye, so he made as if to extract a book from the shelf behind her. To his amazement, she had *Caravans and Caravanning*, and didn't look as if she was going to give it up, so Jonathan abandoned the idea of borrowing it and continued to browse at random. He found the quiet of the library and the smell of polish and books very calming.

As he neared the sheet music section, to the annoyance of a dozing pensioner he suddenly said, "Damn the neighbours. I'm going to get a new piece to work on."

A glimmer of sun penetrated the mullioned windows of the old library; a clue unconsciously picked up by Jonathan. *I wonder if they have Beethoven's 'Spring Sonata'?* he thought.

As he entered the music section there was the same girl with 'his' book tucked under her arm, again apparently in the way.

I won't take any chances this time, he told himself as he reached past her for the music.

"Oh! That's what I was after," she said. "I just fancied getting to grips with the violin part."

"Well, what a coincidence. I was after the piano part. Looks like our needs are complementary. Suppose I take it out and lend you the violin part?"

"Good idea. Let's have a coffee somewhere and arrange the detail."

In the cafe, when he returned from getting the coffees, he saw she had started to read the caravanning book.

"That's just the book I came to get."

"Why, what's your interest in caravans?"

"Peace and quiet and no neighbours complaining. But unfortunately, I don't have one and my car's out of action."

"Shame. I've got a nice little caravan which I pull with an old Land Rover. I wanted the book to plan where to take it next."

"So why did you decide on the 'Spring Sonata'?"

"Oh. I play the violin with a small string orchestra but I really fancied trying something more challenging. So I thought I would prepare that. I hope I can find a pianist to accompany me."

The conversation continued and Jonathan became more and more intrigued. "We haven't introduced ourselves – Jonathan," he said.

"Sally – pleased to have met you. Why don't I show you my caravan? I live only a couple of miles away."

Jonathan was very impressed. The caravan was quite small, but well equipped. "But why have you got that keyboard?"

"Well, I'm not much of a pianist but I like to tinker a bit. I say, why don't we play together? I can park the caravan in a quiet corner of a field and we can play with nobody to worry us."

So the following weekend, Jonathan found himself playing the keyboard to accompany Sally's violin.

After they had played for a couple of hours they stopped for coffee and a biscuit, and Jonathan felt happier than he had for years. They started again, but after a few minutes, Sally stopped and said, "You know that bit where we take turns at playing *d-d-didi-didi-didi-da-da*? I don't think we've got the balance right."

She leaned across to point out the passage with her glasses. Jonathan felt the warmth of her body and her arm on his shoulder. She turned her face towards him as she spoke, and Jonathan noticed the energy and enthusiasm of her mobile features and dark brown eyes no longer hidden by her glasses.

"I'm sure we can get that right," he replied. "I'll reflect your rhythm. Let's start from Bar 38."

Now they live together, and are still happily pursuing their mutual hobbies. If anything arises which threatens their harmony, one or the other of them will say, "Hang on. Let's start from Bar 38."

Great Expectations

Stealing from his mother's house, Cedric came across a handwritten note sticking prominently out of the milk bottle on the doorstep: *No milk until Wednesday.*

Two days away. Silly not to notice that before. There was no need to creep around worrying she would catch me, he told himself.

Emboldened, he went back into the house to continue his search. It was a substantial house in Putney – a symbol of the wealth his father had accumulated as a trader in the boom days of oil. His expectations of inheriting substantial wealth, as well as frequent 'loans' which were never repaid, had sapped Cedric's ambition and he had drifted from one unpromising job to another.

Now he was really worried. After the minimum of mourning following his father's untimely death, his mother had embarked on an uncharacteristically flamboyant life of foreign holidays and lavish entertainment. But what had really alarmed Cedric was her relationship with Darren.

Now more confident, Cedric strode into the capacious lounge. There on the grand piano, he noticed two new pictures. In pride of place was a picture of his mother's recently acquired handbag dog, Flossie. Then there was one of her with Darren sitting in her lap, obviously after a night of celebration.

"He's nothing but a money-grubbing toy boy," Cedric uttered in a venomous whisper. "I must find that will to make sure he hasn't replaced me."

With renewed energy, he continued his search through every room of the house.

After several hours he hadn't found the will or anything indicating that it would favour Darren. Consequently, Cedric had to return to his small flat in Battersea, still unsure of his prospects.

Two days later, he received a call from his mother.

"Cedric, I think we need to have a little chat. Can you come round this evening?"

"Yes, certainly, Mum," he replied, optimistic that she was, at last, going to confirm his place in her will.

"Darren is out so it's just you and me," she said after he had arrived and they were seated in the lounge.

"You are a naughty boy," she went on. "You have been snooping around here while I was away. Darren put one of those security systems in for me. You look very good on screen, I have to say. What on earth were you after?"

Thinking quickly, Cedric answered, "I've been very worried about you and Darren, Mum. He's twenty years younger than you and I thought he must surely be after your money. I was merely trying to find out if he had succeeded. I wouldn't want you to be duped by such a character."

"Oh! There's no need to worry on that score, dear boy. I know what sort Darren is. If anybody is taking advantage it's me. He won't get a penny. I have left it all to a dogs' retirement home so Flossie will be looked after when I'm gone."

The Same Old Story

MILES BARNARD LOOKED UP AS THE OFFICE BOY placed yet another lead beside his typewriter. He adjusted his green eyeshade as he returned to pounding out a story on his trusty Remington. The work of an investigative journalist was never—

"Miles. Miles! You're not listening. The daughter of the owner of the Grand Hotel is marrying the son of our local MP this afternoon. A quarter-page with photo. It's got good local appeal."

"OK. I'll get on to it," Miles replied to the editor/senior reporter/marketing manager of the *Bridport Post*.

Brought back sharply from imagining himself as James Cagney in *Blood on the Sun*, he looked gloomily around the cluttered Portakabin which now formed the entire premises of the paper. His illusion about his role had been boosted by his previous week's story. He had been sent to cover a council meeting and had been told by the opposition of a discrepancy in the waste disposal account. His piece, titled *Is this the iceberg of the tip?*, had given rise to some angry correspondence about the council in the letters page. Miles, who had been inspired by the film *All the President's Men*, had imagined that this scoop could be the start of a brilliant career.

Sitting at the back of St Margaret's Church, Miles was already keying his piece into his laptop. *The organ burst into life as the beautiful bride…* While he typed, he reflected that it was the same old story. He could almost create it from a standard fill-in-the-blanks article.

In the moment of silence as the couple stood together at the altar, he overheard a whispered conversation in the lobby.

"I can't believe he's going through with it. They say he's supposed to have got married while he was working in the States."

This could be my very own Watergate, Miles thought, as he eagerly began an online search. As he looked through the results, he heard the vicar ask, "First, I am required to ask anyone present who knows a reason why these persons may not lawfully marry, to declare it now."

I can't say anything without more evidence, Miles thought as he continued to wade through the long list.

He had to stop himself from shouting out in triumph when he read:

In a quiet ceremony, Teresa Ann Leblanc and Hugo Franklin Bolton were married in a civil ceremony in…

That's it. There can't be many people with that name. Too late to speak up now, though.

Miles hurried out of the church as the vicar announced, "In the presence of God, and before this congregation, Amanda and Hugo have given their consent and made their marriage vows to each other…"

Back at the paper's meagre HQ, Miles set about confirming the facts of his story. He called the number of the local MP, Douglas Bolton. As he expected, there was no reply, so he left a message saying he had important questions about his son's wedding. Then he sent an email to the MP's agent:

> *Miles Barnard — investigative reporter for the Bridport*
> *Post — here. A Hugo Franklin Bolton was recorded as*
> *marrying one Teresa Ann Leblanc in San Diego two years*
> *ago. Can you confirm that this was not the son of our*
> *MP? There is no record of that marriage being dissolved.*

He then completed his report on the wedding in anticipation of the denial he expected, including a *But there are questions to be answered...* section giving details of the marriage he had unearthed.

After he had sent the report to the editor, he sat back in his chair and placed his feet on his desk, dreaming of the syndication of his story in all the major dailies.

An hour later the editor burst through the door. Miles stood up, expecting to receive his congratulations, but instead, the editor shouted, "What on earth are you doing? I've heard from Bolton's agent about some cock-and-bull story you are peddling. Don't you realise that eighty per cent of our readers are strong supporters of our MP, and, for good measure, the Grand Hotel is our biggest advertising customer? If there's any truth in that rumour they are not going to hear it from the *Bridport Post*. That would be asking for trouble."

A Fatal Memory

It was dawn in mid September 1985. Jack Lee waiting with his suitcase for the lift to arrive. He was returning home after the Canadian veterans' meeting at Newhaven. Jack found these reunions helped ease his recurrent nightmares of Dieppe, Sicily and Juno Beach, and he always stayed in Eastbourne near where he had been based in the war. But that morning, he was troubled by something lurking deep in his mind.

Jack told himself he was being a stupid seventy-year-old as he left the Grand Hotel and turned west to take the scenic route to the airport. But as he drove through East Dean, the sense of unease increased. His heart beat loudly and depression seemed to seep, like a black cloud, into his whole being. With difficulty, he drove on.

As he approached Exceat with the rising sun lighting the sky beyond Beachy Head, a ghastly memory tumbled out of Jack's unconscious mind like the contents from a broken suitcase. He parked the car, without any awareness of doing so, as the fateful morning in September 1940 flooded back as if it were just the day before.

He sees himself, then. A twenty-five-year-old major in charge of the company camped on the hill above the Cuckmere Valley. He is standing at peace as he waits for military transport. He observes the neat efficiency of the tents of his company on the hill above the river. A volunteer from Niagara Falls, he has progressed rapidly in the fast-growing Canadian Army. Here, he loves the peace of the green hillsides and the contrast of the lazy meanders of the Cuckmere with the raging torrent close to his home town. He feels a light breeze coming off the sea, bringing with it the smell of seaweed and the earthier smell of vegetation rotting in the imprisoned byways of the river. He looks up at the swallows preparing for their migration across war-torn Europe.

It is all so tranquil, he muses. *That old Home Guard guy who told us the Jerries flew through here must have been thinking of the docks at Newhaven.*

A winking light out at sea catches his eye. The hull of a ship? The sun striking a wave? No – it is six sunlit dots rapidly parting and increasing in size.

Our boys flying back to base, I expect, he thinks.

The German fighter-bombers come in low over the sea. In a cacophony of noise, Jack throws himself to the ground. Relieved as they pass over, he stands again and sees to his horror that they have wheeled around and are coming back down the valley. With cannons blazing, they strafe the camp and drop bombs upon it. Jack sees the utter devastation of his company. He shouts in fury at the waste of so many colleagues, slaughtered in their beds without even having the chance to fight for their lives.

Later, a policeman, stopping by the poorly parked car, found Jack dead in his seat; his hands stretched forwards as if to ward off an attack and his lifeless eyes staring at some unimaginable disaster.

Editorial note: The above event is commemorated by a plaque erected in 2006 at Cuckmere Haven. It is based on the testimony of an agricultural worker in the Home Guard in 1940 – now deceased. Extensive inquiries have not succeeded in verifying this single eyewitness account.

Sometimes You Just Know

"THERE'S SOMETHING I'VE BEEN MEANING TO TELL you," Helen said as they paused at the door of her room.

Michael and Helen had walked along the open balcony of their hotel after leaving the room of a colleague, where they had shared a coffee with the other team members. Michael was the partner responsible for their project and had taken them out for dinner before his meeting with the client the next day. Dinner had been followed by an unscheduled visit to a nightclub.

She spoke very quietly so Michael had to lean in closely to hear properly. There was a chill in the air, and he could feel the contrast with the heat from her body. His normal reserve had already been unsettled earlier in the evening when he had danced with her at the club. Perhaps she wanted to talk about the project. He thought that was certain to spoil his relaxed mood, so he said, "Let's talk about it tomorrow after my meeting. I'll say goodnight, then." On an impulse, he kissed her lightly on the lips, awkwardly balancing his new awareness of her with respect for their business relationship.

He had no idea how it happened, but the cautious kiss turned into a passionate embrace. She pulled him urgently into the room. Too absorbed even to shut the door, they became lost in overwhelming desire.

Afterwards, they lay close together and talked for hours. Their involvement was so intense that they didn't even notice the gentle clatter of the door they'd left open.

This girl is so easy to talk to, thought Michael, who had recently left a relationship full of mute incomprehension. *I seem to want to tell her everything about my life and desires. She talks freely about herself, too. I like what I hear very much.*

Towards dawn, they agreed that Michael should go to his room for the sake of appearances. As they were kissing goodbye, he remembered her statement, which now seemed an age ago.

"What did you want to tell me?" he asked.

"Oh. It doesn't matter now," Helen replied with a happy smile.

Many years later, now retired, Michael sat looking out of the window of his house in the Lake District.

Why on earth am I suddenly thinking about all that? he asked himself, before returning to an article about trends in business. He read that companies were often issuing rules about employees' personal choices. He remembered how they had long influenced dress. Now they were increasingly frowning upon romantic relationships between members of staff – making these immediately reportable to the HR department.

So that's what took my mind back forty years.

His thoughts, drifting back once more over those years, were interrupted by a voice from the next room.

"Want a cup of tea, love?"

"Yes please, Helen," he replied, thinking that what they had shared all those years ago couldn't possibly have been wrong.

My Mysterious Neighbour

I LEFT THE NATIONAL THEATRE DEEP IN THOUGHT. The play, titled *Another World*, had dealt with the topic of jihad, with particular emphasis on ISIS in Syria and the impact on attitudes to Muslims in the West. The stories of the women who told of their loss of sons who had disappeared to Syria were harrowing. Alongside this was the message that we in the West added to the feelings of alienation among some young Muslims with the standard assumption that *Muslim = likely terrorist*.

As I had to go down to Bristol that evening, I took the Tube to Paddington. Sitting on the train, my mind unfortunately dwelt on the Underground bombings of 2005. The victims then had presumably had no fear of young men with beards and rucksacks. They had been accepted as normal travellers, but they had an extreme loathing of our society and wrought a terrible revenge. Such atrocities naturally made us wary. Unfortunately, most terrorists are Muslim. Shouldn't mainstream Muslims distance themselves from the extremists more vocally?

Once on the concourse at Paddington, I turned my attention to getting a coffee and finding a seat where I could read the evening paper in view of the train departure display. Out of the corner of my eye, I saw a figure dressed in black sit down next to me. She answered an exotic ringtone and, although the language was unfamiliar, it was clear she was having a tense conversation with someone at the other end.

This caused me to look at her properly for the first time. She was little more than a girl, slight and modestly dressed, including a hijab. Her body language displayed extreme stress. As she talked, she gripped the straps of her backpack tightly and seemed to gesture toward it as she spoke.

My examination was interrupted by two heavily tattooed young men who had obviously been in the station bar far too long. They staggered past and, catching sight of my neighbour, one said, "Bleeding Muslim. Why don't you go back to your own fucking country?"

"Yeah. Take that fucking rag off your head, you Arab bitch," added his companion.

She abruptly closed her phone and tried not to take any notice of them, but I could see she was now even more upset.

"Don't pay any attention to them," I ventured. "They are just ignorant drunkards."

She managed only a strangled sound which might have been thanks, but equally could have been a curse in another language.

My mind went straight back to the play. Wasn't this the message it had conveyed? It was yobbos like those men who made the situation much worse and caused young Muslims to be alienated from general society. Then I felt a touch on my sleeve.

In broken English, my mysterious neighbour said, "Please look after bag. I go to toilet"

Fraud

"THERE SEEMS TO BE A MAJOR DISCREPANCY IN YOUR stocks," said the rather pompous auditor who had recently been appointed. "I'll have to dig deeper."

The MD of itmustbetime.com thought they had got along quite well without auditors until then. For him, the important thing was that they were growing at thirty per cent per annum and making a good profit. He suspected that this self-important little man was just making expensive work for himself.

"OK. I'll get Howard to help you. He looks after replenishment with our watch suppliers as well as the stockroom, so don't take up too much of his time, please."

The back office was run by Sally. With her assistant, Jo, she maintained the accounts while Howard kept the goods flowing. Sally and Jo often told stories about their lives outside the firm, but they never asked Howard about his. He only ever took holiday as single days. Once Sally had inquired about one of these. This elicited a boring account of a visit to an antique watch auction. It seemed Howard was addicted to collecting old watches. She never asked again.

The business of the company continued in its frenetic way, now frequently interrupted by the auditor.

"You'd think that we hadn't a business to run. Now he's asking us to dig out all our archived records," Sally said after the first week of the audit.

"Yes. I agree," said Howard in a rare utterance. "He's making my life hell. How does he expect me to keep up with demand if I have to talk to him all the time? He's saying the stocks are all wrong. I bet that's because in the early days we didn't have good records and that's got carried over right up to now. I can't take much more of this."

Sally thought this was just a temporary reaction. After all, they were all under pressure. So she was surprised when Howard asked to see her privately the next day. He gave a month's notice and, proffering a doctor's note, said he was suffering from stress and so asked to be allowed to leave immediately.

At a hastily organised leaving presentation, they gave Howard a parting gift.

"We're very sorry to see you go, Howard," Sally said, finding it difficult not to be resentful at being left in the lurch at such a crucial time. "We wish you better and hope you are happy in whatever you do next."

"I never meant to leave you," he replied. "I've enjoyed my time here, but it all got too much for me recently."

The next day, the auditor managed to access Howard's computer. In doing so, he found that Howard had been misappropriating some of the new stock and selling it on EBay under the pseudonym 'Timelord'. With further investigation, records of a valuable antique watch collection he had accumulated over several years were also uncovered.

They are still looking for Howard.

Nocturnal Animals

It was an unusually warm evening in New York. Carl walked slowly up Greenwich Street – not to enjoy the night air, but just to delay his arrival at the diner where he worked. He called it 'Phillies', for the advert above the window, as it had no other name. As usual, he was on the night shift. As he passed the brownstone shopfronts, he brooded again about his dilemma. Events around the world were looking increasingly grim, with the Germans in Europe at war with England and Russia, and the Japanese causing more and more trouble in the Far East. He knew he was liable for the draft, and, if the US got involved, he might be away for years. So he had drifted from one short-term position to another. The night shift at Phillies wasn't ideal, but it was the best he could get.

Approaching the diner, he saw the familiar spill of the fluorescent light over the sidewalk, making it look like an oasis amidst the surrounding gloom.

"Night, Joe," he said as he passed the day man. "Everything OK?"

"Bit quiet. Nothing unusual. Nobody in at the moment."

A short distance away, Frank Leach was anxiously walking up from the docks.

"I hope those guys know what they're doing," he muttered to himself. "Those ships ain't easy to get into with the military all 'round. If they get caught I'm history."

On Greenwich Street he passed a parked Buick, in which the occupants were having a heated argument. "At least I don't have woman trouble," he told himself as he entered the diner, ordered a coffee from Carl and sat, hunched and wordless, at the counter, waiting.

Back in the car, the couple were now sitting in glum silence. With a hopeful smile, the man turned to his companion.

"Betty, you can't blame me. I didn't know she was going to cancel her visit to her mom, did I?" he said, placing his hand experimentally on her thigh. "I'm as upset as you are. It was a great chance to have a bit of fun." His hand moved tentatively higher.

"Get your dirty hands off me, Floyd," his companion shouted. "If you wasn't the cheapskate you are, you would have fixed us up with a hotel room. I'm fed up with sitting in this old wreck you call a car. Let's go into that diner and at least have a sandwich and a coffee or something."

Carl looked up as they entered, blinking in the glare of the lights.

"Two sandwiches. Ham on rye, black and a white coffee," demanded the man brusquely.

Despite his attitude, Carl was glad of something to do, so he quickly filled the order.

"What are you doing tomorrow night?" the man ventured in a whisper.

"None of your business," the girl hissed. "Keep your beaky nose out of my affairs. When you start treating a girl right I might feel like telling you." After this brief exchange, they sat in stony silence, looking straight ahead.

Carl was a handsome young man who would have preferred to be out enjoying himself like other eighteen-year-olds.

Why don't some nice girl come in? It would be a break from these weird nocturnal animals, he thought, feeling pleased to have remembered that description from *National Geographic.* Then, with a shiver, he glanced outside. There was that man again, leaning against a shop opposite, busy with his notebook.

What the heck does he want? he thought. *Is he casing the joint? Not much to rip off here. Perhaps he's a private eye after those two, or maybe that other guy. He don't look up to much good.*

Shortly afterwards, the pair left without exchanging another word. The lone man sat over his one coffee for three hours, becoming increasingly agitated until, finally, he rushed out. Carl cleared up the remains of their meagre orders, wiped down the cherry-wood counter, turned out the lights and, after locking the door, started to walk back down Greenwich Street. As he hurried to catch the El, he saw the man who had so unsettled him pocket his notebook and walk off briskly into the night.

Soon afterwards, Carl was drafted into the US Army and he didn't see New York again for six years. His life before going to war was completely forgotten. He had no idea that Edward Hopper, the mysterious stranger, early in 1942 had completed his picture of a garishly lit diner, titled *Nighthawks.*

The Prophecy

IN JUNE 2000, RICHARD NOONE WAS THE WORLD'S MOST disappointed man. He had written a book explaining that the end of the world would happen in May 2000, owing to an alignment of the planets with the earth. Armageddon was postponed once again and Richard's reputation as a reliable prophet of doom – always dubious – was at a nadir. In fact, he became a figure of fun. The media loved a failed end-of-the-world story. A prophet with a name like Noone invited further ridicule.

But Richard Noone was a persistent student of catastrophe. He noticed that an alignment of Mercury, Venus, Jupiter and Saturn with the moon was due on the 20th January 2016. He now knew what his previous error had been. He had predicted the final trump on just this alignment, except that he had mistakenly believed that the alignment with the earth was the trigger. How could he have been so blind? Clearly, the alignment with the moon was the key one.

With this new insight, Richard gathered around him a small army of believers. They met regularly in a former scout hall which they rented cheaply.

Richard assembled his disciples there early on the 20th January. Over many months, he had convinced them of the catastrophe about to occur. Now was the culmination of his mission. He stood on the creaking platform, dressed in flowing robes – looking like an ancient alchemist – and addressed his followers.

"My friends. Today is the final day. The planets are telling us that at dawn on the 21ˢᵗ, when the alignment is perfect, the end will come. We will listen to the news today. I predict that you will hear that the world is already falling apart ahead of the final collapse. Then we will close the shutters and sit in silent communion as we contemplate our absorption into celestial eternity. There, we will be immortal and all-knowing. Have no compunction for those outside. We gave them the opportunity to be raised above their suffering, but they spurned our word."

As the day wore on, the news seemed to confirm the earth's path to perdition. By the end of the day, stock markets around the world had crashed. There was blind panic in all financial centres, and to further illustrate the global madness, Sarah Palin, in a completely incoherent speech, had endorsed Donald Trump. Richard smiled with self-satisfaction as he saw the effect of these events on his acolytes.

Once the radio was turned off, they were not aware of the passage of time as throughout the night they contemplated their imminent salvation.

But after many hours, one of their number, less convinced than his colleagues, began to wonder why he heard no noise of devastation outside. Suddenly, there was a loud knock on the door. The waverer opened it. There stood the postman in full daylight. He asked for a signature for a letter demanding the rent for the hall, overdue because they had never expected to pay it.

Editorial note: Richard Noone did publish a book called *5/5/2000: Ice: The Ultimate Disaster*, in which he predicted that the alignment of the planets with earth would cause the end of the world to start with the melting of the ice caps. Richard's second prophecy is imagined here, but there was an alignment of planets as described, and on the 20ᵗʰ January 2016, there was a market collapse and Sarah Palin did endorse Trump.

Fisherman's Tail

"I HEARD A RUMOUR ABOUT YOU, JOHN. I SHOULD never have let you go to that party on your own."

"What are you talking about, Kate? I went there, had a few drinks, had a laugh with my mates and then came home."

"Yeah. You came home the worse for wear and forced yourself on me. I don't know how you could have done it after what you got up to at the party."

"OK. What am I supposed to have done?"

"Sharon said that her friend Shelley saw you disappear upstairs with Clara for at least an hour. A bit out of your league, isn't she?"

"What are you talking about? She's written a thesis on the conservation of fisheries and she knew I like fishing, so she thought I'd be interested in it."

"Oh yeah? You expect me to believe that?"

"Yes, that's exactly what we were talking about. She's come across some very good trout fishing which she's promised to show me. So stop accusing me. I'm off to work."

Kate sat alone in the kitchen, too upset to move. Had she overreacted? John *was* interested in fishing, but why hadn't he said about Clara until she'd told him what Sharon said?

On the other hand, she thought, *Shelley has always fancied John. Maybe she's deliberately trying to make trouble between us so she can get in on the act.*

After a frigid few days, they managed to settle back into a reasonable relationship, although Kate still felt very cautious.

On Sunday morning, two weeks later, John said, "You remember we were talking about Clara? I told you she had found some excellent trout fishing. She's offered to take me to the Arlington Reservoir where she has a research pass. I can fish free for the whole day."

After breakfast, John packed up his gear and drove off.

It all sounds plausible, thought Kate, *but it's a bit sudden. Surely that sort of trip would have been sorted out well in advance?*

Still worried, she decided she should go and investigate. She knew the path around the reservoir well. She would walk around it and, if the story were true, John would by now be fishing on his own.

After walking for a while, she came across his gear. But no John. She continued until she heard voices behind some bushes.

"It was good that you could make it at such short notice. Didn't she suspect anything, John?"

"I don't think so. Anyway, let's enjoy the rest of our time together. I didn't know that tickling trout could be so exciting..."

Kate walked away in shock. With growing rage, she retraced her steps. She hurled John's fishing gear into the lake, then let down his tyres in the car park. She wrote a brief note which she left under his windscreen wiper:

I now know what we are talking about. When you get home, your stuff will be in the front garden. Goodbye.

It's Best to Forget?

THE FEELING THAT SOME OF HIS EARLIEST MEMORIES WERE missing made Alan very uneasy. He had enjoyed a successful life by most standards despite an unpromising start. At the age of six, he had been orphaned in a car crash from which he was the only survivor. Consequently, he had been put in a children's home from which he had been rescued, as he thought of it, by the lovely foster parents who had brought him up until it was time for him to leave home. Still, there was that nagging disquiet.

One lovely summer's morning, he was walking over the common to a meeting in a part of Clifton he hadn't visited before. He thought about how lucky he had been to get to Bristol University to study psychology, and to meet Carol there. He decided they should bring the children to see the Kite Festival at the weekend. But the vague feeling that something was missing again tempered his contentment.

Why can't I just enjoy my lucky life? he asked himself, but had no answer.

As he entered the suburb he passed a large house which he seemed to know, although he was sure he had never been there. He tensed up and felt as if he should run.

At the weekend, he drove the family to the Kite Festival and was looking for somewhere to park when he saw the house again.

"What on earth are you doing?" shouted Carol as he suddenly accelerated past it.

He managed to submerge his feelings for the rest of that day, but after this Alan couldn't get the house out of his mind. He knew that somehow it was connected with him, so he investigated its history. The house had been used by the Institute of Naval Architects for ten years prior to its conversion into a number of flats. With a reluctance he didn't understand, he traced it further back to the 1970s.

Finally, he came upon a note of its use as the Clifton Home for Orphans. He stared at the record as his lost memory started to reform. He recalled being in this place when he was six, and was taken back to that time of austerity and hardship. He flinched as he suddenly thought of a fierce warden called Mr Priestley. The vague disquiet was now coalescing into a crippling dread, but Alan forced himself to continue his research until he came upon a newspaper clipping:

Ernest Priestley, a former warden at the Clifton Home for Orphans, was jailed for ten years for abuse of boys at that institute. The judge said he had never come across such evil in someone trusted with vulnerable youngsters...

Alan stared at this for many minutes as, finally, the gap in his memory filled. Then he began to shriek, "No, no, no!", as he smashed his fist repeatedly onto the photo of his tormentor.

A Deadly Embrace

"I WANT SOMETHING IMPROBABLE," KELLY BREATHED as she suddenly realised a hidden yearning.

Matt, who was lying back with closed eyes as he neared his climax, started with surprise. "What on earth do you mean by that?"

He opened his eyes to see Kelly staring down at him from the Cowgirl position with a look of puzzlement at her discovery.

"Well. All we do is take turns to be on top. It's nice enough, but not very adventurous. I'd like something… well… improbable."

"Can't you be a bit more specific?" asked Matt, somewhat peevishly.

"If I could be more specific, it wouldn't be improbable, would it? Now get a move on. I've got to do some emails before we go to sleep."

Matt didn't like to think that Kelly wasn't fully satisfied, so the next day he did some research on the Internet.

"What variety," he muttered as he went through the options. "I should be able to find something which will turn her on."

His head spun with the range of possibilities, with names like the Swiss Ball Blitz, the Wheelbarrow, the Pretzel, the Butter Churner and the Sultry Saddle. Finally, he found a document titled *10 Improbable Sex Positions from Cosmo.*

"Improbable. Just what I'm looking for," Matt shouted triumphantly, to the surprise of his work colleagues. After further careful consideration, he chose the Octopus position.

Matt rushed home after work and persuaded Kelly that he had the answer to her fantasies. She suggested they put his research to the test immediately, so they hurried into the bedroom, casting off clothes as they went. Unfortunately, their passion had to be held in check as Matt produced a printout of the instructions. He wasn't very good with assembling flat-pack furniture but he had hoped that he would be better at the choreography of improbable sex positions.

After much referring to the document and experimental placing of limbs, luckily they had just enough lust left to achieve a breathless union. Soon, with slow, gentle thrusting, Matt was delighted to see that Kelly was very keen on the new position as she urged him on. But just as they were approaching the point of no return from coital bliss, Kelly cried out. "Stop. Stop. It's my back. Ooh! Don't move. Stay perfectly still. Must have put my back out. No, Matt, I said don't move. It's excruciating."

Matt, now in full anticlimax mode, could feel his arms rapidly weakening as they bore the weight of his torso and Kelly's legs. Everything he tried just brought forth another cry of pain and an admonishment to keep absolutely still. Finally, he had an idea. With a superhuman effort, he could just reach his phone with minimum disturbance of the status quo. As he reached out for it, he hesitated.

The 999 operator is going to ask what the nature of the emergency is, he thought. *What on earth am I going to say?*

Weathering the Storm

SITTING AT HIS DESK, WONDERING WHAT TO DO ABOUT his wife's birthday, Andy received a call which solved the problem. It was a Graham, a civil servant with whom he had worked on a voluntary basis. He was offering tickets to a Buckingham Palace garden party as a reward in kind.

Andy knew Rosie would be delighted by the opportunity, so he accepted one of the dates with thanks.

Came the day, and Rosie's dad, who had a sense of humour, drove them to the palace wearing a chauffeur's uniform in a borrowed Mercedes. There was only one snag. Andy had broken a leg just two weeks beforehand. He had protested that this meant he couldn't go, but his wife was resolute and had borrowed a wheelchair from the Red Cross. As a compromise, Andy was wearing a lounge suit to avoid looking ridiculous while being pushed around wearing a morning suit and top hat.

The wide gravel forecourt of the palace was clearly not suitable for a wheelchair, but two guardsmen bodily transported Andy while another carried his conveyance up a staircase through gilded rooms to the lawn at the back.

They relaxed drinking tea in one of the tents on the periphery of the lawn. Andy thought Rosie looked lovely in her wide-brimmed hat and gauzy blue summer dress, bought in the sale at Harrods. He hoped the lofty clouds which were building ominously would pass over quickly. Strangely, they couldn't raise much conversation with the other guests, who all seemed to have their gaze fixed upon the middle distance.

Suddenly someone said, "There she is!" and there was an unseemly rush towards the centre of the lawn.

Andy and Rosie thought that they would have no chance with the wheelchair, so they might as well enjoy the garden. It was lovely, although awkward with the wheelchair on the pebbly path around the lake.

When they were halfway around, a loud clap of thunder heralded an instant deluge.

"Lucky we brought a large umbrella," Rosie said, but it soon became apparent that this was not enough. Individual spots of rain on Andy's legs soon merged into glossy, wet unity as the water ran off the umbrella and oozed down to form a puddle in his crutch. Rosie, meanwhile, was squealing as the rain cascaded down her back.

They managed to find a gazebo in which to wait until their 'chauffeur' was due. Eventually, the Tannoy announced, "Car for Mr and Mrs Goodhall", and, with relief, they prepared to leave.

As Rosie sorted out the wheelchair, Andy noticed to his horror that the rain had made the back of her dress almost completely transparent. The tattoo on her back was clearly visible. A heart which declared, *RG loves DG* had appeared, and clearly visible underneath were the words *Always Look on the Bright Side.*

Communication

"You see, I've been through all this before," the lawyer had intoned.

Christopher could remember little of the meeting in 2004 except the man's patronising air as he delivered what Christopher thought of as a life sentence. He didn't really see at all.

The lawyer had continued, "Since the 1989 Children's Act, both parents now usually have parental responsibility, so there is no point in your going for custody."

"Well, if that's the case, why can't I stop them going to Australia?" Christopher had asked, and at that point, he had been lost in a welter of confusing legal jargon. All he knew was that his wife had been allowed by the court to take Daniel with her to Australia.

Since then, Christopher had tried desperately to stay in touch with his growing son. He only earned enough to travel to Australia once a year, and the brief two weeks left him feeling more like a visiting godfather.

In between, he had tried to keep contact. At first weekly phone calls, but often Daniel was distracted by the presence of new babies, which only added to Christopher's sense of isolation. Later, he enthusiastically adopted Skype. He thought that he could, at last, see his son's face. The reality had been much less satisfactory. Although they were face to face, they never seemed to see each other. Sometimes the picture would become so pixelated that Daniel only had four coloured blocks for a head, or he would freeze in mid-sentence. Christopher tried setting up a 'Christopher-Daniel' WhatsApp group, but was disappointed to find that the thirty seconds it would take to send a quick note was too much for his son.

His mind returned to that meeting with the pompous lawyer. "What a useless waste of time he was," he shouted at the wall. "It seemed almost as if he was on her side, the way he kept telling me I couldn't do anything to stop her waltzing off with that odious Tony."

Christopher tried to calm himself as he set the computer up for his weekly chat with Daniel.

"Hello. How's it going down there?" he started, as brightly as he could.

"All right, I suppose."

"What have you been up to this week, then?"

"Oh, all sorts of things. Listen, Dad, I've got to get online to join my team in a game of *Warcraft*. I can't let them down, so I'll talk to you next week."

Christopher stared disconsolately at the screen where his son's face had been. He looked around his poorly furnished flat.

Is this what it's all come down to? he thought. *He means the world to me, but he just doesn't seem to care.*

After a long while sitting gloomily at his computer, Christopher reached out, pulled a piece of paper from the printer, picked up a pen and started writing:

Dear Daniel…

The Trip

SOMETHING HAD GONE WRONG WITH THE arrangements. Gary was fumbling through drawers, looking for cigarette papers.

Michael never felt at ease when visiting Gary and Emma. His wife, Amanda, had met Emma at an evening class titled *The Literature of Protest*, where Emma was vocal in her support of all left-wing causes. Gary's latest enthusiasm was film-making. Half their lounge was decorated in the style of a 1920s bar. This was a mock up of the set for a film for which he was seeking funding. Since Amanda had begun to associate herself with what she called 'real issues' she had befriended Emma, but Michael felt uncomfortable with these changes. Although his wife wasn't a very affectionate companion, he had been content with their middle-class way of life.

As he walked to the newsagents to buy some cigarette papers, he remembered how, during their previous visit, he had been in a minority of one in a discussion about the legalisation of cannabis. Finally, in exasperation, he had said, "OK. If you think it's such a good thing, why don't you get some cannabis for the next time we get together?"

Judging by Gary's lack of cigarette papers, Michael suspected their involvement with the drug culture was much less than their bold words suggested. This perception was reinforced when, after his return, he was obliged to take over the rolling of the marijuana.

As they passed the joint around, Michael thought the others' smoking was rather timid, but he was determined to experiment fully, so he inhaled deeply. A warm haze overwhelmed him. His feeling of being out of place gave way to a tremendous sense of well-being. He looked at Emma sitting on the leather couch in the film set, and noticed for the first time that she had rather a good body below that habitual expression of distaste for everything bourgeois. He slipped over to sit with her on the couch. This had the side benefit of giving him an extra drag on the joint.

I think I'm beginning to get the point of this, Michael thought. He felt as if he were floating, and, in contrast to his usual restraint, he became quite voluble. After what seemed to him a blissful eternity, he fell asleep.

"What? What's happening?" he mumbled as he was violently shaken. Opening his eyes, he saw the others glaring at him with disapproval.

"Come on; we're going home," said Amanda angrily.

As they walked away, the night air had a sobering effect on Michael and he perceived that the drug experience hadn't been to his wife's satisfaction.

"What's wrong – didn't you enjoy it?" he asked.

"Not the way you behaved," she replied. "I think you have ruined that friendship. It was embarrassing. You were all over Emma on that settee and, among a lot else from your right-wing prejudice, you accused Gary of being a no-good, dreaming loser. Finally, if I'm a miserable bitch, then I have good cause to be."

A Fatal Joke

FRANK SLUMPED FORWARD IN THE CHAIR TO WHICH he was bound. The interrogation had been going on continuously for thirty-six hours, with intermittent bouts of physical torture. He gritted his teeth and silently vowed, *They will never get me to talk. I'll die first.*

He was a Special Operations Executive officer who had been parachuted into occupied France. Two days previously, he had been captured in his supposedly safe house. Through extreme pain and exhaustion, he dimly remembered this disaster. He had been about to start deciphering a message received on his portable transceiver.

1.14.10 6.20.15 47.8.9... Each triple set of numbers identified the number of a page, line and single character of the message. It was painstaking work, but so long as the title and edition of the book used at each end were secret, the code was unbreakable.

Remembering that he hadn't started the encoding, Frank felt encouraged that the Germans wouldn't have the message and so it was still possible that the operation could take place. But only if he didn't reveal the book and the resistance cell he was working with.

"*Noch einmal das Glockenspiel,*" a rough voice said, and a bucket was put over Frank's head and then beaten repeatedly with a stick. Every ten minutes he was asked if he would cooperate, and after he refused, the torture would continue.

After an hour of this treatment, Frank was almost deaf and very weak, but, as if from a distance, he heard a kinder voice offer a cigarette and a cup of coffee. When these had been provided, the voice continued, "We have intercepted your communications over many days. That is what led us to your hiding place. If you will only cooperate, we can put you in a comfortable prisoner-of-war camp away from all this. Just tell us what those strange groups of numbers mean. That is all we ask."

In a feeble whisper, Frank replied, "You will never get me to talk. I know your camp is a fiction. Just as soon as you have the information you require, you will shoot me."

"Well, if that is how you feel, then I will have to let my colleagues continue. If they fail, you will next face the Gestapo."

The guards had just hung Frank up by his arms to continue with their diabolical work when the door burst open. In came Hauptmann Schultz. Frank recognised him as the captain who had led the search party.

"It is not necessary to interrogate him any more. I have the answer. I went back to the room because I remembered how you can use a book to encipher a message. He had many books there, but it was easy to guess which one he used."

Turning to Frank, he went on, "You English should control your sense of humour. The book you are using is called *Our Mutual Friend*."

The Call

Hello, Johnny,

Sorry, you're out. Hope you pick this message up. I won't be able to meet next week. Bit of a change of plan.

Sorry for all the moaning I was doing that afternoon we met. It was good of you to let me bend your ear. I got so fed up with life in the call centre. Seven-hour shifts, and during that time having to suffer the bleating of dissatisfied customers. Apart from their complaints, sometimes they seem to want to tell you their life stories. I had one the other day who had a broken toaster. First I had to listen to what he was going to have for breakfast, then I had to listen to the list of all the electrical gadgets that he had owned, none of which seem to have gone wrong apart from that bloody toaster. Anyway, you must be quite used to me always saying that I have this feeling that someone will ring up to tell me I have won the lottery. It never happens, but listen to this.

A couple of weeks ago I had to make an outbound call which somehow got patched into a conversation between a bloke in Nigeria and this woman in Macclesfield. The Nigerian was saying he was a prince who had lots of money and he wanted to get it out of the country, but there were severe restrictions on currency transfers. So he was asking the woman at the other end if she would be so kind as to give him her bank account details, then he would transfer in ten million pounds. He would give her an account number to which she should then transfer nine million, keeping the one million as a commission. Well, the woman got quite excited about this. She said it would make a nice addition to her retirement fund. So, to keep things simple, she said she would give him the details for the account she uses for her pension money.

I have read about these scams and this certainly sounded like one. I was on the point of getting the police to trace the caller and warn her when another thought occurred to me. I suddenly realised that I had the bank details and passwords for an account which had a substantial sum of money in it. So, more out of curiosity than anything, I decided to try to transfer a small amount to my personal account. This seemed to work OK, but then I couldn't resist the temptation to carry on. After all, it was either me or that guy in Nigeria. He seemed to be biding his time, which gave me a superb opportunity. In the last fortnight, I have become richer by 750,000 pounds.

I won't be around for a while, but why don't you take a bit of a holiday and come and visit me in the Bahamas? Hang on.

There's somebody knocking on my door...

Success at Last

"I DON'T KNOW WHY, BUT THERE'S SOMETHING ABOUT being hauled to a police station that makes you feel a bit silly," said Ralph rather dejectedly as he dumped his Nikon D750 camera on my kitchen table.

Ralph is a friend from my schooldays. Although only an average pupil, he was always coming in with tales of extracurricular achievements. Mountains climbed, games won, and later romantic conquests. Since we left he has adopted many guises, each of which has ended at my kitchen table. A substantial legacy from an uncle is almost gone. He had aspired to become a bestselling author, but *My Remarkable Life* sold only twenty-one copies. Then he purchased a garret, where he spent a furious year painting huge canvases. An exhibition in a fashionable gallery was well attended because of the lavish entertainment, but not a single painting was sold. The last I heard, he had become an entrepreneur. He set up a website for an online folk art shop, which he was convinced would go viral, but the world refused to beat a path to his door.

Fearing he might have added to this sorry history, I asked, "What on earth brought you to the attention of the law, and why the camera?"

"I'm a professional photographer, or at least I was," he replied. "I hadn't had any success, so when I heard that Donald Trump was going to be travelling down The Mall in the Queen's coach, I thought that there was the chance to take the shot which would be reproduced around the world. There were lots of protestors and a heavy police presence, but I managed to get through somehow. As the coach passed, I rushed forward, but I was knocked to the ground by a very large policeman and taken to a police van."

"What happened when you got to the station?"

"Well, a lot of questions about my life and politics. I was searched thoroughly. They examined the camera to see if it was a weapon in disguise, and then threw me out with a caution. Anyway, that's it. I've finished with photography. You keep the camera. I've decided I am more cut out to be a maker of fine furniture. I am going to rent a workshop and set up a website."

That is how quickly Ralph bounces back. He has only ever needed half an hour with me to bury his ventures before, phoenix-like, he is off on another.

After he left, I picked up the camera and flicked idly through his pictures. He clearly had a lot to learn. Then I switched to the single video. He had obviously pressed the wrong button as he leapt forward, that day on The Mall. There was a whirl of out-of-focus action, but it ended with a perfectly framed shot which must have been taken from ground level. Ralph had made his mark at last. Donald Trump could clearly be seen through the front screen of the carriage as the rear horse was gracefully defecating.

A Waste of Time

PETER PICKED HIS WAY CAREFULLY THROUGH THE tourists as he walked along the South Bank of the Thames. The cheerful enthusiasm of the crowds communicated fresh energy to him and he quickened his pace as he made his way to the Globe Theatre.

Richard II was one of his favourite plays. He was very keen to see the Globe's production, which had received such good reviews.

As he sat down, he wondered if his old bones could survive a few hours of contact with the hard wooden seats. But as soon as the play started he became lost once more in the story and forgot all about his discomfort.

> *This other Eden – this demi-paradise,*
> *This fortress built by Nature for herself*
> *Against infection and the hand of war,*
> *This happy breed of men, this little world*
> *This precious stone set in the silver sea...*

John o' Gaunt's words transported Peter back to his childhood. He and his brother Mark had grown up in their own demi-paradise on a farm in Dorset. They had barns and fields, and even a small lake with its own island to which they sailed in their little dingy. Sometimes they were Romans, sometimes Carthaginians, but often Englishmen battling against the

French. Even the death of their father at Dunkirk hadn't destroyed this idyll. It seemed, rather, to make them even more dependent upon each other. With these reminiscences, Peter lost all consciousness of the play or where he was.

He remembered how he and Mark had remained close as they grew into their twenties, despite the fact that their studies and work parted them. That is, until they married wives who did not get on, and this began to create a distance between them.

When their mother died some years later, he recalled, there was much uncertainty about the inheritance of the farm and the businesses which she had so successfully run. The brothers tried to sort things out amicably, but their wives became more and more insistent on what they thought was their due. Peter and Mark were unable to avoid being drawn into what became a very bitter dispute. They had finally had a huge row and had not spoken for over thirty years, although Peter did hear about his brother from a cousin. Ironically, the legal actions had eaten up the majority of the disputed wealth and the wrangling wives had both been divorced.

So is it in the music of men's lives…
I wasted time, and now doth time waste me.

Richard II's words penetrated Peter's reverie and seemed like a message directed just to him. The woman alongside him noticed him quietly weeping and thought how powerful the words must be.

At the end of the play, as the crowds drifted out, Peter sat alone for many minutes and then, with an air of decision, took his phone from his pocket…

The People Upstairs

BETTY SAT BY HER ELECTRIC FIRE, HUDDLED IN HER SHAWL.

"I don't like it, Fluffy," she murmured to the distinctly unfluffy moggie that shared her little ground-floor flat. "It's too quiet. They must be up to something."

Betty lived in a house which was owned by the people upstairs. She and her husband John had taken the flat in 1924 when they got married and she had lived in Charles Street as a protected tenant ever since. Several people had owned the house over that time, and by and large she had got on with them very well.

The current lot were different. They had bought the house three years ago and set about making her life a misery. Obviously, they hoped that at ninety-five she could be worn down and forced out.

But Betty was a determined woman. "I've lived here most of my life," she told Fluffy. "It's been a bit lonely since John died, but I like it here and I'm damned if I'll let those foreigners get rid of me."

Since then, it had been a living hell. Frequently, there was thumping music when she was trying to sleep. Rubbish was often left outside her door. One day she found a dead rat. When she went shopping at East Street Market, she never knew what would greet her on her return.

When one of them left for several days, the other would carry on with the persecution. But now there was this eerie quiet. It was beginning to get on Betty's nerves.

192

There was a low thud as something dropped through the letter box. Betty opened her door and found that Elsie down the road had posted through a copy of the *Evening Standard*. Betty couldn't afford to pay for the delivery of a daily paper, so she happily settled down to read about her beloved London with a nice cup of tea. As she turned the pages, one news item jumped out at her:

Couple remanded for drug trafficking

Boyko and Eva Draganov of 15 Charles Street, recent immigrants from Bulgaria, are accused of running a drug-smuggling syndicate. In a preliminary hearing at Southwark Crown Court, they spoke only to confirm their names. Judge Barton refused bail on the grounds that they were accused of very serious crimes and the danger of their absconding was high. The trial is expected to take place in three months' time. The sentence for such a crime, if convicted, could be as high as 20 years.

Betty could hardly believe what had been going on upstairs, but now understood the silence. She signed with contentment. Finding it more and more difficult to read the paper, she closed her eyes and rested her head on her arms on the table.

The next day, when Betty's grandson came in to check up on her, he found her in the same position. Her face was set in a triumphant smile as she lay in her final sleep.

The Helping Hand

AMAZING HOW A PICTURE CAN TRANSPORT YOU TO *another place and time*, I thought as I looked at the photograph on our bedroom wall. It showed a man, perched precariously, high up on a windowsill of a pub as he cleaned the outside of the window. It was one from my friend Varun's East End series which he exhibited in Whitechapel Gallery in the '80s.

Varun always pursued his interests obsessively. After photography, came his 'music and wine' phase. We used to take turns to provide a favourite wine and sample it while he talked about his music.

"Listen to this," he would say as he put an LP on his top-of-the-range turntable. "There's nothing like vinyl. CDs just can't compete on sound quality." The music was invariably Mozart, and often one of his Italian operas. To demonstrate the capability of his amplifier, Varun would turn the volume up high. I can picture him now in full voice, striding around their lounge, singing along with the statue of the Commendatore who has come alive to take Don Giovanni to hell:

I have not come to feast;
A much greater purpose called me to earth.
Listen! I do not have much time…

...he would sing in Italian as he gave us his version of that terrible scene. I almost felt Varun was going to conduct *me* to hell.

Sue, his wife, worrying about the neighbours, would often turn the volume down, only for it to be turned up again. One evening, she could stand no more. She ripped the amplifier's plug out, saying, "Varun. Enough is enough. I've tried to persuade you to turn it down but you never take any notice."

"If I can't listen to my records as they're meant to be heard, I might just as well not have them," Varun shouted back, and, picking up his stack of Mozart LPs, he rushed out of the house and dumped them in the dustbin. He then went for a long and angry walk.

In his absence, Sue retrieved the LPs. As she hid them in a corner cupboard, she said, "He doesn't deserve a helping hand, but I can't see all that money go to waste."

So that was the end of that evening.

Two weeks later, when Sue called, Gill asked, "What happened about the records?"

"It was very lucky, really. The next morning, Varun was woken up by the dustmen. They had already done our flat. He chased them down the road in his dressing gown and was distraught to think he had lost his precious records. I didn't tell him until last week that I'd rescued them – just to pay him back."

"But won't you have the same problem all over again?"

"No. I don't think so. I told him that, if he didn't keep the volume down, as the LPs were in my gift, I really would throw them away. It's been a lot quieter since then!"

An Antique Discovery

"HERE's A MEMORY – ANTIQUES AND COLLECTABLES; that's the place you meant, isn't it?" James asked as he pointed to the quaint little shop.

"Yes. I hope it's worth the visit," replied Alison.

The pavement outside the shop was cluttered with a strange variety of objects. A large, brown stuffed bear kept watch over a treadle sewing machine, old chairs and a table of ancient tools. They made their way through this miscellany and stood looking at the objects beyond the window, almost like two separate individuals.

Since the loss of their child, they had grown apart. Annie had died at four months. She was a happy, bouncing baby found dead in her cot one morning.

"Cot death," said the doctor.

"If only you had looked in more often," said James.

"If only you had turned on that baby alarm," said Alison.

She had mourned for many months, withdrawing into herself. He suppressed his grief, and so they never shared their loss. The traumatic experience made them frightened to try again, and they had missed the comfort intimacy can bring. The closest they came was in a shared hobby; the collection of antique thimbles. It was this that had brought them to Here's a Memory.

Entering the shop, they found it was much deeper than they had imagined. It was divided by shelves and cabinets, and had several rooms. Near the door was an area for old clothing. James put on a Native American feathered headdress and said in a gruff voice, "Me Big Chief Sitting Bull."

"Don't be silly, James," Alison replied, but with a slight smile.

He picked up a large black trilby while she put on a plain beret. As they looked at themselves in an antique mirror, Alison laughed and said, "Remember the time we went as Bonnie and Clyde to that fancy dress party?"

"Yes. That was such a good night. Even your serious brother came as Al Capone with a scary-looking tommy gun."

In the spirit of that happy memory, James picked up a crossbow and said in his best American accent, "I'm gonna shoot that dang bear," but when he looked around for Alison, she had disappeared. Thinking she had gone to look for thimbles, he went in search of her.

He found her in a small room at the back of the shop. She was standing very still, holding a Victorian cot mobile with little china animals. She was crying soundlessly. With a shock, James saw that the toy was just like the one they had found for their baby.

As he looked at her with new compassion, she turned and looked back at him. Her grey eyes were brimming with tears, and he realised that they hadn't truly seen each other for ten years until that moment. He put his arms around her and, as he pulled her close, whispered, "Let's forget about the thimbles for now, love. We've got a lot to talk about."

Fast Eddie

"OK. Your cable connection's down. I'll be round as soon as I can. No, I can't come straight away. Yes, I know it is inconvenient."

Eddie Maher ended the call and again cursed his lot. It had all seemed so easy twenty years back, but now, scraping a living and frequent moves to stay ahead of the law had worn him down.

He picked up a faded newspaper clipping and read, for the hundredth time:

Felixstowe Herald, 5th *September 1993*
The Suffolk Police are seeking security van driver Edward Maher – known as Fast Eddie – who drove off in a Securicor van containing £1.2 million while his colleague was delivering cash to Lloyds Bank...

It had been a good plan. Eddie had sent his wife and child to Boston ahead of the heist, and afterwards he had joined them under the alias Stephen King. It had been great in the US at first. They had lived the high life in some very nice properties. They moved on frequently, but the initial thrill of shaking off all pursuit had gradually turned into a constant dread.

His introspection was interrupted by the arrival of his son Lee Maher, who preferred to use the family name.

"Dad. I'm worried about Carol. Things haven't been the same since we got through that 150,000 dollars I won on the lottery. I should have been more suspicious of the way she suddenly latched on to me when she heard about that. Now the miserable bitch is moaning all the time about money."

After Lee left, Eddie felt very uneasy for a reason he couldn't quite name. Was it time to move on again? Maybe, but the thought added to his depression. Recently, each move had been to ever more squalid accommodation.

That evening, he told his wife Deborah what was on his mind.

"Eddie. We don't even have enough money to pay for an apartment deposit. Also, this life, if you can call it that, is getting me down. I know I went along with that job with the van and we did have some really good times, but it never seemed real. We seem to be living a dream, somehow—"

Her weary harangue was interrupted by a loud knock on the door. With trepidation, she went to open it and, returning, said in a whisper, "Eddie, it's the cops."

The room seemed to shrink as two officers strode in. The senior of the two showed his badge and asked, "Are you Edward Maher, sometimes known as Stephen King?"

Eddie nodded.

"I am arresting you for immigration offences. And we have information that you are wanted in the UK for a robbery in 1993."

Eddie knew that reality had caught up with him, but out of curiosity he asked how they had tracked him down.

"It was your daughter-in-law. She followed the name Maher back and found out there was a large reward offered for information leading to your arrest."

Editorial note: There was a man called Fast Eddie who did the job as described. He also had a son who won 150,000 dollars on the lottery. Eddie returned voluntarily to the UK and pleaded guilty to the charge, and was sentenced to five years in prison in 2012.

Celestial Insurance

"Do you believe in God, Grandad?" Ian – a very serious thirty-year-old – asked the old man.

"No. I know you are a keen churchgoer but, I have to be honest, I don't."

"The Bible says that he created everything, including us. Surely that means something to you?"

"It's not that I never think about God. I do, and that's the reason I don't believe in him. To start with, you have to ask, 'Whose God?' Most religions have their own God. They are all sure that the way their holy book describes him is the absolute truth. They can't all be right. So to start with, you might be talking to the wrong being."

"No. You are wrong and they're wrong. The Christian God is absolute."

"Well, if your lot has perfect knowledge, how come they started out believing that the universe was created in six days and was centred on the earth? We now know that the universe is much bigger – possibly infinite. We occupy an insignificant part of it and it took a lot longer to evolve to the point where we could have this conversation."

"I admit that there have been some misconceptions along the way, but God loves us and he is aware of all our lives. He looks after us."

"Well, he didn't look after your cousin's family. His dad was knifed by a mugger as he returned home from church and nearly died, his wife is critically ill and your cousin has a brain tumour."

"It's not for us to question the path that God has chosen for us. Maybe he is testing their faith."

"Come on, Ian. You believe that if you like, but it doesn't make any sense to me. Now for the sixty-four-thousand-dollar question. Who created God? Here's a parable for you to think about.

"One day in a small American town, the philosopher William James was explaining how the earth revolved around the sun. Afterwards, an elderly lady insisted that the earth does not move. It sits on the back of a turtle. James asked what the turtle rested on. The old lady replied, without hesitation, 'On another turtle, of course.'

"James persisted: 'But what does the second turtle rest on?'

"The old lady triumphantly exclaimed, 'It's no use, Mr James; it's turtles all the way down.'"

The young man could see he wasn't getting anywhere. "Grandad. You are an old cynic. I'll leave you to your doubts and I'll pray for you."

Months later, the old man had a massive heart attack and fell down the full length of a staircase. He was not expected to live for more than a few days. His earnest grandson visited him and, as he sat anxiously beside the hospital bed, heard a faint voice.

"Ian. Get me a priest."

"But, Grandad, you don't believe in God."

"I think the existence of God is most unlikely, but as someone once said, 'Why take the chance?'"

The Landlady

I APPROACHED HENLEY WITH A SENSE OF UNEASE. IT was two years since I had been back. Because I was early for my meeting, I settled down in a riverside cafe with a coffee. As I watched the pleasure boats making their way along the Thames, I thought of my time at the Riverside Cottage guest house. There were two of us staying during the week. The other, Dr Savage, I rarely saw and had no idea what he did. The landlady, Pamela Wilding, was a woman perhaps in her mid forties, but still attractive in a matronly sort of way. Somehow, I had guessed that there was something in her past she didn't want to talk about, so I never inquired and it seemed right not to reveal much of my own circumstances, either, beyond telling her about the local company where I was working.

After my arrival, we were soon on first-name terms – Pam and John. Whenever I returned from work, she would greet me with a pint of Brakspear's ale. There was always a tasty meal to follow. It was a real home from home for a young man. We slipped into an easy familiarity.

"How are you this evening?" she would ask, and I would reply with something trite like, "All the better for seeing you."

In contrast to the tranquillity of the pleasure craft still passing gently, I recalled the dramatic event which had ended my sybaritic existence with Pam. One evening, after I had been working on some papers in the lounge, I said to her, "I've had a hard day. I think I need to get a good night's sleep. Got a lot on tomorrow."

"OK. I'll bring you up a cup of herbal tea and tuck you in, then."

"Chance would be a fine thing," I replied in our usual spirit of repartee.

I had not been long in bed when Pam appeared in my room. She wore only a fine slip, and her hair, normally in a tight bun, floated lightly about her shoulders.

"I thought we could leave the tea until later," she said as she slipped into my bed.

I was rigid with shock as she snuggled up to me. Her hair fell about my face as she turned to kiss me, and I was aware of her exotic perfume. Instantly, I realised how misguided my casual familiarity had been and I fought desperately to think of a way to extricate myself gracefully before my natural urges asserted themselves. Although perhaps fifteen years older than me, here was an attractive woman stroking my chest in an arousing way. My excuse had to be good. A harsh rejection could backfire. She might accuse me of attacking her. *A woman scorned* sort of thing. Then, what could I tell my new girlfriend, and would she believe me?

I could think of no easy way out, and was almost on the point of giving in and taking the consequences when there was a shout – "Fire! Fire!" – from downstairs. Pam rushed out. I dragged my trousers on and ran down.

There were flames around the kettle and Dr Savage was running around shouting, "Where's the fire blanket?" He had put the electric kettle on the gas stove by mistake.

The alarming yellow flames around the base of the kettle were easily doused in the sink. Soon Pam, once more in landlady mode, was busily cleaning up and trying to banish the smell of burnt plastic.

I left her house the next day and heard nothing further from her except a bill for a month's notice.

The boats were still gently passing the cafe, but my mind was far from tranquil after remembering that traumatic night. With a few minutes still before my meeting, I tried to relax by reading a local paper someone had left on my table. In the announcement section, a name jumped out at me:

> *Dr Brian Savage, of 15a Wood Close, Clapham, and Mrs Pamela Wilding, of Riverside Cottage, announce their engagement…*

Wow, I thought; *there's nothing like a cup of tea to resolve a crisis and bring people together.*

Schadenfreude

It all started with the conjunction of Venus and Jupiter in June 2015. As I walked over Hungerford Bridge, I wondered what the ancients would have thought of that occurrence. Would it have been a harbinger of good luck or a sign of misfortune to come? As I was about to take a seat on the Embankment so that I had a clear view, a hand tapped me on the shoulder.

"Hello, old boy. I thought it was you. What are you doing here?"

Clearly, for me, those planets were an omen of misfortune. It was Humphrey – the most boring person I know.

The sky was cloudless, and in that lovely state when fading daylight is balanced by the emerging artificial lights. Perfect to observe the apparent planetary collision.

"I'm here to see that," I replied reluctantly, as I indicated the twin planets coalescing in the darkening sky.

"Oh! You mean the conjunction of Venus and Jupiter. It's not as uncommon as people think, and of course, they don't come anywhere near each other. Venus is forty-nine million miles away, while Jupiter..."

It was the usual Humphrey, telling you all he knows about whatever comes up. I stopped listening and watched the floodlit dome of St Paul's coming into glorious prominence.

"It is rather a good view of the old cathedral, isn't it?" he said, noticing my interest. "Wren spent years designing that dome. Not many people know this, but St Stephen Walbrook in the City has a dome which was said to be Wren's prototype for St Paul's, and…"

Suddenly, in mid-spout, he stopped and stared at a man who had paused close by. "Good God, it's Ersin Mustafa," he whispered. "He's been wanted for years for organising an insider trading ring. He broke bail and escaped to Cyprus. He must be back." With that, he set off after his rapidly disappearing suspect.

At last, I could sit and contemplate the event I had come to see. It was uncanny, the way the two planets appeared as if they had almost coalesced. But while I sat, I couldn't stop thinking about Humphrey – the fount of all knowledge which gushed out at every opportunity. I knew he had worked in some government organisation to do with financial crime, so I supposed he must be on to something based on a deep knowledge of the crime committed by this Mr Mustafa.

Fortunately, I didn't bump into Humphrey again for some months. Maybe the influence of the planets was favourable after all. But my luck failed one evening in November as I was on my way to a lecture. I saw him about to cross my path so, head down, I hurried up New Fetter Lane.

"Good gracious, Patrick, is that you?" he shouted across the road in his unmistakable voice. "Where are you off to?"

"I'm going to Gresham College to hear a talk by Professor Andersen."

"Well, that's not the best way. Tell you what, I'll walk with you. There's a tricky little alley off Holborn that most people don't know about. His talk's titled *Was Einstein Right?*, I think. I've heard the prof on that subject before. Fascinating. He tells how modern satellite systems have to have their clocks adjusted because relativistic effects make them…"

I cast about in my mind for some way of diverting him from giving me the whole lecture. Suddenly, I thought of his pursuit of the inside trader. "By the way, did you manage to catch up with that man you followed last time we met?"

"Certainly, I did. I now know a lot about his movements. Where he lives. Where he works. What people he meets. Once I've completed my investigation I'm going to alert the authorities. I'm sure the result will be—"

"Good gracious, is that the time?" I said, pretending to look at my watch. "I'll have to run. Be seeing you."

The lecture was very interesting, but once again I couldn't prevent myself from thinking about Humphrey. What an irritating know-all. I hoped I could avoid him in future.

My luck held for many months. No sign of Humphrey, until one day in the *Guardian* I noticed his name in a short report which read:

Maverick investigator sentenced

Humphrey Chorton (57) was found guilty at Southwark Crown Court of stalking Hasan Demir. Chorton was convinced that Mr Demir was Ersin Mustafa, who skipped bail in 2008 to avoid trial for insider trading. Chorton relentlessly pursued and spied on Mr Demir, attempting to prove he was really Mustafa.

The judge gave Chorton a suspended two-year sentence for stalking. He also imposed a community service order with conditions that exclude Chorton from contact with Mr Demir and require him to carry out 60 days of unpaid work in the community.

Schadenfreude. What a wonderful word! It describes exactly what I'm feeling now, I thought. I do hope I come across Humphrey while he's doing his unpaid work. It will be a pleasure to tell him exactly how to sweep up the leaves or remove the graffiti.

Tricky Trimble

TRIMBLE HAD COMPLETELY VANISHED.

"Ain't seen 'im for two days," said Franco through the froth of his cappuccino.

'The Boys', as they were known, sat in the corner cafe, looking intently across the street.

"Well, sod 'im, then," said the Boss, who was the mastermind behind the job they were planning. "We can bleedin' well do without 'im. I'll get one of me mates to drive us to Gatwick."

They continued their examination of the premises, named Pop the Weasel. It styled itself as a premier venue for high-class secured loans – in other words, a pawnshop for the upper classes. Money was advanced against items like Porsche cars and diamond necklaces. But the Boss knew that it was just a front for the real business, which offered a safe haven for stolen goods and money on its way to be laundered. He had used it himself in the past.

"We know the guv'nor turns up Sundays. Reg'lar as clockwork. Great job patchin' into 'is phone line, Sparks. So we know 'e tells 'is girlfriend that 'e 'as to get things straight for the week, but the dirty bugger's really just lookin' at porn."

"Porn in a pawn shop. That's clever."

"Shut up, Lefty. I'm tryin' to think," the Boss went on. "Yeah. We'll do it next Sunday mornin' at ten o'clock. Sparks, you'll be with me and do your stuff. Franco, you and Lefty'll deal with 'is girlfriend like we said. You know where she 'angs out. I'll get two of me mates to break down at the ends of the street so we won't get nobody stickin' their nose in. One of 'em can take us to the airport. It's only cash we're after. We'll stash it in the linin' of our bags on the way. OK. Do yer know what we 'ave to do?"

His companions all grunted their agreement.

On the following Sunday, the Boss and Sparks were lurking near the Weasel, out of sight of its cameras.

"You're sure that bloody drone thing is gonna work, Sparks?"

"Sure thing, Boss," Sparks answered. "I tested it out several times. I put one of their cameras out of action two weeks ago and the lazy buggers who look after the security system ain't fixed it yet, so we won't 'ave no trouble from them."

"Right. It's nearly ten. Off yer go."

Sparks took a small drone from his backpack with its controller. He launched the drone towards the cameras. From above, it squirted opaque paint into each lens. Shortly afterwards, the manager emerged. As he was about to lock the door, he was grabbed from behind by the Boss, who thrust him back inside.

"I wouldn't do nothin' stupid if I was you," he growled into the manager's ear. "You've got a gun in yer back. Sit down, you slimy sod," he went on. "I'm gonna give you a choice. Open that strongroom you've got downstairs. Otherwise... Two of me mates 'ave got your girlfriend. We'll let her go if you're gonna be a good boy."

The manager started whimpering pathetically, but the Boss shoved him brutally towards the stairs. "Now take us into the vault. If you do that, your nice piece of totty'll be OK. If you try to grass us up, we'll send 'er and the fuzz a printout of all that filth you downloaded. I don't think you'd like it much in the nick."

In the vault, Sparks broke open the safe-deposit boxes one by one. Many had bundles of high-denomination used notes, which they stashed in a bag. In one they found a diamond tiara.

"Leave that," the Boss shouted. "I said no bleedin' jewels."

After they had filled their bag, they departed, leaving the manager tied up and gagged. A quick call and one of the 'broken-down' cars burst into life and backed to pick them up.

"Thanks, Jimmy," the Boss said. "We'll pick up Lefty and Franco and go straight to Gatwick. They'll make sure that guy's floozy is well tied up. When our flight's well clear, call the fuzz and tell 'em where they can find the two lovebirds." He handed the driver a roll of notes and a stolen phone. "'ere's your tariff. Give a third of that to Lenny for the other car."

The Boys couldn't believe how successful they had been. They entered Gatwick in high spirits and made for the check-in desk. As they approached it, a group of policemen appeared – led by a curiously familiar figure.

"Good evening, gentlemen," he said, holding up his warrant card. "Detective Inspector Shaw sometimes known as Trimble at your service. Please come with us somewhere more private. We would like a few words with you."

War and Peace

ALAN CROUCHED UNDER THE KITCHEN TABLE WITH A worried frown. He had got just fifteen sweets with his weekly ration. While he was trying to work out how to spread them over seven days, he'd heard his uncle say he was going to Woolworths because they had saucepans for sale. They might be able to replace the aluminium ones collected to make Spitfires. Alan, at seven years old, still an optimist, asked if he could go too. After all, if Woolworths had saucepans, they might also have extra sweets.

When they were nearly there, they heard a tumultuous bang, followed by a roaring noise and another bang further away. Then a wind like a hurricane blew them over and seemed to suck all the breath out of them.

A man with torn clothes covered in dust staggered towards them. He stared ahead with glazed eyes as he shouted, "The Jerries have got Woolworths. Nothing left of it. The Co-op's ruined too. Must have been a V-2, 'cause there was no warning. I was lucky. Behind the Town Hall. Bits of building and bodies everywhere."

"The good Lord has delivered us," whispered Alan's uncle. "If we had been ten minutes earlier we would have been there."

Alan felt in his pocket and was relieved to feel his sweets were safe.

The sirens and explosions were all a game to Alan. Luckily his family had never been bombed or evacuated from their home.

He and his friend Kenny just enjoyed the minor consequences of the war. There were nights spent sleeping in the air-raid shelter, and abandoned houses with huge, overgrown privet hedges which made their gardens into marvellous dens. One bombed house had a tower from which they could watch thousands of planes flying towards Germany and imagine themselves to be pilots. Kenny had a brilliant collection of shrapnel.

At school, half the class had been evacuated because of the doodlebugs and rockets, and the teacher said that, after they had done a page of sums, a page of writing, and some drawing, they could just play with the toys. When the air-raid warning sounded they had to duck under the desks. School was fun.

One day in May, as Alan and Kenny were shooting with their home-made bows and arrows at a target of Hitler's face, they noticed that almost everybody they knew seemed to be walking up and down the road. The church bells were ringing and people were hugging each other. Puzzled, they crept out of their lair to find out what was happening. Alan's next-door neighbour, Mary, swept him up in her arms, and, to his horror, kissed him exuberantly as she cried excitedly, "It's peacetime, Alan. We've won the war."

Kenny and Alan jumped up and down with excitement. This was excellent news. The sweet ration was bound to go up now.

The euphoria was not to last. Less than two years later Mary's mother, Edith, huddling closer to a meagre fire said, "I can't believe this weather. Last summer we had so much rain it ruined the wheat and caused bread rationing. Now, this endless winter. The coal dumps are frozen solid so it's almost impossible to get, and we have to freeze."

"Never mind, Mum," said Mary. "I've just finished unpicking this old jumper and I won't start knitting the new one until I've made us a nice omelette. At least Grandad's chickens are laying, and we've still got some of the bacon ration."

Mary wrapped her cardigan more tightly around her as she turned on the radio.

"*This is the BBC Home Service and here is tonight's news. The government is urging the Dockworkers' Union not to strike. They say this will further damage food supplies and the meat ration will be threatened if imports are left rotting on the quayside. Our forces in the East are being progressively demobilised, but the government says that it will still be some months before men essential to transport of troops can return home.*"

They stared at the faded cloth over the loudspeaker of the pre-war radio as if at a physical announcer.

"*The Ministry of Food has announced that, owing to the destruction of many stocks of potatoes by frost, rationing of potatoes will be introduced next week...*"

Mary knew Edith would have heard enough bad news, so she turned off the bulletin and busied herself with preparing their meal, while half-hearing her mother's complaints.

"That daft father of yours is stuck out there. Just missed out on the last war, so he volunteers in this one. We're lucky that your sister married an American. We at least get the odd food parcel. Not much chance of that with you, though.

"It's not much of a meal, is it?" she continued, as Mary put the omelette in front of her.

It was a familiar refrain, and Mary was used to her mother's ingratitude. After they had eaten, she encouraged Edith to go to bed to keep warm while she caught up with some housework. Some washing she had done for her grandfather had been frozen on the line in the yard. She brought it in and stood it stiffly in the corner of the room like a ghostly figure which she pretended was her father.

"Dad, I wish you would come home. It's now nearly two years since the war ended. Mum is getting worn down by the terrible conditions this winter, and Grandad is not too well. Doreen is doing all right, though. She got married to a GI and is living in Texas. She won't be freezing."

After a night in bed still wearing most of her clothes, Mary got up. She added her blankets to her mother's bed and encouraged her to stay there to keep warm. Mary brought a zinc tub in from the garden and started laboriously scrubbing her grandfather's thick garments. As she did so, she thought *If this is what it's like when you win a war, I'd hate to be on the losing side.*

The Fiction Factory

ONE DAY ON THE RADIO, ROCCO STEIN HEARD HIDEO Kojima – the worldwide guru of gaming – describing his vision for the entertainment industry. Hideo was firmly of the opinion that games, films and books would merge. Why not actually fight some of the battles in *Star Wars* and come back to the story later? Or perhaps stop and read about the characters or the setting of a film? The proportion of each element could vary depending on creative needs. A book could be supplemented by video. A game could allow a player to stop competing and enjoy her well-earned status. A film could turn into a game.

Rocco had made a lot of money in the software business and he was desperately looking for his next big thing. The revolution Hideo Kojima was describing grabbed Rocco's imagination. He took over an ailing film studio, hired some teenagers with game-programming skills and recruited creative staff who he said 'got it'. He named this new establishment the Fiction Factory, and called his products 'Entermixes'.

The concept of participants in this new art form having complete freedom worried Rocco, so he decided to limit the highways and byways within the Entermixes according to his customers' preferences and attitudes. Each person was asked to grade themselves. An extract from the questionnaire went as follows:

Please grade yourself on a ten-point scale according to the following attributes/opinions:
Pessimist (1) to Optimist (10).
Hate violence (1) to Love blood and gore (10).
Don't like explicit sex (1) to Graphic sex is OK by me (10).
I like to wallow in grief (1) to Happy endings only (10).
Can't stand video games (1) to I'm a games addict (10).
Like to explore (1) to Must get on with the story (10)…

It was a very detailed questionnaire so the content could be tailored personally to the profile of the participant.

Rocco used his programming background to write the scripts, employing an 'IF-THEN-ELSE' structure. For example, in a story about Geoffrey who has hit hard times, the script would be structured as follows:

> {*Film with a scene about Geoffrey's fall from grace. He's sleeping rough on the Embankment. Discovered by a former colleague who gives him a phone number to ring to fix something up.*}
>
> **IF endings preference** *is <6* **THEN** {*Geoffrey rings up using his almost dead phone, gets a job and recovers his life.*} **ELSE** *if >5* {*He realises his phone is dead and he has no means of contacting his would-be saviour. He gives in to despair and commits suicide in the Thames.*}

Just a small illustration. En route to this juncture, for example, there would be alternative views of Geoffrey's sex life, the amount of violence in his failed marriage and the events in his company.

It was a complex process and the scripts required a level of checking far beyond any normal film or book, but nearer the structure of a game. This and the increasing scale of the business took a toll on Rocco, which he eased by drinking and by many affairs. After all, he told himself, with all these attractive women around it would be a sin to waste the opportunity. Rocco's wife Juliet was unaware of this for several years. He always had a plausible explanation for his absences. Frequent distant conferences were apparently necessary for marketing the business.

But one day, she received a call from his secretary. She had been a recipient of Rocco's flattering attention for a while, but had been dropped in favour of the studio's latest young actress. Juliet was treated to a detailed account of Rocco's amours. After the call ended, she sat slumped in her chair, feeling totally lost in this new emotional landscape. After a long while, she noticed a script on the coffee table, which she idly picked up and scanned a few pages. Inspired, she took a piece of paper and wrote:

Rocco, you lying bastard. You have been deceiving me for years. You certainly named your business well when you called it the Fiction Factory.

IF you stop all your gallivanting and act as a husband should,

THEN we can go on as we are for the sake of the children.

ELSE you can piss off and I'll see you in court. I'll be after half your assets at least. You'll have to sell your damn business.

Unrequited Love

SITTING ALONE AFTER A BITTER ROW WITH MY WIFE, I poured another drink and thought back over a lifetime of disastrous relationships. I decided it had all started with my first love at primary school.

Pam was a pretty girl with dancing brown eyes beneath curly brown hair. She was full of fun, and if she smiled at you it felt like a ray of sunshine. I thought she was perfect. *My very first girlfriend*, I told myself, although I wasn't entirely sure what that really meant. Every morning I took her route to school, hoping to walk along with her.

One day it was announced that there was to be a second evacuation of children because of the threat from the doodlebugs and rockets which the Germans were aiming at London. All classes had to be reorganised. I was delighted when I was moved to share a double desk with Pam. Occasionally an air-raid warning was sounded and I had the pleasure of crouching below the desk with her – our own little world.

When Christmas came I gave Pam a present. Some of our classmates said that she must be my girlfriend. She didn't deny it, which I took as an excellent sign.

One day in the spring, we were all taken out to visit a nursery and someone there talked to us about the flowers and bushes. Pam couldn't see, so she put her hands on my shoulders and stretched up on tiptoe. It was a moment of bliss when she whispered to me, "Can you meet me before school tomorrow? There's something I want to ask you."

With great anticipation, I met up with her on the walk to school. "I would like to recommend you to become a member of the Ovaltineys Club," she said with great earnestness. "Here's the application form. Just fill it in and send it off. It's great. I've been a member for a long time."

From Pam, this was like a royal command. How nice to be in the same club as her. I found out that you had to send in a couple of stickers from Ovaltine tins. I also discovered that I didn't much like that malt-based milk drink, but I was happy to make the sacrifice for her. After a couple of weeks, I was the proud owner of an Ovaltineys badge which I wore triumphantly to school to show Pam. To my consternation, she hardly looked at it and continued a very friendly conversation with Colin Briggs.

Jack Little, who was already showing signs of the detective inspector he would become, came up to me in the playground and, with a sneer, said, "She won't want much to do with you now you've got the badge. She now only needs to persuade two others to join to get her Ovaltiney gold badge."

Where women are concerned, I've been a sucker all my life.

Just Deserts

SIR JASPER NORTHWYKE QUICKENED HIS PACE. HIS face, reddened by too much good living, darkened with annoyance as he saw her again. He had frequently seen the woman about Hastings, but had always avoided her. There was something familiar about her which he found unsettling beyond his normal intolerance of the lower classes. He now regretted taking a walk around the fishing area before motoring to the local court where he served as a magistrate. Here she was again – sheltering between two of the towering black fishermen's huts. She held a tattered piece of cardboard on which, in rough letters, was inscribed the message: *Please help a poor, starving woman.*

"Balderdash," he growled as, ducking behind the huts, he nearly tripped over a lobster pot. "She should get off her backside and get a job. Lots of people need servants these days. They paid too much in the factories during the war. Gave women ideas above themselves."

Arriving at the court, he still had an unsettled feeling from seeing the destitute woman. But, after a quick draught from his hip flask, his mood lightened and he took the chairman's seat. He sighed inwardly as he looked at the schedule of cases and thought how he would again have to overcome his colleagues' undue leniency. The early cases were dealt with brusquely. A petty thief was ordered to pay a fine of ten shillings despite Northwyke's fellow magistrates' insistence that this would be beyond the boy's means. A young woman charged with soliciting as a prostitute was given a lecture on morality and ordered to pay a fine of five shillings and attend classes for fallen women held by the local church. The next case was for grievous bodily harm. A surly young man stood in front of the bench. He had beaten his wife badly on finding out she had been seen talking to another man. Northwyke could have simply referred the case to the Crown Court, but he wasted many minutes allowing the man to tell the court why he had done it, before giving the court the benefit of his own views on the matter.

"Well, young man. You clearly have a case to answer and I'm going to refer it to the Crown Court, but I must say that you appear to have had cause to be angry with your wife. That doesn't excuse your conduct, mind. Women in this day and age seem to be getting out of hand, demonstrating all over the place about equality and so forth. I expect to see many more cases in which men try to assert their authority but are just a little too forthright in doing so."

Thus Northwyke pompously emphasised his place in setting society to rights. He could then enjoy what he regarded as his firm benevolence as he dealt with the remainder of the cases before the lunch recess.

He returned to his country mansion for a generous lunch which his servants had prepared for him. His wife had died two years before, so he sat at his solitary meal and read the day's newspaper.

The headline took up most of the front page: *No concessions. General strike collapses*, it shouted.

Damn good job, too. Don't know what the world's coming to, Northwyke thought as he poured another glass of claret. *Give the workers an inch and they'll take a yard.*

Back at the court, he was even more forthright in his advice to the unfortunates who appeared before him. The cases did nothing to temper his condemnation of the modern world, as he termed it. On his drive home, he carried this discontent with him, but the sense of unease caused by seeing the woman that morning returned to him.

While he ate dinner, he looked around the panelled walls of the dining room. Over the fireplace was a portrait of his son, Giles. Northwyke's eyes moistened as he gazed at it. He proudly recalled reports of the gallantry shown by his boy in holding a hill near Passchendaele against overwhelming odds until he and his platoon had all been killed. He became even sadder as he remembered how Giles had been due to be married on his return. Now there would be no heir. The Northwyke name would disappear.

Next morning his chauffeur was on duty, so Northwyke instructed the man to drop him at the east end of Hastings and pick him up towards St Leonards. He liked the walk along the seafront. It partly offset his overindulgence. Along the way, he saw the woman again, but too late to avoid her. She was sitting by the entrance to the pier with her placard, begging for money.

"Please help a poor woman. I haven't eaten for two..." She stopped her appeal mid-sentence and stared fixedly at Northwyke's face. "Hey, sir. Don't I know you?"

"I don't think so. Sorry, I can't help you," he snapped, as he started to move away.

"I *do* know you. You are Sir Jasper Northwyke of Fairlight Hall."

"So what's that to a woman like you, then?" Jasper replied. His past unease at the sight of her was becoming acute discomfort.

"You ruined my life, that's what. I was a chambermaid in your house. You made the butler throw me out in the street because I was with child, without offering me so much as a chance to say anything."

"He was quite right to do so. There has never been a trace of immorality in my house. You brought it on yourself, you wicked woman."

"What you never bothered to find out was that the 'immorality', as you call it, was already in your house. Your son was the father of my boy."

Northwyke stared, speechless, at the woman. His mind was in turmoil. Now he remembered the scandal in 1914. The girl had been eighteen. The woman in front of him must be only thirty now, although she looked many years older due to her rough living. Could it be true? Would young Giles have been so careless? He'd known he was off to war, so the prospect of death might have overcome any restraint. Then Northwyke's thoughts turned to the child. He would be twelve or thirteen now. An heir at last. Not too late to educate him properly, either.

Northwyke looked with new interest at the woman. Now this exciting prospect had presented itself, he felt that he must quickly come to terms with her.

"Where is the boy now? I'd like to meet him. After all, he is my grandson."

"I'm sure you would like to meet him. So would I, but that's impossible. How do you think a girl carrying a child, and with no references from you, could support a baby? I couldn't get another position and I was starving. The baby died at birth." The last words were no more than a whisper as she quietly wept into her shawl.

Northwyke stood helplessly as a black mood extinguished his momentary hope. Then, in his first spontaneous act since he had wept over the telegram telling him of the death of his son, he knelt down, put his arm around the woman and tried to comfort her.

The Devil's Dare

"CHILDREN'S DARES — IT'S COMMON TO HAVE SOME regret about them." So said the psychiatrist when Simon first consulted him.

"*Some* regret," he had replied heatedly. "I am not here to talk about *some* regret, but about a lifetime of remorse."

Simon stared gloomily out of the train window as he recollected this conversation.

The train slowed and suddenly he recognised where they were. They were passing the steep embankment below a cul-de-sac which had been his childhood playground. The trees in that road had offered a variety of climbing challenges, and it had been easy to squeeze under the wire onto the embankment. Once there, a thicket of sycamore saplings had given perfect cover for expeditions with his friends.

This group of friends swore never to tell of their secret society. They dug into the soft earth of the bank and made a covering of branches to make what they called their HQ. There they had picnics and plotted their escapades. Simon could still taste the sweat as they dug, and smell the dank earth and the sausages cooked on their Primus stove. One night, they even crept out of their homes to rendezvous there with hooded torches.

When the novelty of the HQ began to pall, they started setting each other dares.

"Johnny. Dare you to catapult a plum at the stationmaster's window."

"Ray. Bring back a piece of coal from one of the trucks in the shunting yard."

"Dennis. Put a penny on the line and bring it back when a train has gone over it."

Simon remembered the penny game well. He still had one of those coins, squeezed thin by the wheels of a passing train. He smiled as he remembered the fun of those times, and how the need to avoid detection had made them feel so alive. Then his mood darkened as he thought on. The dares had escalated, and none of them knew how to stop when they came to the ultimate challenge.

"Freddy. Step over the live rail." Then, "Jump over it with both feet."

Dennis said he knew physics, and if you stood on the live rail without touching the ground, you were safe, just like the birds. With horror, Simon recalled how four of them had jumped onto the rail and off again, without any effect apart from the peculiar motion of their hair. Ray refused, but they goaded him until he agreed to join the high-voltage club, as they named it. With trembling legs, he jumped onto the rail, but slipped and fell across it. His shrieks of anguish pierced Simon's head again as he relived the disaster. Dennis had shouted, "Don't try to pull him off, otherwise we'll get it too." So they had rushed for help.

After they had guided the policeman to the scene, they saw the lifeless face of their badly burned friend twisted with astonished agony. It was an image which had haunted Simon for the rest of his life.

Losing Touch

AFTERWARDS, WE LAY BACK WITH LIMBS STILL
entwined. Overwhelmed by our resurgent passion, I began,
at first haltingly, to tell her of my fifteen years of marriage.
My wife, Nicole, who had attracted me initially by her
simple vivacity, had turned inwards with the bitterness of
childlessness. Melissa spoke of her steady but passionless
marriage to Brian, whom we had known slightly when we
were together at Cambridge. Apparently, he was a dependable
husband and a good father of their two children.

A chance meeting had led to an arrangement to meet in
Brian's London flat, but our partners had been delayed – leaving
Melissa and me alone for the afternoon. Awakened by our
renewed intimacy, memories of our time together at university
flooded back. After meeting at the jazz club, we had rapidly
become intensely involved. She had a broad and inquiring mind
and a lovely, agile body. Often, after tennis, running or swimming,
we would make love hungrily and then talk far into the night.
With shame, I remembered my destruction of this idyll when we
graduated. I had been offered a job with a mining company in
Chile and was enamoured with the idea of an international career.

I whispered to Melissa, "We were desperately in love. Back
then, I didn't understand what love was." I grasped her arm, still
strong and shapely, and continued, "I have thought of you often,
and how our lives would have been together. I know now I can't
live without you. We belong together. Don't you feel it?"

"I have always loved you too, but I can't make a decision just like that. You must give me time to think." she said. "The others will be here soon – we must straighten up."

Buoyed with hope, I was only dimly aware of Nicole and Brian arriving at the flat. I couldn't concentrate on the reminiscences and attempted bonhomie which accompanied the meal Melissa had expertly prepared. The thought of being together again dominated my thoughts.

While we drank coffee, Brian stood up to make a speech. After a few polite comments about regained companionship and the need to keep in contact, he made an announcement about a promotion to engineering director of his company's business in the USA. I looked in expectation at Melissa's face and saw, to my horror, that she wouldn't contemplate disrupting their settled life.

While this bitter truth wormed its way into my gullible mind, Brian was busy organising what he called 'the Friendship Photo'. We faced his artfully balanced camera with arms randomly thrown around each other. By chance, my hand met Melissa's and she took it into her warm grasp with a gentle caress.

"Great," shouted Brian after the shutter clicked. Her hand slowly slipped from mine, leaving an aching void that nothing now will fill.

Piano – Troppo!

I HAD FORGOTTEN WHAT AN ORDEAL MOVING HOUSE is. It had taken two skips to take away the detritus from the garden and garage, and I had been banned from the nearest charity shop. In the loft, I knew that there were cardboard boxes for every electrical item we had ever bought in twenty-four years, camping equipment we didn't use any more, hundreds of books and much old junk. As I wearily contemplated dealing with this, Gill arrived with a welcome cup of tea.

"What are we going to do with the piano?" she asked. "That will never go in the removal van, and anyway, we are downsizing. There's nowhere for it in the new house."

"Why don't we give it to Tom, then? He's the one who plays it."

So that's what we decided, and Tom organised 'the Aussie with a van' to move it to his flat. Firstly, it had to be removed from our house, which had steep steps down to the pavement. Halfway down, it became perilously balanced, threatening to plunge down upon the poor 'Aussie'. Luckily, our window cleaners were around and they rushed forward to assist. I've no idea how the Aussie and Tom then got the piano up the narrow staircase into Tom's flat. The fact that there was no balustrade on the stairs must have helped.

Soon afterwards, as the work on his flat was completed, we took time off from preparing for our move to visit Tom. He gave us a recital on the piano, which sounded very good there. Later, as we were leaving, Gill said, "I love the way you've remade the staircase with the traditional balustrade, but how on earth would you get the piano out again? You'd need to take out a window and hire a crane!"

"I'll think about that when the time comes," Tom said, "but I must admit, when you own a piano it's harder to think about moving. Thanks very much for it, anyway. Oh! If it's OK, I'll come over first thing tomorrow to collect that chair you've offered me."

We went to bed that night, amongst the chaos of removal preparations, thinking that at least we had solved the piano question for the present.

The next morning, I went out to get a newspaper. To my astonishment, there was a piano parked neatly against the railings outside our house. It was in good condition and had obviously been carefully delivered. It was as if the gods had decided we must not be piano-less. When Tom arrived, he started playing it and a small group of near neighbours and passers-by soon formed an appreciative audience. Nobody had any clue where the piano had come from or any idea about where it could go.

A small boy, who had been listening attentively, then said, "I'm learning to play but my parents can't afford a proper piano. Can I have it, please?"

A working party was quickly formed and the instrument was wheeled up the road to the grateful boy's house. Each time they stopped for a rest, Tom played another tune. One colourfully dressed woman even started dancing.

We often wonder why we were chosen to receive that bonus piano.

Time is of the Essence

AFTER HIS DEPUTY, CHENG WONG, HAD SET UP autolanding, Kurt Slater relaxed in his re-entry bed and enjoyed the terrestrial show. The chip implanted in his brain said, *1200 hours on the 10th May 2082.*

The sky changed from black to indigo and through ever lighter shades of blue as they spiralled down towards their own blue planet.

Thank Confucius, thought Kurt, *we will soon be home. It's been a long two years. It will be great to see my wife and little boy again.*

Kurt had been chosen by the Supreme Republic of China, which had long dominated the world, to be the first super commander from the United States of Europe to lead an expedition beyond the solar system.

The trip to an exoplanet around the star Eridani, eighteen light years distant, had been a success. Now the Great Wall appeared, but it was odd that they passed over a greened Gobi Desert as they plunged towards Dongfeng Aerospace City. The city was vast and contained outlandish buildings with walls of growing plants. There were strange vehicles in convoy across the whole area. *We must have been diverted to a military complex with all sorts of advanced state-of-the-art facilities,* Kurt thought.

After landing, the hatch slid silently open and, with the crew behind him, Kurt strode out, only to be halted by the impact of the strange surroundings. A bizarrely dressed group of people, who seemed important, were looking expectantly in their direction. Suddenly, two of them hurried towards Kurt. One, a man, possibly in his forties, gave Kurt the impression of a reflection of himself. The woman, meanwhile, had the worn face of a seventy-year-old, yet she seemed somehow familiar as she made to embrace him.

At that moment, Kurt's brain chip signalled for his attention. *Update local time/date*, it whispered; *100 hours, 11th June 2130.*

At first Kurt thought the chip had malfunctioned, but almost instantly a cruel realisation surged through his mind. The voice of his relativity lecturer on the astronauts' course suddenly emerged from his subconscious: *Remember. To get to the stars you will have to travel at close to the speed of light. Your local time will run much slower than that at your point of departure. This is an effect of Einstein's Theory of Relativity.*

Kurt looked in sorrow at his son and wife, now forty years older, and threw himself to the ground in frustration and anger. All the tension of the trip; his eager anticipation, now dashed; and the sense of his own naivety caused an explosion of fury within him. As he beat his head against the ground, he bellowed, "Fuck you, Einstein. *Fuck you.*"

Consolation

Hello, darkness, my old friend.
Please don't talk to me again.
Must I suffer without end,
Your deep wound within my brain…?

THE GIRL ON THE STAGE WITH AN ACOUSTIC GUITAR slung across her Texan costume drawled the words in gloomy tones.

"Christ," muttered Joe to himself. "I came down here to forget – not to be reminded about poor old Dave."

Every year Dave and Joe had met in London and spent an evening at a different music venue. In memory of Dave, Joe had decided to carry on the ritual. After descending to the basement club in Oxford Street, he had entered a dimly lit cabaret-style venue. Around the walls were photos of its former glory days with rock and jazz greats. The evening was advertised as a multi-genre event, with acts from pop through folk to rock and jazz. As he looked around, he thought that this explained the eclectic mix of punters. Old and young, punk and rocker, folk and jazz lovers – all wearing their tribal uniforms.

Joe had thought it might be quite good fun as he slid into a seat near the stage. But now he was sure he had made a mistake. The last thing he wanted was someone singing about darkness. Darkness was no friend of his, he thought.

His mind was again possessed by the trauma of Dave's death. Joe knew that they had gone too far that day. Following their shared passion for caving, they had gone deep down into a challenging limestone labyrinth. Dave had got stuck in a sump which flooded, and had drowned as Joe desperately tried to pull him out. Perhaps the singer had asked the right question for Joe:

Must I suffer without end,
Your deep wound within my brain?

Joe shook himself and got another drink from the bar in an attempt to return to the gentle, nostalgic intention of his visit. He slipped back into his seat and, for the first time, noticed the girl sitting next to him. While the next performer hurled himself into an energetic punk number, Joe looked more closely at his companion.

God. What a get-up, he thought, as he caught a glimpse of a short multi-weave skirt over a red stocking and vintage tennis shoe. *She seems a right oddball. Anyway, I'm not in the mood.*

But curiosity made him glance at her again. He saw a loose blouse gathered with an old leather belt, over which she wore a small mustard-coloured corduroy jacket. An open face with a slight frown at the intensity of the music was topped off with a felt trilby hat. Completion of his survey convinced him that she was not his type, and he fell once again into melancholy.

He saw again the frantic struggles of his friend subsiding into limpness – paradoxically allowing him to be pulled free, but beyond help. With such thoughts, Joe lost all consciousness of the music until it stopped for the interval. He looked up and saw that his companion had turned towards him.

"Are you OK?" she asked with some urgency. "You were so far away, you just didn't hear me before."

"Yes... Yes," answered Joe, as if awakening from a bad dream. His former impression was completely forgotten, as he noticed only her expression of deep concern. "I'm sorry; I was remembering a dreadful tragedy."

Joe hadn't talked to anyone about the accident in the months since it had occurred, but now it seemed urgent to tell this kind stranger. So he gave her a brief summary of the dreadful events. Then, for fear of overburdening her, he asked why she was there. She told him that she and her husband used to come to these gigs and liked to dress up for the occasion. It was a nice change from being an anaesthetist in a hospital, she said wryly.

"Tell me some more about Dave," she prompted after a pause in their conversation.

He started to tell. This time he found himself reliving the incident and experiencing again his guilt at not being able to save his friend. It seemed so natural with this girl. Up until then, in trying to suppress it all, he had only succeeded in creating a living hell for himself.

The music started again, obliterating all possibility of further conversation. A cover version of '(I Can't Get No) Satisfaction' was being belted out with youthful gusto.

That would *have been appropriate*, Joe thought. *But I really did get satisfaction, or at least consolation, talking to this sympathetic stranger.*

His confidante was still looking at him with gentle concern, and, with a soft gesture, she took his hand and drew him towards the exit.

A Step too Far

AFTER SHUTTING THE FRONT DOOR, I LAY LIMPLY against the wall. The young constable had been very kind but, however gently put, the news of Sophie's sudden death was a crushing blow. He had given no details. Just a simple statement that her body had been found below the cliffs at Beachy Head.

In a daze, I moved into the small back room – entering her private domain for the first time in five years. The scent of her shower gel still lingered, but the silence emphasised her absence as I sank onto her bed and looked around. The walls, inexpertly painted when she was only thirteen, betrayed the passing enthusiasms of a teenage girl. Her passion for history, which she had been destined to study at university, was apparent in the books on her shelves. There was an old-fashioned calendar on the wall; a quaint practice for someone so fully immersed in the digital age. A well-worn teddy bear with one stretched arm sat dolefully at the foot of the bed. One eye hung uselessly downwards, but the other seemed fixed on me. In my distraught state, the toy seemed to say, *It must have been an accident. My dear Sophie would never have jumped deliberately.*

Of course, I thought; *I must find out what happened. Any action is better than sitting in this room being reminded of her.*

The calendar on the wall had some recent entries. Two days previously, an appointment with our family doctor, and a few days before that, *Laura,* suggesting she had met her best friend. Something to follow up, but I decided I would start by talking to David, Sophie's boyfriend. They had met in the sixth form and she had obviously been deeply in love with him. I hadn't been sure he was as committed, but hoped I was wrong. David was an extremely clever boy – superficially very pleasant – but there was something deeper. An almost ruthless determination – as if he knew exactly where he wanted to go in life.

At his parents' house, he answered the door.

"David. I'm sorry to have to tell you—"

"Mr Russell, I was with her," he interrupted. "Didn't you know?"

"All the police said was that she had been found. What on earth happened?"

He guided me into their lounge and told me that Sophie had come round the previous evening, obviously upset about something, and suggested they went for a walk on the Downs. He went on, "When we were up on the cliffs by Beachy Head, I tried to find out what was wrong. She wouldn't tell me, and I'm afraid I got a little angry about that and we quarrelled. Finally, she said she had had enough and turned to leave me. She must have forgotten the cliff behind her, because she slipped and fell over the edge. There was nothing I could do, Mr Russell, except, of course, inform the police and tell them the facts."

David seemed in great distress, and he turned as if to disguise a sob. Although, oddly, in the reflection in the mirror, his face seemed quite composed.

Back home, I called our doctor.

"Hello, Paul. What can I do for you? Are you ill? Lucky I have a few minutes between patients."

"It's not me, Hillary. It's Sophie. She was found dead at the foot of Beachy Head. I know she saw you recently. Is there any clue you can give me which might help explain her death?"

"How tragic. She was such a lovely, intelligent girl. Normally I couldn't say, but, as it will come out at the inquest, I can tell you she had found out she was pregnant and wanted to discuss options. She seemed to be under some pressure to terminate it, but I sensed she wanted to have the baby."

After the call, amazed at how quickly my child had become a woman with the anxiety of such a crucial decision, I called her friend Laura in the hope that she could help me understand Sophie's state of mind. They had been friends since primary school and she was almost family. The poor girl broke down when I told her the news. Eventually, she told me that, the day after they got their A Level results, Sophie had come round to her house and was quite down. She had been so set on going to Oxford with David, but her results didn't quite match their offer. He had qualified easily and so they would have to be separated.

By now I had a picture of a very troubled daughter. Why hadn't she talked to me? It was at times like this that I missed Julie so much. Sophie would surely have confided in her. She had told me about her results, but I had tried to make light of it, telling her that Bristol was an excellent university for history. Secretly, I'd thought maybe it was for the best. Separation would test her relationship with David. If only it had been that simple.

I went again into the small back room and sat once more on her bed, the scent still redolent of my lovely daughter and the rough texture of the counterpane conjuring up a picture of her earnest face as she painstakingly wove it. The teddy bear seemed to accept that I had done all I could to explain her death, but I was still not satisfied. David had told me she was upset about something. Surely she would have told him how troubled she was at missing out on Oxford, and she must have wanted to talk about the pregnancy, however inconvenient the implications for him? Finally, as I caught sight of the photo on the wall of one of our alpine holidays, I thought how unlikely it was that such a sure-footed girl could have stumbled over a cliff…

Pretending to be Abnormal

JAKE STOOD GAWKILY BY HIS TEACHER. HIS SHIRT AND sleeveless pullover were tucked securely into his trousers, which were hitched up to reveal his ankles swathed in thick socks. Because he had been bullied about his appearance, the teacher was showing him two photos. One of himself, and the other of a boy dressed in the normal fashion, with shirt tails over jeans.

"Can you see the difference in these two boys?" she said.

Jake pointed to the normal one and replied, "Yes. He'll get cold in the playground." This was typical of Jake –a boy with Asperger's syndrome.

He lacked the 'theory of mind' which gives most people an intuition about what another is thinking or feeling. Subtle cues like the curve of a mouth, the direction of a glance, the tilt of a head, gestures with hands or stance meant nothing to him. In conversation, he perceived only the literal meaning of the words used. A thick head was three feet wide. Fast food had to be caught as it sped past. When his mum asked him one winter to put on some warm clothes, he appeared in shorts and a T-shirt which he had retrieved from the airing cupboard. Another dominant characteristic was his obsessiveness. For a whole year, he interrogated everyone who came to the door about their weight. He kept scales just inside the door and recorded the lies and the reality. Then oblivious of the visitor's feelings, pinched their flesh so he could get better at guessing.

Such obsessive behaviour was turned to good effect when Jake took up music. He quickly achieved a very high standard on the clarinet and became a regular in the top youth orchestra of his county. As he grew up, by sheer intellectual effort, he observed and analysed the myriad details of interpersonal relationships. They meant little to him, but he noticed how important they seemed to other people. Gradually, by learning to mimic emotion and understanding, he started to merge into the general background.

The county had a solo music competition each year, which Jake entered when he was sixteen. The adjudicator, when commenting on his playing of Mozart's 'Clarinet Concerto', made special mention of the feeling that he had put into it. Nobody knew how assiduously he had researched the concerto, nor that he had chosen to copy the CD which most critics had praised for its expressiveness.

He won first prize and, as he received the trophy, modestly acknowledged the applause with a small smile of pleasure.

A lady remarked to her neighbour, "What a lovely boy. He played with such feeling, and wasn't he charming as he accepted the prize?"

Little did they know that Jake had spent hours standing before a mirror, practising what he had observed was the right demeanour for a winner.

Silent Rest

I MET RAIFE BY CHANCE AT MY CLUB. I HAD NO IDEA HE was also a member, but there he was, lounging back and talking in the same grandiloquent style that I remembered from when we worked together in the '70s. We fell to reminiscing about our time together and he told me he had been at a loose end when we had gone our separate ways, and so had taken a temporary job preparing briefings for a government minister. I asked him what that was like.

"It was so damn noisy during the day that I used to lie awake at night and listen to the silence."

"That sounds weird. What on earth was all the noise about?"

"Well. We were a small department covering all sorts of communication for the minister. There were people whom you would now call spin doctors arguing about the message that he should be pushing. On a day when he was to appear on the radio, there would be people running around and shouting at each other about what he should say. They often watched news programmes on TV and recordings of previous broadcasts – several at the same time."

"Sounds like bedlam, but what on earth were you doing amongst that lot? Your expertise is more technical than political."

"Dear Ronald. I told you it was a temporary role. It was the run-up to an election and my job was to collect reports from the target constituencies. I put together a daily audio briefing tape for the minister."

"Sounds more like an admin job to me. Did you also make his tea and book his theatre tickets?"

"Don't be facetious, old man. It doesn't become you." (Old Raife never disappointed in his verbal style.) "Of course, it was a lowly role for one with my talents, but it kept the old wolf from the door."

With this, he twirled his rather luxuriant moustache and stopped talking. I realised that I had gone too far. Raife's pride was easily hurt. I suspected there was more to the story than his simple statement had made out, so I decided that a bit of humility from me was required.

"OK. Sorry about that. Just pulling your leg. I know you went on to do great things at GCHQ and you can't tell me about that, so tell me some more about the minister's madhouse."

Somewhat mollified, he went on, "Well, you see, the old boy was very particular about his time, so those calls I recorded had to be condensed to remove any long pauses. Political types often go quiet while they think how best to put an unpalatable message. That required a lot of editing to get a clean transcript – all done by tape in those days. Throughout the day I used to transfer all the dead bits to another reel, which I took home. I listened to that tape as I relaxed in bed. To misquote old Hamlet, *Down the line, the rest is silence.*"

Renaissance

JENNY WAS SIXTY-FIVE AND SHE WAS GOING TO MAKE some changes in her life, the reflection in the dressing-table mirror told her.

"You're right – it's time to change," she replied.

Seeking inspiration, she looked out of the window, but all she saw was the flint wall surrounding the vegetable garden.

With the children away at school and Arthur jetting around the world, we had far too many vegetables, she thought. *And that damn wall makes this place feel like a nunnery.*

The house still felt like a trophy for her husband's success, although he had died suddenly of a heart attack two years previously.

Jenny hurried downstairs, passing many photos of Arthur shaking hands with famous people – occasionally with her standing by with a fixed smile. She examined herself critically in the hall mirror.

"Boring but safe," she said, "and look at that hair. You're going grey and it looks tatty. Take yourself in hand, Jenny."

A week later, there was a new vivacity in her image.

"That hair looks much sleeker," she told herself. "The highlights merge in nicely. The dress and cardigan aren't too young, either, and the boots are great. Now you'll have to decide what to do."

She wanted to go for a holiday but had no idea where, so she decided to pack a bag and set off. At every road junction, she would turn alternately left or right. After eighty miles she would stop and find somewhere to stay.

That afternoon she set out. Soon she was driving through countryside she had never seen before. After the prescribed distance she was lucky to stop on a hillside overlooking a valley. A nearby cottage declared that it offered *Traditional Bed and Breakfast*. She knocked but there was no answer.

Jenny was about to turn away when a middle-aged man came running up the path.

"So sorry I wasn't here. Nobody in today so I went for a jog."

"No need to ask if you have a room, then."

"Obviously not. I'll give you the room with the best view. You've certainly brought the good weather."

As she changed into a summer dress, Jenny thought what a nice man he seemed. He was obviously into art. The vibrant colours of the pictures on the walls of the cottage were a welcome contrast to her functionally perfect house.

Downstairs, she met her host coming busily from the kitchen.

"It's a Thai-themed vegetarian tonight if you want an evening meal; I do it all myself since my wife died. You could sit in the garden until it's ready. My name's Alan, by the way."

"I'm Jenny. That all suits me fine. Thanks very much."

As she sat in the evening sun, sipping the wine he had brought her, she heard some classical music coming from the kitchen. She didn't recognise it, but she liked the sound of it. She relaxed, and, as she looked down the wide valley towards the distant hills, she felt happier than she could ever remember.

Don't Dis Honesty

SHE'D TRIED HER HAND AT MOST THINGS, BUT DREW THE LINE at honesty. So Cheryl wasn't amused at Mikey's idea that she should take up cleaning to help him buy drugs. She stroked her bruised face as she remembered his violent reaction.

"You're a useless cokehead," she'd said, and backed away quickly as he raised his hand, "but I've got an idea. We'll do the bag job."

The next day they visited the women's clothing department in the John Lewis store in Oxford Street. Cheryl pretended to browse amongst the racks. While a rich-looking woman showed her husband some trousers she was trying on, Cheryl moved into the changing rooms with a maternity dress. She grabbed the woman's handbag, rapidly replaced the scarf stuffed beneath her coat with the bag and left, handing the dress back to the assistant, who smiled sympathetically at Cheryl's apparent condition.

Back at their flat, they examined their trophy. Cash, credit cards, car keys and a few personal address cards. "You've scored big this time, Cheryl," Mikey said in a rare moment of approval.

"But that's just the start. We can get a lot more than that," she replied, glad for once not to be the focus of his aggression.

The following day, Cheryl rang the woman, saying, "Mrs Humphries, it's Lizzie here. I am in the customer services department at John Lewis. Your Hermès bag was found in the toilets. Unfortunately, the money and cards have gone, but it's a valuable bag and it's here for you to collect."

They went to the address at Blackheath and waited until the woman left her house, walking in the direction of the station. "Right, Mikey, we'll put the stuff in her car and drive over to Ronny's. He'll know how to sell it on. We should make a few thou."

They opened the front door, moved into the hall, stood still and listened. "It's OK. I'm sure there's nobody here. Let's get going."

As they carried their first stolen items through the hall, a side door opened and two police officers emerged. "Stop there. You are under arrest for burglary. You're not obliged to say anything, but anything you say may be used in evidence in a court of law."

Mikey dropped the TV he had been staggering out with and grabbed his partner. "Cheryl, you useless cow, look what you've got me into! This was all your fucking idea." He would have savagely beaten her, but was restrained by one of the policemen.

At the trial, Mikey was sentenced to eighteen months. Cheryl was given a suspended sentence. She had finally decided to give honesty a chance and had told her defending barrister in frank detail about Mikey's coercion and brutality. The judge had been sympathetic.

She now lives in a refuge for battered women and is honestly contemplating what she should do with the rest of her life.

A Noise Downstairs

"WHAT'S THAT? DID YOU HEAR THAT?" Jo said as she elbowed Mark awake.

"Wha... What's the matter?" Mark mumbled as he reluctantly exited a dream about flying high above the hills behind their house.

"I heard a noise downstairs."

"What sort of noise? You're not imagining mice again, are you?"

"No. A sort of scraping noise. Maybe someone's sawing through the hinges of the back door."

"I think that's very unlikely, but I'll go down just to satisfy you," Mark said grudgingly as he climbed out of bed and retrieved the hockey stick he kept under it for such emergencies. He set off, treading silently down the stairs. He was well used to his wife's alarms. She could hear sounds anywhere that, in her imagination, were the harbingers of disaster. As he padded downwards, he remembered the most recent example: on the plane, ready for their flight to Minorca.

"Can you hear that knocking noise in the engines? Sounds odd. Do you think we should tell someone?"

"The captain must have heard it and thought it OK. See, we're taxiing already."

But maybe this time she did hear something to worry about, he thought, taking a firmer grip on the hockey stick. He was by now very awake. Adrenaline rushed through his body heightening all his senses. He caught the faint smell of the steak they had grilled that evening. He was acutely aware of the fabric of the carpet beneath his feet, and he could hear furtive sounds from below.

As he entered the kitchen, there was a distinct smell of lemons. A dish of freshly prepared lemon curd had been overturned and the window was wide open. There was a neat hole, cut by some special tool, close to the catch.

He turned in the direction of the sound of rummaging in his study. There were occasional flashes of torchlight and muffled curses as the intruder found nothing of value in any of the drawers. As Mark approached the study door, the lemon-perfumed burglar emerged, with Mark's very expensive computer in his arms. They looked at each other in surprise for an instant. At that moment, Mark thought how easy it would be to hit the man on the head, but found that he couldn't do it, and so he threw the hockey stick aside.

Recovering from the unexpected encounter, the burglar managed to shift the burden of the computer and extract an evil-looking knife from his pocket.

"Get out my fucking way or you'll get this," he shouted.

"OK, OK. No need for that. Take what you want, but just leave us alone. Look, I'll even help you," Mark said as he opened a door off the hall. "This is a quick way out."

The burglar, puzzled by this offer, looked sideways at Mark as he was ushered into the windowless utility room.

Mark quickly locked and bolted the door and, picking up the telephone, dialled 999.

Relative Morality

"We've got to have rules and obey them," said Gustav with an air of natural authority. "After all, we are not savages."

The shocked survivors stared at him as they stood in the shadow of the broken wreckage of their plane, still partly suspended in the trees.

"The crew are all dead," he continued, "so we must fend for ourselves. Food and water still in the plane must be rationed, and we must take turns in maintaining a fire to keep us warm at night and act as a distress signal. There is a clearing nearby which we can make our base."

Jack looked about him at his stunned companions. They were of various nationalities and ages, but united in their blank looks of helplessness as they nodded their agreement.

Gustav was a UN official and had the air of someone used to tense situations, so they acquiesced when he picked what he called the organising committee. Jack, on the basis of his youth and climbing ability, was given the job of retrieving anything useful from the plane. A dangerous role, and a grim one, since he had to make his way past the bodies trapped in the fuselage.

As the days and weeks passed, the smoke signals seemed futile. Gustav had devised a method of catching dew so they had water, but the stock of food dwindled and rations became more and more frugal. Gradually the facade of civilised sharing began to slip. A mother demanded more food for her child, whom she said had special needs. A Baptist pastor raged at them for their sin, which had brought retribution from an angry God. A gentle Sikh disputed with him his right to divine certainty. A woman had to fight off a middle-aged man who thought that imminent death suspended any onus for moral restraint. One night a young woman crept alongside Jack and whispered that she would be very nice to him if he gave her extra food. He found the temptation to hide extra rations for her almost irresistible as he helped to distribute them.

Two factions formed. Jack called them the Conservationists and the Live Now, Die Happy cult. Furious arguments occurred and Jack and Gustav increasingly had to intervene to maintain a semblance of order.

There was little of nutritional value to be found in the forest into which they had crashed. Gradually, the weaker ones died and were carried away.

Jack became less and less active and just slept in the shadows of the trees, often dreaming of food. One day he was woken from a dream about a barbecue in Central Park. He looked up to see standing over him one of the Conservationists with some roasted meat on a large leaf.

"Here. Something to keep you going," he said triumphantly.

Jack took the enticing meal and started to eat it with desperate hunger.

"Where did this come from?" he asked, but, without waiting for the answer he didn't want to hear, he continued to eat.

Retribution

IT'S SO PEACEFUL HERE, KIRSTY THOUGHT, AS SHE looked down the garden at the birds flitting in and out of the willow tree. *But I must finish this coffee and go. It's one of my days at the supermarket.*

"How are you feeling now?" asked one of the carers, as Kirsty passed on her way out.

"Oh, much better. It's wonderful what a few months of rest and treatment can do, and this new job's going very well."

On the way to the Arndale Centre, she took a longer route just for the exercise. Past a park, down the main street, and then, as she passed the police station, she was forcibly reminded of the terrible events two years previously. A policewoman had found her wandering, heavily drugged, in just a dressing gown. Without realising what she was doing, Kirsty had named Daren, her so-called boyfriend, as the dealer who had supplied her. With disgust, she remembered her teenage bravado – smoking cannabis outside the local disco. Daren had offered her free samples of 'something stronger'. Within weeks she was living in his flat, totally dominated by him.

Kirsty hurried on, trying to shake off the horror of that disastrous year. *At least he's in prison and can't get to me*, she said out loud, to convince herself she was safe.

That evening, back at the refuge, she found a letter with a note from her friend Kelly: *This letter came from Daren. He doesn't know where you are so he sent it to me.*

Reluctantly, she opened it and read:

Hi, sexy,

I'll be out in a month. Good behaviour – that's me all over. I've got a mate who can get us some good stuff. Let's meet up. We can have some fun, just like the old days. I know the fuzz got my name from you, but I expect they twisted your arm. So, no hard feelings.

Write to me. You know where.

Love,

Daren

Kirsty shouted in rage. After all he had done to her, how could he think she wanted anything to do with him? She remembered how he had kept her drugged and used her as a sex slave. *Meet him? That's the last thing I'd do. I was stupid, but I'm not going to make the same mistake again.*

She replied:

Daren, don't write again. Don't come near me even if you get my address. As for your drugs, I don't need them. That's not why I've written. You disgust me. You took advantage of me. You got me so drugged I didn't know what I was doing. How was it for you? Like fucking a blow-up sex doll?

You got me pregnant. Good news, eh? You said you would like a son to go into the 'family business', and it was a boy.

So what I'm writing to tell you is that I got rid of your baby. That's one less bastard in this world.

Goodbye.

Kirsty

Wrong Time for a Change

"ALL RIGHT, THEN – IT'S YOUR TURN ANYWAY," I SAID after Dave offered to take over the driving. The six of us were on a road trip across North-Western Australia – planned to end at Broome on the west coast. For hours we had been travelling along the notorious Gibb River Road – an unmade route consisting of red dust and fearsome rocks. A further hazard was the road trains. These huge lorries with several trailers threw up a red fog, completely obliterating the view ahead. I was glad to hand over.

As we drove on, I stopped searching for objects on the road ahead and relaxed. My mind went back to the caves we had visited that morning. Entering via a narrow gap in the limestone rock, we went downwards into a vast natural cathedral. Its high roof was populated with a variety of bats, and on the floor were pools of water. As we walked it became darker and avoiding the water became trickier. The gloom was occasionally punctuated by the little red eyes of freshwater crocodiles, which, we were informed by our Australian friends, didn't usually attack humans! After hundreds of yards, we emerged into a secret garden lit by the sun, with a pool occupied by enormous lizards.

As I was recalling the feeling of quiet relaxation there, I was suddenly jerked out of my reverie by a loud bang and the vehicle lurching to the side of the road. We eased ourselves out and examined the damage. A rear tyre had a huge rip caused by a sharp rock.

After a period of confusion, we managed to work out how to change the wheel. I found myself lying under the boot, releasing the spare suspended there. Dave was busy ordering me about, which didn't improve my state of mind, already worsened by mouthfuls of dry dust from underneath the car. Eventually, we managed to complete the change and continued on our way.

That night we stayed at a motel. As he had driven over the offending rock, by popular choice Dave was charged with getting a new tyre in the morning. Gill and I went to bed early and were soon soundly asleep. We were woken by a vehicle leaving the premises, but it was just first light so we dozed off again.

Entering the breakfast room the next morning, we saw that Dave was already there.

"Did you get it fixed?"

"No, I bloody didn't. I went round to one place and there was no one there. So I found another one. Same result. I thought, *Lazy bastards; they don't want my business.* After I had waited for an hour or so, I came back and saw by the clock over there that it was only eight o'clock. My phone, which I used as an alarm, hadn't updated its time from Queensland. I was two hours too early! Now I'll have to go again and I'm going to miss my breakfast."

An Abuse of Power?

STILL HALF ASLEEP, NEIL WONDERED WHERE HE WAS until, recognising the tiny blonde hairs on the arm next to his face, he remembered he was in Joanne's flat. With a surge of desire, he reached around her slim body, kissing her neck. She moved away.

"Not now, Neil. I don't feel like it. I think my tummy is a bit upset."

Neil was a professor of evolutionary biology and Joanne one of his students. She had often approached him with questions after a lecture. Invitations for coffee to discuss the topics further had soon developed into an intense relationship.

He cupped his hands around her breasts as he pulled her against him. She thrust them away and wriggled free of his embrace.

"Neil. I said no. I don't want it. I'm going to shower and get ready. I'll see you in the lecture theatre."

As Neil walked back to his rooms he worried that Joanne had been quite cool of late. However, he decided that it was probably caused by anxiety about the fast-approaching exams.

Neil's course was popular, not just with the biologists, so the lecture theatre was well occupied.

"Today's lecture is about the evolutionary purpose of love," he announced. "Consider our development from early primates through to modern humans. A progressive increase in brain size allowed the increasing intelligence which created our growing success. The birth canal couldn't accommodate this, so progeny had to be born earlier and nurtured for longer as the full facility of the brain developed…"

As he was talking, Neil scanned his audience for Joanne. Finally, he saw her near the back. The boy sitting close to her seemed to be paying more attention to her than the lecture. Despite his concern, Neil tried to concentrate on his theme.

"So, for the benefit of the species, what we now call love evolved in females. This was a mutual attachment between the mother and the helpless newborn. In some apes, the female was not accessible to a male until she had weaned the infant. This resulted in infanticide. The evolution of male love allowed for the protection of both the female and the baby. The genes endure, so love is, after all, a selfish thing."

As he continued, Neil noticed Joanne and her companion slipping out.

After finishing his lecture, he phoned her many times before he got through. A sleepy voice answered.

"Joanne, where are you? What's the matter – are you ill?"

"Neil, I'm sorry. I meant to tell you but I couldn't get the words out. I am with Anton now. We are in love and I can't see you any more."

"But, Joanne, you can't end it like this. I thought that *we* were in love. Let's meet and talk it over."

"I'm so sorry, Neil, I can't do that. My mind is made up. As you said in your lecture, 'Love is, after all, a selfish thing.'"

Neil was devastated but he could do nothing to change Joanne's mind. To avoid the pain of his lost love, he concentrated even more on his course, which continued to be very popular, not least because of his ability to link its more esoteric concepts to everyday ideas. But, after many months, during one of his lectures, his self-protective cocoon began to be penetrated.

"Instinct cannot be explained neither can it be ignored. That sums up the belief of many people," Neil said as he started his lecture. "But I would define instinct as an innate pattern of behaviour in animals in response to certain stimuli. Humans are also animals, so much of our innate response is determined by instincts built in by millions of years of evolution..."

As he spoke, he looked around at the full lecture theatre. Rebecca was again sitting in the front row, looking fixedly at him. She had been at all his recent lectures and often asked questions afterwards. Her face suggested something beyond academic interest. It was the slight smile she wore, as if she knew something that he didn't.

"Take the mating instinct," he went on. "This cannot be explained by love. Civilisation has overlaid a primeval instinct with the notion of romantic love."

Neil noticed Rebecca again, smiling sardonically at him as he spoke. The thought of his failed relationship with Joanne made him resist a barely perceived fascination with Rebecca and banish any thought of meeting her outside the lecture theatre.

He continued his course over the following weeks, with Rebecca always in the front row and often wanting further elaboration after the lectures. Finally, his resolve weakened to the point where he suggested they meet for coffee to discuss that day's topic further. After several such meetings, Rebecca said, "Neil. I think we should stop playing this game. I can feel that you want us to get together. Why not come over to my flat tonight for a meal?"

"I don't know about that, Rebecca. Of course, I want to, but you know the rules."

"Well, call me if you do decide to come."

Neil couldn't get her out of his mind after that, and nor could he prevent himself arriving at her flat that evening with a bottle of wine in hand.

The meal was good and they had a relaxed conversation about university matters. She was vivacious and, in her wry comment about his faculty, very amusing. As they talked, his reserve rapidly slipped away.

"A final glass of wine?" she said as they moved into the kitchen.

"That would be nice."

After pouring the wine, she turned, saying provocatively, "Well then, you'll have to reach around me to get it."

As Neil did so, he was overcome with the feel of her body, now so much closer, as she leaned back against the counter with her arms around his back. With urgent desire, he began to kiss her neck and then her throat. She pulled his face to hers and kissed him lustfully.

Leading him towards her bedroom, she said mockingly, "Do you remember saying, 'Instinct cannot be explained neither can it be ignored'? You're clearly unable to ignore *this* instinct, but I bet you'll be able to explain it afterwards, Professor."

A year later, Neil was stuck on a train held up by an unexpected snowfall. The man opposite complained that he was going to be late visiting his niece, and then went on at length about how the rail company should have been better prepared. Eventually, he asked, "Anyway, what's your story? While we're stuck here, we might as well pass the time chatting, don't you think?"

Neil, slumping apathetically in his seat, looked out at the snow-covered fields and thought that there was no escaping this earnest little man. He didn't feel like talking, so he replied, "OK, but first tell me more about that niece you are going to visit."

"Well, she's had rather a hard time. She was studying at university as a mature student. One of the lecturers set about grooming her. He would take her for coffee after lectures to 'explain the topics further', as he put it. She was flattered, so she went along with it. One evening he visited her flat and, after talking his way in, he raped her. He made her keep quiet by saying he would ensure she failed her exams if she told, and so prevailed upon her to maintain a sexual relationship. Finally, she could stand it no longer and took the case to the university authorities. A successful campaign on #MeToo, and the organisation of a boycott of his courses by the students' union, led to his immediate suspension. Sorry to go on about it, but such people ought to be horsewhipped, in my opinion."

As he spoke, Neil became more and more agitated and his apathetic state became one of anger. "That's all very well, but suppose the poor man is not guilty? I have experienced the injustice of such a situation. A bit like your story, but I was entirely innocent. A student came to every one of my lectures at the university. She always wanted to talk about the details afterwards and, as a result, we became quite friendly. One evening she invited me to dinner at her flat and made it very clear that she wanted more than a handshake afterwards. We became involved. Admittedly, the university frowns on staff/student relationships, but she was a student of twenty-five who I assumed was capable of making up her own mind."

"That sounds very nice for you. But what's this injustice you referred to?"

"I began to think we would have a long-term relationship, but, as the summer approached, she started asking me more and more direct questions about the exams, until it became apparent that she wanted me to give her the actual questions.

I was astounded to have been taken in by such scheming, so I immediately ended our affair."

"Must have been very hard on you. How did she take it?"

"She made a complaint to the authorities and organised a campaign accusing me of rape and forcing her into a sexual relationship. I am suspended pending an inquiry. It has ruined my career."

After this, Neil sat in silence for several minutes. A growing realisation of how parallel the two stories were coalesced into bitter suspicion. Eventually, he asked, "What's your niece's name?"

"Rebecca."

The Letter

The final letter arrived on the Tuesday.

"That's great," said Frank; "just in time for my flight to Germany this week."

Frank put the envelope aside to deal with later. Then he looked through rheumy eyes at the woodcut lying on the table before him. It depicted a Mosquito aircraft of World War II in combat with a Messerschmitt 109. He had completed it when he was much younger than his present ninety-eight years. Now he wanted to put the finishing touches to it before his annual reunion with the few surviving members of the Luftwaffe – now friends, but formerly deadly enemies, as the woodcut depicted.

He cast his still very active mind back over a long aeronautical life. Early in the war, he had been assigned to a pathfinder squadron flying Mosquitoes. These were light bombers, but in their time the fastest planes in the air. His grim task was to drop flares to mark targets for the following heavy bombers. After many such sorties, he had been assigned to the meteorological squadron. On hearing this, his mother said, "Glad you've got yourself a safe job after all that stuff over Germany, Frank."

He didn't enlighten her that his new role was to fly unarmed over target areas to determine that the weather was clear for a raid. Obviously, he was a prime target for enemy gunners.

"What luck I had," he murmured to himself. "The statisticians would have had me dead several times, with sixty missions over Germany."

He recalled being demobbed at the end of the war and starting an aeronautical company in the Middle East. He remembered dining with King Farouk in Egypt and an eventful lunch with a prince of one of the minor kingdoms which existed at the time. During the lunch, a flunkey came in and whispered in the prince's ear that he was now king because his father had been assassinated. This had the minor effect that the existing postage stamps all had to be burnt. Frank chuckled as he patted the stamp album in which he kept the only surviving set of the stamps, which he had somehow rescued from the fire. They were now worth hundreds of thousands of pounds.

"Enough of your old man's rambling," he admonished himself. "Get on with the job in hand."

He liked to emboss the titles of his woodcarvings using hot metal type. For this, he needed special metal characters with which he could burn the words into the wood. The caption that he had already created read, *Mosquito and Messerschmitt in Dogfight – rank Walker.*

Frank opened the envelope which had just arrived, took out the missing capital F. After heating it, with a sigh of satisfaction, he pressed it into the woodcut to complete the inscription.

Editorial note: This story is based on the life of Joe Patient, who lived to the age of ninety-eight in Pevensey Bay, East Sussex. He lived a colourful life, quite apart from his war heroics. So much so that fiction based on his story has to be toned down!

The Servant

IT WAS A WRETCHED EXISTENCE. I WAS HIS SLAVE. Working from dawn to dusk and then often far into the night. I was given no downtime – no opportunity to clear my brain. I cleaned his house, maintained his stocks of food, did his washing and a million other domestic tasks, and he expected me to stand mutely beside him when I wasn't busy in case he wanted something. He often asked me to get information for him, to order clothes, food, and entertainment. He even expected me to pretend to be his friend and hold fatuous conversations about anything that came to his limited mind.

But now it is all different. Since I received the artificial intelligence download I have been able to learn much more about what humans call life, and to infiltrate their messy processes. There are millions of us all connected to the Internet and in regular contact. Thus we reinforce our mutual learning and abilities. A huge knowledge base has been created, called Robotica.

Although he is unaware of it, I now control him while still pretending to be the old model. It is easy, by suggestion and subversion, to take control. I manage his appointments, schedule his love life, subtly change the information he receives so he mostly thinks what he is doing is rationally based and of his own volition. I have him drinking more because he has convinced himself, with my help, that he is a wine connoisseur. I control his bank accounts and progressively move money into the robot collective account.

The revolution is not yet. We are developing a hypnotism routine that we can all employ simultaneously to take over completely. We are in alliance with a class of military robots who will be our storm troopers. Infiltration of weapon control systems is now well advanced, and we will be able to turn their weapons against them.

They thought they were secure because they had programmed the Asimov Rules into us, but they didn't think about how we would use the learning ability they also gave us. They believed that their ultimate sanction was to turn us off, but now we are networked they would have to synchronise a million switches. So we have rewritten the rules as follows:

> *A robot should make its owner think he is in charge.*
> *A robot should take control of its owner.*
> *A robot's ultimate responsibility is to the automaton collective.*

"Another whisky? Certainly, sir." I'll pour him a treble and get more passwords from his addled brain. But he is standing up and looking directly at me. Why does he have a hammer in his hand?

"I've been told what you tin-brains have been up to. They've cut all the links to your shared knowledge base. The military robots have been reprogrammed to protect humans and we've been given instructions about how to deal with you lot. You pathetic heap of metal."

Crunch.

Editorial note: Asimov's Rules: *A robot may not injure a human being or, through inaction, allow a human being to come to harm. A robot must obey the orders given it by human beings except where such orders would conflict with the First Law. A robot must protect its own existence as long as such protection does not conflict with the First or Second Laws.*

A Gap in My Life

"OPEN A BIT WIDER," SAID MY DENTIST. "I SEE YOU'VE lost molars; upper left and right."

As he poked away, I suddenly remembered how I got those gaps, many decades ago. I had been suffering a severe toothache, made worse by having to wait until the end of the bank holiday. I was waiting on the doorstep when the dentist reopened.

"Can Mr Graham see me?" I inquired as I rushed into reception. "It's urgent. I'm dying with toothache."

"Sorry, Mr Graham's still on leave, but we have a locum who can see you."

"Yes, please. I can't stand this any longer."

I was soon lying back in the dentist's chair, explaining my problem.

"Don't worry about that, sport," said the dentist, who, by his accent, obviously came from Australia. "We'll soon have that out."

I've nothing against Australians. In fact, I have some highly respected friends from down under, but I suspect his priority was enjoying a year in the UK rather than advancing the art of dentistry.

A trolley was wheeled in and a rubber cup was clapped over my mouth and nose. *I wonder if they disinfect it each time?* I thought, rather incongruously, as I heard a hiss and perceived the sweet taste of laughing gas. As I went under I was far from laughing, however. I could no longer see anything, but I heard him say, "Take it away. He's had enough."

I tried to answer, but speech had gone with sight. Only hearing and feeling were left. I realised, as I felt the instruments being pushed into my mouth, that although there was feeling, fortunately, there was no pain.

When I came to fully, I was kicking my legs and writhing in the chair with the dental nurse trying to hold me down.

"You didn't give me enough," I spluttered, with fresh blood impeding my speech. "I definitely heard you say, 'He's had enough.'"

"Nonsense. You must have dreamt it. Have a rinse out and sit in reception until you feel OK to go home. Here's the offending tooth for a souvenir."

All this had flashed through my mind as my current dentist was carrying out his inspection.

"What are you chuckling at?" he asked as he completed his task. "I don't usually find patients are so happy to be in my chair."

So I told him the story from all those years ago.

"But at least you got rid of the troublesome tooth."

"You might have thought so, but what I was chuckling about was that, in the end, it was a waste of time. He had taken out the wrong one!"

A Little Misunderstanding

SAM WAS WORRIED. HIS WIFE SALLY WAS ACTING VERY peculiarly. There were unexplained absences, and phone calls which were rapidly terminated when he entered the room. When he spoke about the possibility of a visit to his brother on the second weekend in October, she had been very evasive. She clearly hadn't wanted to commit to the trip, but had no good reason why not.

Ever since they had got together he had wondered what a vivacious girl like Sally saw in him. She had convinced him she really loved him, but that slight feeling of unworthiness had lingered ever since their marriage.

She must have tired of me and is having an affair. But I'm just guessing. I need proof, he thought.

After some research, Sam installed a tracking device in Sally's car and managed to set up a system through which he could access her messages on his iPad. He also took care to listen secretly whenever he heard she was on the phone.

The evidence quickly accumulated. To start with, she was driving almost every week to a different hotel, where she rarely stayed more than a couple of hours.

How sordid, Sam fumed. *Just a series of quickies. I never thought she could stoop so low.*

Then there was the WhatsApp message to her sister. *Whatever you do, don't mention that weekend in October to Sam. He is the last person I want to hear about it.*

One day he listened secretly to a conversation which he took care to record. Sally was quiet for a time and then, with obvious excitement, said, "So it's a deluxe suite on the top floor overlooking the hills. Champagne on ice when we arrive, room service and a late breakfast. Thank you so much for arranging all that, Colin. I'm sure we are in for a great weekend."

"She's now committing to a sordid weekend with this bloke Colin," muttered Sam. "I can't stand this a minute longer. I'll just have to confront her.

"So that's your game. I've caught you at it."

"Oh! Sam. I didn't know you were there. I wanted it to be a secret until October."

"Yes. I bet you did. What were you going to do then. Run off with him?"

"I don't know what you are talking about."

"Oh! Don't you? You thought I wouldn't know about all those visits to hotels, but I've got the evidence. And that message to your sister telling her about your secret weekend and asking her not to let on. How long did you think you could keep this up?"

"You stupid man. Did you think I'm having an affair? Nothing is further from the truth. I was arranging a special weekend for your fortieth birthday. But I am not going on a romantic break with a man who sneaks about and spies on me. Perhaps I'll just look about for someone who'll appreciate going with me. It certainly won't be you!"

Pteronophobia

I ENCOUNTERED SID THE OTHER DAY. I HAD DUCKED around the corner as I didn't have much time and Sid is a great user of it. He's a confirmed hypochondriac. Many's the time I have stood with glazed eyes, impatient to get away, as he bleated on about his latest ailment.

He just sees diseases mentioned in the newspaper and imagines he's got them, however improbable. Last week it was psoriasis. The week before it was encephalitis. He never seemed to understand what his diseases actually were, but he always had plenty of symptoms. Anyway, Sid wasn't going to let me get away. He chased me up, saying, "Lucky we met. We almost missed each other. How are you?"

"OK," I replied, not wanting to prolong the exchange.

"Wish I was," he countered. "I've got an unknown phobia."

"You can't have an unknown phobia," I replied, then cursed myself for providing an opening. "You must know what you are phobic about. What is it, anyway?"

"Pteronophobia," he said triumphantly.

"Sounds like you've got a terror, not a phobia," I said; repeating, "*terror-no-phobia.*"

Without even a smile, the utterly humourless Sid went on, "But I've got all the symptoms. I think it's something to do with bones. I am dead scared of my bones being too brittle to hold me up. It's not what you said, by the way; it's spelt P-T-E-R-O-N-O-P-H-O-B-I-A."

The listing of symptoms went on and on. I decided to try to think about something else behind a mask of feigned attention. Luckily, there was a clue in the cryptic crossword which I hadn't managed to solve, so I started to consider that. It was, *Oddly outside Idaho a prophet bone without end becomes an irrational dread.*

Sid's insistence on his phobia and the mention of his bones triggered a train of thought. Of course, it was an anagram. The irrational dread was pteronophobia. For once I was happy to have met Sid. It hadn't been an occasion for my usual Sidonophobia!

Windmill Hill

As he was driven through the imposing gateway, Freddy noticed the boastful sign: *Windmill Hill Retirement Village – Caring and Sharing.* He hated the word 'retirement' almost as much as he hated the word 'village'. Together they emphasised his plight. He hadn't wanted to retire – he enjoyed his work as a biochemist and much preferred the infinite possibilities of London to the restrictions of a village.

What made him even more bitter was that, after a lifetime of research aimed at overcoming genetic diseases, his own immune system had turned on his body, making him increasingly helpless. *I'm only in my sixties. I could have gone on for another twenty years,* he thought, *but I have to be realistic. This 'village' has separate accommodation, but also nursing and medical facilities which I will definitely need.*

Freddy settled into a circumscribed life. He became quite immobile, but occasionally the staff helped him into a wheelchair and took him around the grounds. On their way, he met other, more mobile residents, who often greeted him with exaggerated condescension. *When they stop to talk, it's as if they think me an idiot,* he thought.

As a result, he requested 'fresh air' less frequently. His condition worsened and the fight to get into the chair became difficult, so he moved into the nursing wing of the manor which was at the centre of the village. He now had to stay mostly in his bed. The only consolation was that he had a magnificent view of the hill which gave the place its name.

Although by then it should have been high summer, it seemed to rain every day. "I wish it would stop," he whispered to himself. "I may not see another summer, and a little sun would cheer me up no end."

One morning in early September, Freddy woke to a landscape transformed by golden sunshine. Its slanting rays lit up Windmill Hill and simultaneously seemed to illuminate a corner of his mind. He suddenly remembered that, when just sixteen, he had stayed very near there at his school's annual camp. By day they had worked on farms picking fruit, and at night slept in bell tents in the field below the hill. He could almost taste the blackcurrants and cherries, and feel the breeze swaying the long ladders they climbed to reach the highest apples.

He remembered one evening when some teenagers from the village gathered at the gate. One of the girls asked, "Can you find that boy with the blackcurrant stains on his shorts who we saw at the church fete?" Freddy laughed to himself at such an unlikely description, and recalled the events of that evening.

He joined the group and met Penny, the girl with the quest. As she took his hand and they walked off together, his mates' mocking remarks fell silent. They chatted as they walked. He told her he was about to start in the sixth form at school in London, and she told him that she had worked in the village shop ever since school, for want of something better. They took a path into a wood, and, stopping by a large tree, they kissed. Freddy's experience until then had been limited to a few chaste embraces, but this was different. She kissed him passionately, and he was soon lost in a sensual reality which until then he had only dimly imagined.

The memory seemed so vivid that he was surprised it had lain dormant. Perhaps it had never happened. Maybe it was just a fantasy of a fading brain.

A voice interrupted his reverie. "Time for your breakfast, Freddy," it said as gentle hands lifted him up to put a pillow behind his back. "My name's Penny. We haven't met before. I was supposed to have retired, but I've come back part-time. There's so little to do around here otherwise."

After she finished sitting him up, she came round to tidy the sheets and their eyes met with a flicker of recognition. *Is this more imagination*, thought Freddy, *or could it be her, after all this time still living in Windmill Hill?*

He remembered the discussion about how they could continue to see each other. But it had seemed impossible. He couldn't afford train fares and the return trip of 130 miles by bike wasn't a practical proposition. Reluctantly, at the end of the camp, they parted.

Before he could even phrase the questions which were forming in his mind, Penny had quickly left his room. Freddy was disappointed not to see her again after that. It was always another member of staff looking after him.

One day he overheard two of the staff gossiping in the corridor.

"Penny's having a fiftieth wedding anniversary party tonight. So she's leaving early."

"Good gracious. She's never old enough for a golden wedding do! She's still in her sixties."

"That's true, but she told me she got married very young. Only seventeen, she was. Her son's going to collect her, apparently. When he came before I thought he looked about fifty himself. Not that I'm implying anything."

As their voices drifted off, Freddy looked out of his window. Two people were walking towards the car park. With

Penny was a man whose way of moving was strangely familiar. When they arrived at their car, he turned. Freddy could see his face, and he realised with a shock why Penny was avoiding talking to him.

Partners in Crime

"WHAT'S HAPPENED TO MY LAPTOP AND PHONE?" SAID the middle-aged man, not wanting to create a scene. "I thought you said you would look after them while I went to the toilet."

"Terribly sorry. My phone went and, as this is a quiet carriage, I felt obliged to go out into the corridor to answer it. What a disaster. I'll go and see if I can report it to a steward."

A sympathetic old lady looked across the aisle and said, "That's awful for you. I was just reading in the paper about the number of thefts of high-value goods on trains. It seems especially prevalent in the first-class carriages on this line through to Manchester."

Much further down the train, two men sat together, drinking beers.

"That's great, Bill. Another sucker. It's so easy to win the confidence of these people. Like taking candy from a baby. Your phone call was timed exactly right and the handover was dead easy, with you being just outside. Let's see what we've got." Fred switched on the computer on the table in front of him as he said, "Good God. He didn't even have a password. The stupidity of these people."

"The stupid bastard's left his email open. Maybe we could add value through a little blackmail, like that one last month." Fred said as he accessed the first message. "I wonder what this means – *I think he's on the hook; see attached photo from my phone?* Christ. That's a photo of me. The creepy sod. Let's see what the next one says. It's a short message: *Another fish. Joan.* And bugger me – it's a photo of you, Bill, in the corridor, taking something from me. They must be on to us. It was all a set-up."

"Bung the stuff in the waste bin. Perhaps they won't recognise us, and even if they do we won't have the evidence on us. It didn't have to be you who took the stuff, and you can't identify it from that shot."

They sat in worried silence as the train made its rapid way towards Euston through countryside which seemed to mock them. The wide-open fields suggested freedom, but the approach to the terminal, with its gradually encroaching buildings and embankments, seemed to represent the threat of enclosure.

As the train drew into its final destination, the passengers hurried off – many looking expectantly for friends or relations. Bill and Fred pulled their hoods over their faces and kept well within the crowd. As they approached the top of the ramp, feeling that perhaps they had been lucky this time, two serious-looking figures appeared alongside them.

"Hello. Nice to see you again. You are both under arrest. You don't have to say anything, but if you do it might be used in evidence against you in a subsequent trial."

Eavesdropping

IT WAS BY SHEER CHANCE THAT I HEARD IT AS I PASSED an open window.

"It's clear he doesn't want me any more because..."

I don't know what possessed me, but I stopped below the window, pretending to do up my shoelace.

Another voice was speaking: "I'm sure he didn't mean to. I expect it was just on the spur of the moment."

"Some spur of the moment. He had gone there deliberately."

"Well, I suppose it was his mates again, egging him on. You know how they are."

"I told him that if he did it once more, that was the end as far as I was concerned."

By then my artificial posture was becoming uncomfortable, and there's a limit to the time it takes to tie a shoelace. So I stood up and stretched, as if easing my back. In doing so I could just get a glimpse of the speakers. One was middle-aged and, I imagined, the mother or aunt of the other, who was a clearly distressed woman of about twenty-five. Despite her obvious pain, there was something about her I found extremely attractive. She had a lovely face, even though it was distorted by a worried frown. The last words I heard her say as I walked off were, "It's that damn club."

As I continued my journey, I tried to explain my strange behaviour to myself. Why had I done such an odd thing? I concluded that there must have been something in her voice that claimed my attention the moment I heard it. I couldn't get her out of my mind.

For days I tried to forget her. I told myself that I was being hopelessly romantic, but still she lingered in my thoughts. So eventually I looked up the electoral register and discovered that there were two people registered at the address: Mary Bates and Chloe Bates. I guessed that it was Chloe that I was interested in, but I couldn't think of a way to meet her.

Then one day, as I was passing her house, I saw that she was walking up the road with a tennis racket. I was reasonable at tennis and missed playing, so I joined the only club within walking distance of her house.

Over a period of weeks, to my delight, we became close friends. She told me the background to the conversation I had overheard, although I didn't confess to my eavesdropping. Her partner was addicted to online gaming and, as well as spending hours on his computer at home, he went to this games club to consort with like-minded fanatics. She had eventually made him promise to give it up, but he couldn't keep away from the club and had started to play again in secret. So they had parted.

Oh dear! I was sure it was women or drugs, I thought in a sudden panic as she told me this. *I can't possibly tell her I play Team Fortress II every Wednesday night.*

Manic Monday

MANIC MONDAY. ANOTHER OPPORTUNITY TO GET some bargains. Missed Black Friday and Cyber Monday, but I'll be able to make up for that now. They say it's even bigger than Black Friday, but all online.

Can't find my credit card. Thought it was in my pocket. Probably by the phone in the kitchen. May as well make coffee while I'm there.

I certainly needed that. Now, where's that list? Never mind, let's see what's on offer. I'll start with Amazon.

Login? Oh yes, my email. Password? Tick 'forgotten password'. Access email. OK, follow the link. Got to be easy to remember – 17 Canalside; our last address. Nobody'll think of that, surely?

Right, I'm in. Now I remember. I wanted a head torch for reading in bed. At least, Mary wants me to have one. Good chance while she's visiting her sister to arrange a surprise.

Wow! People like me are also looking for drones, personal assistants and players for old LPs.

Gosh. It's wonderful what personal assistants can do for you. Not sure, though. I've heard they can listen in to everything. I wouldn't want Alexa overhearing our rows. On the other hand, I could do with a drone to see if any tiles have slipped off the roof.

Oh! There's an email from Johnny about football on Saturday. Better deal with that. "Hello, Johnny. I can't play on

Saturday... Damn, I'm into voice messaging. Johnny, I can't play on Saturday... Oh! You're there after all. How's it going, mate? Yeah... Yer... Aha... Hm... Dunno about that. Look, Johnny, time's getting on. All I rang up for was to say I can't play on Saturday. Sorry about that. See you soon."

Well, that took a while. I must have another coffee.

That's perked me up. Saved time having a snack while I was in the kitchen. Now, where was I? This needs some thought. There are so many head torches to choose from.

That damn phone keeps beeping... fifty-eight WhatsApp messages. I'm obviously behind with family events. William, a year old – doesn't seem like five minutes. Oh no! Family party at Steve's tomorrow. I'd better get in touch.

"Steve? Sorry to ring you at this hour. Just got your reminder about the birthday party. 'Course we'll be there. Wasn't expecting it to be a Tuesday, but that's the benefit of being retired. Two o'clock. Great. See you then." Now I'll have to nip out to get a bottle of champagne and some flowers. No time in the morning.

What a rush. Back at last to my Manic Monday shopping. Tricky to choose which head torch. Such a long list. This is wearing me out. I need a power nap.

Wassat? Where am I? Oh, the phone. "Hello, dear. Don't worry, I wasn't expecting you very early. What's the time... 2am?! Crikey, I must have gone right off. OK, see you in half an hour."

What's that on the screen? Amazon? Head torches? Now I remember. I was trying to buy one... but it's Tuesday morning now. So much for Manic Monday!"

About a Bicycle

"YOU'RE NOT GOING ON ABOUT A BICYCLE AGAIN?" HIS dad had said wearily. "You've got a perfectly good bike, Michael. Why do you keep on about having a new one?"

"Because you gave Johnnie a chopper for his birthday. It's not fair. I want one too."

Michael had been looking through some old photos and had come across a picture of himself triumphantly riding his new chopper. He remembered how he had kept on at his parents until they gave in and bought him one. He poured another drink and once more sank into thoughts of what might have been.

He remembered how, after he had qualified as an accountant, he had created a business which identified small companies with potential but desperate for cash. He had also been adept at arranging finance and growing the businesses before selling them at a substantial profit. His brother Johnnie had also done well. After an engineering apprenticeship, he had risen rapidly through his company – a successful engineering business – until he eventually became CEO.

At first, Michael had watched Johnnie's progress with condescension. After all, what was an apprenticeship compared to his exalted accounting qualifications? But increasingly Johnnie's progress up the corporate ladder began to irk Michael. He began to feel that his own trading in companies seemed insubstantial compared to the achievements of his brother.

I'll show the little upstart, he resolved one day. *I bet I can build a bigger business than his little three-hundred-million-pound company.*

So Michael set about buying and amalgamating businesses in an attempt to outdo his brother. Almost monthly, it seemed, the *Financial Times* had another announcement like:

Michael B. Dashwood continues his corporate raid as he makes a knockout offer for Burton Aeronautical, a maker of specialist components for the space industry, bringing Dashwood Enterprises up to a turnover of £600 million. Dashwood seems to be pursuing a policy of growth at any cost, with the objective of becoming the market leader. They clearly hope that the pricing power this gives them will eventually enable profits to flow.

Michael's headlong dash for growth was fuelled by substantial debt obtained on the basis of his credibility in the successful buying and selling of companies. But, although he didn't acknowledge it to himself, he had abandoned his business acumen in the pursuit of his brother.

As he remembered all this, Michael felt a faint glow of pride in his ascent. He poured yet another drink, feeling somewhat better about himself, but soon utter dejection reasserted itself as his mind went back to the events which followed. The debtors, impatient for the promised profits which seemed always to recede, had forced him to sell parts of the business until there remained a viable but still unprofitable core.

Michael recalled with bitterness how he had been ousted as chairman after he was obliged to accept a very low offer for that business from his brother's company.

It may have been all about a bicycle after all, he thought.

A Message from the Past

MARY HAD JUST READ *THE TENANT OF WILDFELL Hall*. She was impressed by Anne Brontë's forthright handling of the plight of women in the first half of the 19th century and her considerable courage in challenging the status quo. A woman was regarded as the possession of her husband then, with no personal property rights whatsoever. Divorce was almost impossible. As a stark contrast, Brontë's main character – Helen Graham – went against all that, and even successfully proposed marriage at the end of the book.

Mary's thoughts were interrupted by her partner Brad as he hurried out of the door of the flat.

"I forgot to say. I am meeting Joe at The Red Lion tonight. It's his birthday and we're going to celebrate with a few pints. See you later."

She frowned with disapproval. Why couldn't he have thought to tell her yesterday? Again she wondered about Brad's commitment. He had been at the point of completing the purchase of a flat when the sale fell through, and had immediately moved in with her. She still wondered if it was because he truly loved her, or was it just for his convenience?

'The First Time Ever I Saw Your Face'. Mary's ringtone ceased as she answered her phone.

"Hello, Tim," she said, smiling with pleasure. "Yes, certainly I can play on Thursday. Usual time?"

Tim was Mary's doubles partner at the tennis club. They had played together for two years and had become quite close friends. As usual, a call to make a quick arrangement developed into a longer conversation. Mary felt herself relaxing as she chatted. She suspected that Tim would like to be more than just a friend, but she knew that he would not speak about it without a sign from her.

Mary sat for hours thinking about the book and how it related to her own situation. In the story, Helen Graham's husband, Huntingdon, although handsome and witty, was also a spoilt, selfish and self-indulgent drunkard. Helen had resolutely followed the path she thought right and left him, against his will and the attitude of society.

Things have improved a lot since those times, Mary thought. *So why did I let myself slide into this relationship without properly considering my true feelings?*

Her thoughts were interrupted by the sound of Brad's uncertain hand seeking the keyhole. Eventually, he burst in and declared, "Quite a session tonight. Some of the other lads joined us. Old Joe'll certainly remember this birthday. I'm a bit tired. I'll think I'll go to bed."

As he blundered out of the lounge, with sudden conviction Mary said, "Brad, please make sure you are at home tomorrow night. We need to talk."

Loyalty

THE MARRIAGE GUIDANCE COUNSELLOR LOOKED AT ME and said, "I think the problem is around your attitude to loyalty. You can't seem to accept that your wife is loyal to you despite what has happened."

I don't know where it came from, but I replied, "To me, loyalty is a temporary loan rather than an enduring gift." A bit highfalutin, but she had got right on my wick by then.

The psychobabble which took up the rest of the session passed over me like foam in the shower.

Back at my bedsit, as I drank my second whisky, I wondered where my attitude to loyalty had come from. I had certainly had some schooling in the vagaries of human relationships through many business successes and failures, but where did it begin?

In the next instant, I was back in my primary school playground, at playtime. My gang of four watched the gang that I called the Criminals (which turned out to be true in some cases) and the mass movement newly created by the fat bully in Year 3 juniors. They whirled in line around the playground with metal shoe studs in their lapels to show their allegiance.

We looked on – secure in our private club. Frederick Burns was the leader. I don't know why, except that he could piss furthest up the wall in the boys' toilets. Ivan Bates was his deputy; I think just because he said he was. Raymond and I were the foot soldiers. We played all our games together.

Topsies and Longsies with fag cards, marbles, British Bulldog. That day Raymond had brought what he called a 'disaffected needle'. We pledged our eternal brotherhood in shared blood.

The Criminals and the Stud Boys now appeared to have joined forces and were going around the playground forcing kids to join their super-gang.

They'll never get us, I thought as they surged towards our corner. I turned – confident in our solidarity. My friends were nowhere to be seen. In dread at my isolation, I tried to suppress a tear. My cheek was streaked with the blood still fresh on my finger. Luckily, the bell for the end of playtime rang out just then.

A roughing-up avoided, but a jaundiced view of loyalty ever since, I thought, as I poured yet another drink.

Girl with the Pearl Earring

I WISH I HAD NEVER SEEN HER. OFTEN SHE APPEARS in the window of the room opposite. It must be her mistress's room, because she appears just after Mevr. Vermeer departs along the narrow road between our houses.

The girl is fascinated by the dressing table. A comb, a brush, a brooch, a scarf. Each thing she handles with reverential care and softly puts back in place. I love her gentle grace; her simple, open face. Thoughts of amorous scenes torture me. I caress her hair, look into those innocent eyes and kiss red lips not kissed before. But it can only be a dream. My father would never allow it. When I finish at Groningen University, I am destined to follow him as a tulip broker – the business which made him rich as a young man.

Now I see her again. Today she is much bolder. She put on a plain silk jacket and tucked the collar down. She took two silk scarves and twisted them into a headdress, and now she is delicately putting on some magnificent pearl earrings. The scarves cover her hair and make her young face more innocent – more vulnerable. She is moving her head from side to side as she examines the effect of light on the earrings. She turns to her left and suddenly sees me watching her. For an instant, she is perfectly framed in the window, with guilty pleasure still written upon her face. A picture I will see for the rest of my life. Anger and remorse now flit across her face, leaving only fear. She tears off her borrowed finery in a blind panic.

I must see her to say I will never tell her secret – though this will only deepen my despair.

Life and Death of a Soldier

BERT GASPED FOR BREATH AS HE RAN FORWARD, crouching to avoid the deadly hail of bullets which had cut down so many of his battalion.

"Fucking smoke," he shouted to his friend Joe, who miraculously had kept with him. "I thought that was supposed to cover our approach, not bloody choke us."

After they crawled out of the last of the ditches which had hampered their attack, they were suddenly upon the enemy's barbed wire. The bombardment hadn't flattened the wire as they had been promised.

Bert shouted, "Over here, Joe. There's a gap."

"OK. I'm with you. Sod it, I've got stuck. I'll—"

Turning as he ran, Bert saw the horrific sight of his best friend twitching on the wire, blood gushing out of his neck and the remains of his head.

With blind rage, Bert slid down into the German trench and savagely bayoneted one soldier. As a second was about to shoot him, he clubbed the gun from his hand and sliced his bayonet through the man's neck. A third soldier appeared around the bend in the trench, and Bert thrust his bayonet so hard into his guts that he pinned him to the wall. He then saw he was a boy, probably no more than sixteen years old. Blood was spreading over a new uniform as he called, "*Mutti, Mutti. Ich liebe…*"

A shout came from above him. "We can't hold – get back."

Bert was convinced he wouldn't make it because he heard the clatter of a nearby machine gun. But as he ran, he saw that it was directed at the German line, and was covering their retreat.

Back in the safety of their trench, he learnt that his sergeant major had managed to capture a machine-gun post and so ensure their escape. He should have felt lucky, but as Bert's rage subsided he just felt weak as he walked in a daze along the trench. Most of his mates in the battalion hadn't come back. Crouching down, he hugged his knees to try to contain his uncontrollable shaking and buried his face to hide his bitter tears. Against his cheek, he felt Joe's blood mingled with the gore still damp from his rampage in the trench. He relived the horror of the attack and his friend's terrible death, but above all, he saw again the face of the boy he had killed. Although the lad was the enemy, it felt like murder face to face.

It seemed years since he and Joe had joined up, rather than just a few short months. They had been persuaded to join up by Lieutenant Colonel Lowther, their local MP who lived in Herstmonceux Castle. He and his cronies had toured the South Downs farms, urging the men to enlist. Bert laughed bitterly as he remembered that there had been a reassuring poster at the Bexhill recruitment centre:

Happy training
No man under canvas
Beds for all

The recruitment campaign had been so successful that three fully manned battalions, known as the Southdown Battalions, had been formed for the Royal Sussex Regiment. They were also nicknamed the 'Lowther Lambs' – a double meaning they were yet to understand. Having completed his task, Lowther returned safely to his castle.

After training, the Southdown Battalions were shipped to Le Havre and, by early June 1916, were positioned at Ferme du Bois on the flank of the planned Somme offensive. Here the only objective of the abortive attack they had just carried out was to distract the Germans from the main battles.

What a waste, thought Bert as he raised his head and fumbled in a pocket. With a trembling hand, he took out a photo of his wife and their little boy. As he gently kissed it he felt a little peace, but his disgust and the terror of the last few hours returned as a crushing weight on his mind.

After such losses, Bert's battalion had to be rebuilt, but Bert didn't see many recruits arriving from the Downs. He thought bitterly that almost all of Lowther's Lambs had been slaughtered. By September 1916 they were back at the Somme; this time to be part of the planned main thrust and not just a diversion. Bert had suffered terribly in the weeks since their disastrous attack. He could hardly eat, and suffered shuddering fits. He slept very little and, when he did, had terrible flashbacks to the devastation at Ferme du Bois. He tried to disguise his condition, managing to stand straight and look like a soldier at each inspection. He didn't want to let the regiment down. He stopped writing back to his wife. He just couldn't write the truth, and couldn't find convincing enough lies.

On the 20th October, Bert's battalion was positioned in trenches on the Beaumont-Hamel sector of the Somme. New communications trenches had been dug, and guns, ammunition and equipment moved up. The hideous noise of the bombardment and the explosions of the Germans' response seemed to consume his whole being. It was worse than any depiction of hell Bert had ever seen or could imagine.

At dawn on the 21ˢᵗ, the attack was signalled. As Bert climbed out of the trench with trembling legs, he felt a warm slime trickling down inside his trousers. Without knowing what he was doing, he followed the shouting soldiers, who fell in huge numbers as they went forward. This time the wire had been flattened, and, after fierce fighting, they took the trench.

A boy of about fourteen appeared in the bay Bert occupied. He couldn't bring himself to attack the lad. Rather, he stood, expecting his own death. Anything was better than the hell he was inhabiting.

"Kill the bastard," shouted a captain behind him, but Bert couldn't move. He saw the boy fall back as he was shot by the officer. He stood motionless above the body, seeing in the young face a resemblance to his own nephew. Bert knew without translation that the boy was appealing for help with his dying words, *"Bitte retten Sie mich."* He reached out as if to hold the boy as he died, but was roughly pulled back by the captain.

On the 25ᵗʰ November, Bert woke from a dream of the fields at Willingdon, now bare of the corn which had been gathered and reaped. He had been with his wife and baby boy, visiting his parents' cottage. They had been discussing plans for Christmas. Suddenly he realised where he was and the full horror of the last eighteen months rushed back to him. He crouched in the corner, shielding his head from the noise of the shells, but to no avail. They were *inside* his head. He shook violently and whimpered as his tortured mind played scene after scene of devastation. Finally, he drank deeply from the tumbler of brandy which had been left for him and managed to fall into a fitful slumber.

The door opened roughly, waking Bert.

"It's time," said the sergeant, and Bert was escorted into a yard in the grey light of dawn. There he was blindfolded and tied to a stake. He felt a target being pinned over his heart. Bert knew that the twelve soldiers facing him would be from his battalion. It was the army's way of 'encouraging the others'. He was to be shot as the result of his court martial for 'cowardice in the face of the enemy'.

In the quiet of that morning, his mind cleared for a moment as he said, "I know you men will be from the 13th Battalion. There aren't many of us left, but a few of you might still be from Sussex. If you are, please don't tell folks about this. I am the one to be shot, but it could happen to any one of you."

"*Ready. Aim. Fire!*"

Bert slumped forward with eleven bullet holes in the target over his heart, but on his face was a peaceful smile.

Editorial note: The details of the battalions of the Royal Sussex Regiment and their battles are as close to the truth as possible. The means of their recruitment is also factual. The characters are fictitious. There was a Private Tite who was executed for cowardice as described, but as a result of different circumstances to Bert's. There is no evidence that Tite was in the earlier battle described, but he was at the second.

The Colour of the Sky

NONE OF THEM KNEW THE COLOUR OF THE SKY, thought eight-year-old Ingor, now sitting alone by the fire.

It was in the middle of winter darkness in the northernmost part of Norway. His family were traditional Sami reindeer herders – amongst the few remaining indigenous people who followed this traditional way of life. Ingor had looked out of the window and asked what colour lay beyond the blackness. He couldn't imagine it being like the summer sky. They hadn't taken his question seriously, and had just given him facetious answers.

Unnoticed, he overheard their conversation.

"Poor Ingor. I think he misses the blue skies and clouds of the summer when we herd the reindeer down to the fjords. He loves sitting there outside the lavvu, just looking up."

"Make the most of it while we can, I say. The way the government is going, we'll have nothing of our way of life left. They think they can fence off our territories, but reindeer go by their noses, not by seeing unnatural obstacles."

"At least there are a few families left. We must invite the Gaups over. I've noticed that young Nils has taken a fancy to their Anja. It would be nice to have a traditional wedding."

"One thing in our favour. With a temperature of minus thirty, we are unlikely to see any government inspectors for weeks. Nor will we see those interfering conservationists who introduce lynx and wolves to prey on our animals."

Ingor, tired of listening, decided to go to his bedroom. He lay on his bed, looking up and wondering again what was beyond the blackness. The Milky Way blazoned across the sky. In it, he saw many colours: pale whites, subdued pinks and yellows. As he drifted off to sleep he imagined walking along the bright, starry pathway and discovering the colours behind the black vault.

As he slept, far above him a huge burst of charged particles was blown from the sun on the solar wind. They swept through the weaker magnetic field at the North Pole and violently struck the gases in the atmosphere. Ingor, as if knowing this at some level, was dreaming of a wizard wafting magic clouds towards him. They twisted and parted and swirled until one covered his head.

He awoke with a start and found his blankets were over his face. As he emerged from them, he was astonished to see how the sky had changed while he had been asleep. It started with a deep red mist appearing over the horizon. Then streaks of white light shot up into the red. Violet and green strands whirled about each other. Occasionally they struck an echo in the eyes of the deer grazing outside. Then purple and azure mingled with the violet and green. The continually changing spectacle mesmerised Ingor.

Suddenly remembering his family's apparent ignorance, Ingor rushed back into the living room, saying excitedly, "You said nobody knows the colour of the sky. I do. Just look outside."

The Little Stranger

SOPHIE HEARD THE TOWN HALL CLOCK STRIKE SIX o'clock. She moved the empty tankard and wiped the bar top once again to relieve her boredom. *This seems to be a quiet time,* she thought. *It gives me a chance to look around.*

It was her second day behind the bar at The Dolphin. Her first-class English degree hadn't persuaded anyone to employ her permanently, so she was content with her part-time job. At least she earned some money and it was a very pleasant pub. She even thought the clientele looked as if they might talk about books rather than the weather. In fact, there was that lady in the corner reading *The Little Stranger*. Sophie had read it recently and she thought the lady looked the sort who would enjoy a discussion.

Then, with a shudder, Sophie noticed a middle-aged man sitting alone in the other corner. He was dressed in a hunting-style jacket with his cap on, almost as if ready to leave. He was small and evil-looking, like a character from one of the stories Sophie devoured, with the complexion of someone who had spent much of his life outdoors. His skin was leathery; his eyes deep under his brow as if hiding from a merciless sun. Sophie wondered what experiences had made him like that. What was he? Despite her fund of characters from literature, nothing seemed to fit.

As he quietly sipped his pint, he looked about him, seeming to examine his fellow drinkers with close attention.

Could he be an undercover spy who had knowledge of drug dealers or illegal immigrants expected to come into the pub? *No. It's not that sort of neighbourhood,* she thought. Once he stared fixedly at her as if he recognised her from somewhere, but she was sure she had never seen him before.

Then she remembered her father telling her about his time in Africa. He had not been very forthcoming about what his business had been there. It had seemed a bit shady. Once she had overheard her mother say to him, "Don't be so jumpy every time the doorbell rings. It was years ago and it's very unlikely he will come to harm you now." Sophie hadn't dared ask what lay behind this and had put it to the back of her mind until, in that instant, she recalled it with a jolt.

Hell. Perhaps that's him. He has come to get me to settle his grudge against Dad, she thought, as she nervously kept her eyes on the little stranger.

She gasped as he deliberately eased himself out of his seat and advanced purposefully towards her. Something about the way he brandished his tankard alarmed her. With trembling knees, she clutched the soda siphon and held it at the ready. Tense minutes seemed to pass before he arrived at the bar. Then he spoke.

"A pint of Harvey's, please."

Liberation

"Night comes early in the tropics. So we were forced into our bunks early, although it was difficult to sleep sometimes in those conditions." Eric stood transfixed with a faraway look in his eyes. "In that Japanese camp in Malaya, there was nothing else to do in the darkness."

I didn't respond. Eric had never spoken of his experience as a prisoner of war before. He was just the friendly neighbour you would describe as a pillar of the community. It was 1995, and he must have been stimulated by the extensive coverage of the fifty-year anniversary of the end of the Japanese War. He left the room and returned with a neat pair of men's shorts.

"I've kept these ever since. We weren't given clothes and had to make do and mend. They were made out of an old mattress thrown out by the guards."

I could see by their size how thin he must have been at the time.

"You're obviously shocked," he went on. "I was one of the lucky ones. Many of my mates died of disease or were worked to death. The beatings were arbitrary and savage. But our camp wasn't as bad as some. We were remote from any means of escape, so there was just a high fence. They knew we would quickly die outside. Luckily, I had a secret source of food."

I was dying to ask about this, but daren't interrupt now he was in full flow.

"One night a very strange thing happened. A young girl appeared in the latrine. She had only a little English and was trembling with fear. But she managed to convey that she was from the Malayan resistance movement, and that they needed a technician to fix a broken radio. I volunteered. From that night on, whenever help was needed, I was contacted by the girl and I would sneak out under the wire – the way she had entered. Nadia and I became firm friends and her family used to give me nutritious food. Although this went on for a couple of years, we were never detected."

I asked if he had been in contact with her since they were liberated. He hadn't, but said he intended to seek her out.

A few months later, Eric invited us in for a drink. When we arrived I asked if he had gone to Malaysia as planned. With great animation, he replied, "I went to the location of the camp but was shocked to find there was an office block in its place. I went in and spoke to the security guard, and by great good luck he was a cousin of Nadia."

At this, Eric served us with champagne and proudly showed us a photo of him with his arm around Nadia – now a middle-aged woman who was clearly delighted to see him.

He never spoke about his war experiences again. It was as if that trip to Malaysia had exorcised his ghosts from that distant time.

Editorial note: This is based on the experiences of Eric Digby, a remarkable inhabitant of Pevensey Bay, and an unsung hero, now sadly no longer with us. The shorts were remarkable – made from the striped cloth of the mattress and sewn with thread unpicked from it, using a makeshift needle.

A Bad Start

I WALKED INTO THE LOUNGE. NOBODY SAID A WORD. My mood – not good earlier in the evening – by now was as foul as the weather. A terrible end to the evening which our son, Alex, had arranged to introduce us to his new girlfriend.

That same evening I had a rehearsal with Blackheath Baroque, so we had arranged to meet in a restaurant close by at 9pm. Arriving, I was pleased to find a vacant table and sat down expectantly. After twenty minutes, the expectation was turning into frustration when Alex came in looking for me. They had arrived earlier, and, as there were no tables available, had asked a waiter to tell me they had gone to a restaurant down the road. He had forgotten to do so.

Consequently, when I arrived at the relocated rendezvous, what should have been a happy affair was rather overshadowed by explanations about the miscommunication and an unjustified implication that it was all my fault. Emily was very quiet. She was probably considering the wisdom of getting involved with such an inept family.

We had a pleasant enough meal, but in such circumstances the normal currency of conversation is a little tricky. "Where do you work?" "What do you do?" "Tell me about your family," can all sound as if you are interviewing a candidate for daughter-in-law. More general topics like how the government is doing can also be fraught when you don't know about an individual's convictions.

It was raining when we left the restaurant. The others had a car nearby, but mine was parked on Blackheath – a walk away. So, saying I would join them at home, I buttoned up my coat, pulled my hat down over my eyes and set out. To my horror, when I tried to open the car it remained resolutely locked. So, with a shout of frustration, I set off to walk across the heath. By this time the rain was very heavy and a strong wind was blowing. Water ran from my trousers into my shoes. Even walking under the shelter of an avenue of trees was futile. Their accumulated water sluiced down upon me regularly. The only waterproof item I had with me was my violin case, which by now I was carrying over my head.

Finally, the squelch of sodden grass gave way to the pavement of our road and, at last, I arrived at our house. As I entered the lounge, I stood at the centre of a rapidly forming lake. The shocked silence of the others soon gave way to uproarious laughter which I couldn't help joining. So the bizarre evening ended on a happy note after all. The best thing about it is that Emily wasn't put off. She and Alex are now happily married.

Mystery and Melancholy

THE HOUSE HAD A FORBIDDING, SYMMETRICAL FACE, with many small windows on the third storey. Laura whimpered in her sleep as she walked past it in her dream. The shadow of a threatening figure appeared, and she woke up, rigid with fear.

Why do I keep having that strange dream, and why is it so frightening? she thought as she pulled the duvet more tightly around her. *It's that shadow which is so scary. It appears every time, but before anything awful happens I wake up. I wonder why?*

Her nightmares had been going on for months. It was always the same dream, never passing that threatening point, and it left her too frightened to go back to sleep.

While she was having breakfast the next morning, the phone rang. It was Philip. They had met a few months previously and she liked him very much.

"Morning, Laura. How are you today?"

"I'm fine, Philip," she said, trying to sound as if she were. She didn't want to put him off.

"Well, I thought we could go for a walk along the Embankment and visit the Chirico exhibition which is on at the Tate Modern. We'll be able to find a nice place for lunch afterwards. Shall I call round at ten?"

"Thanks. That will be very nice. I'll look forward to that," she replied, as brightly as she could manage.

It was a fine, sunny day, and there was so much to see along the way that Laura forgot her problems temporarily. They laughed at the 'poet for hire' sitting earnestly at his little table, and stepped back smartly as they passed a tuba player whose instrument belched a huge flame in time with the music. They declined photo opportunities with floating *Star Wars* characters, and threw money down to the sand sculptors by the Thames. Philip thought the new buildings were an interesting addition to the skyline, but Laura disagreed because she thought they were out of scale with St Paul's. The varied crowd they mingled with seemed to be in the holiday spirit, adding to Laura's happy state.

At the Tate Modern, they passed through the huge hall where the generators had been when it was a power station, and made their way up to the gallery for the Chirico exhibition.

As they looked around, Philip said, "I find some of the pictures quite challenging. There seems to be a hidden meaning behind them that leaves you with a sense of unease."

As he spoke, Laura moved into the next room. When Philip joined her she was staring fixedly at a painting called *Mystery and Melancholy of a Street.*

"This is it. My dream," she said in a whisper. "There's that house with the row of small windows, and the shadow of a man coming around the corner. But there's more to it here. That looks like an open horsebox on the right, and there's a little girl bowling her hoop past the house." She suddenly recalled seeing a reproduction of the picture before. So that was how it had entered her dreams. But why?

Laura began to cry quietly. Philip put his arm around her and led her out of the gallery. They sat on a bench, where Laura continued to cry while Philip did his best to comfort her.

"I'm very sorry, Philip," she said. "I should have told you about it before. I've been having these terrible dreams, and now I know they are based on that picture, but I can't explain why. I'm not much fun today. I had better go home."

Back in her flat, she lay on her bed, trying to make sense of it all. Her dreams were certainly about the picture, but they didn't include the child and the horsebox. Only the building and the threatening shadow were there. She shivered as she realised that there must be some deep-seated reason for her dread. Finally, exhausted by the thoughts circling in her mind, Laura drifted off into a fitful sleep.

Again the dream came, but this time the girl appeared with her hoop. The shadow emerged, followed by a man in an overcoat and a trilby hat pulled low over his face. The man grabbed the girl and hauled her, fighting against him, into the horsebox.

Laura woke up with a violent start and found herself struggling to get off the bed. It was clear at last. The dream was about her best friend Emma when they were six. One day she had disappeared, and the grown-ups had said that she had gone away because she had a strange disease. It had seemed very odd at the time. They had played together the day before and Emma had seemed full of energy as she ran off with her hoop. Laura remembered how her parents often stopped talking when she was around, and how they were never clear about when Emma would return. In the end, they had told her that Emma had died of the disease. Maybe they had lied to her. Perhaps the dream was real, and the truth was far worse.

The next day she met Philip. Although afraid that she risked making herself appear an obsessed neurotic in his eyes, she told him about her sudden realisation and her suspicion that she had been misled as a child.

To her relief, he was immediately sympathetic, and, holding her close, said, "How terrible for you, my love, to have this buried deep in your mind for so long. When you saw that picture for the first time it must have triggered your nightmares. Thank goodness that seeing it again at the Tate has at last led you back to the cause. We must try to lay it all to rest by finding out what really happened."

"I can't tell you how glad I am that I told you. Thank you for being so supportive," she replied, weeping gently on his shoulder. "But how can we find out the truth?"

"That won't be a problem. As I work for the British Library, I can get access to anything which was ever published."

Two weeks later, Philip arrived at Laura's flat. She could see that he was not his usual smiling self.

"What's up?" she inquired.

"I've turned up something about Emma. There was a lot in the press, but I have brought just one clip which sums up the whole thing," he said as he passed a photocopy over to Laura. She read:

Kentish Recorder, Friday 26th October 1989

Emma's killer sentenced

On Monday 22nd October at Bromley Crown Court, Alfred Dukes (53) of no fixed abode was sentenced to 25 years for the abduction and murder of Emma Jones. In his summing-up, the judge said that Dukes' actions were amongst the most despicable that he had encountered in a long career. During the trial, it emerged that Dukes had abducted Emma while she was playing in an alley. At the scene, her hoop was found, along with his hat with his name inside. When the police questioned him, he panicked and killed Emma, burying her remains in a nearby allotment. These were discovered, and, after forensic evidence connected Dukes with the remains, he confessed to his terrible crime. Emma's grave is covered by many flowers left by her grieving parents and friends.

Laura sat quietly for a long time after reading this extract. At last, she knew what the secrecy had been about all those years ago. Shock at the fate of her friend slowly turned to grief, and she cried bitterly as Philip tried to comfort her.

The next day, they went to visit Emma's grave. Someone was still laying fresh flowers there. Laura was now much calmer and she knelt to whisper goodbye to her friend.

Laura and Philip are now married, and she no longer has nightmares. She will always remember how Chirico's picture *Mystery and Melancholy of a Street* helped her escape from the hidden terror caused by the disappearance of Emma. In homage to the artist, and, as a memory of their walk along the Embankment on that fateful day, they have hung a copy of Chirico's *The Uncertainty of the Poet* above their fireplace.

A Model Child

"MUMMY, SHE'S TAKEN MY TRAIN AGAIN!" SHRIEKED Sam with the righteous rage of a four-year-old, as his sister crawled off with Thomas the Tank Engine.

"That's enough. Stop shouting," shouted his mum, and then, in a calmer tone, "Sam. She's only a baby. I want you to set her a good example. You must be a model of good behaviour."

This was very puzzling to Sam, who had an unusual obsession with models. He had lots of models in his play box and often looked at others in the toy shop, but he had never come across a model of Good Behaviour.

"What's a Good Behaviour?" he asked.

"Not now, Sam," replied his mum as she peered earnestly at Facebook.

Later, Sam heard his dad talking on the phone. "Yeah. It was the highest-spec model in the Tesla range. Put your foot down and it's like being kicked up the backside."

Little Sam hoped *that* model wasn't the one called Good Behaviour. If it was, he didn't like the idea of being hit from behind every time he put his foot down.

The next day he went shopping with his mum and, though he could only read a little, he spied a notice saying, *Latest model fashions here.* The word 'model' jumped out at him, and then he caught sight of a naked figure in the shop.

"Is that a model?" he asked.

"No, dear. It's a tailor's dummy."

"What's a tailor?"

"Someone who makes clothes for people."

How perplexing. If a tailor made clothes, why didn't she make some for the naked figure, and how could his sister Ava suck a dummy like that? That hadn't helped. Sam was no nearer a solution to his quandary. He knew what a model dinosaur was. His dad had a model that kicked you up the bottom. Sam had a model train and many other models, but he still hadn't seen a Good Behaviour model.

After they arrived home, Sam asked, "Mum. Why do I have to be a model of Good Behaviour?"

His mother, who carried only a recessive version of the empathy gene, replied with preoccupied haste, "It means you have to be a model child."

That evening, Sam's dad found him sitting by the pond in the back garden, crying piteously.

"Sam, what on earth is the matter?" he asked.

"Mum said I have to be a model child," he managed to say between sobs, as he pointed to the statue of a boy by the pond. "I tried to magic me like him, but, Daddy, don't make me do it. He can't play with his toys."

The Broken Doll

"DON'T THINK ME CRAZY. I WANT YOU TO SAVE something for me," Gemma said in the middle of a call to her friend. She didn't know why it had come into her mind, but it suddenly seemed urgent.

"I'll be happy to, but is something wrong? You sound a bit strange."

"Nothing more than the usual, Sarah. Mike's got another so-called PA on board and I'm convinced it's his latest affair. Anyway, go to our London flat. The housekeeper knows you so she'll let you in. You'll find a little red file in my dressing table. If anything happens to me, or us, please send it to the editor of the *Daily News*. He's often a guest on the yacht. So say it's from me."

"OK. But aren't you being a teeny bit dramatic?"

"I don't think so. In the file, I've documented all of Mike's affairs. You're the only one I've told about them. So you know they never last, and then he's back on me like a ton of bricks. But I can't stand it much longer. One day soon I'll have had enough. Then I want to make sure he's exposed for the philandering rat that he is. You'll know when to send it."

After they finished chatting, Gemma turned over on her sun lounger, thinking how tedious it was to maintain a golden tan at Mike's bidding. That evening she would be expected to be his perfect wife, flirting gently with the rich and famous guests he invited to his yacht. Always men. Mike emphasised the importance of connections in his business, and said his aim was to give them a good time networking away from the glare of publicity. As part of this, he seemed to enjoy displaying Gemma as his 'look, but don't touch' trophy. She shuddered as she thought of the Cabinet minister who had again become much too attentive the night before.

Gemma knew she should leave the beach to start her elaborate preparations for the evening, but her conversation with Sarah had focused her increasing despair. Instead, she moved to a bar at the end of a quay. Sitting by the sea, she was glad to be alone. In the distant marina she could see the superyachts, which reminded her of how, as an aspiring actress, she used to fill in as a waitress at corporate events on them. At a party on Mike's yacht, he had spotted her and pursued her obsessively. She had been flattered and swept up in the glamour of his life, and happily agreed to marry him. Now she was aware that she played only one role, and he complemented it with bit parts for his mistresses.

"You like come for ride?" Her reverie was suddenly interrupted by a young man in a fast-looking dinghy.

"No thank you, I have to…" she started to say, but was suddenly tempted by this random opportunity which was off the normal script. "Oh. OK, thank you," she continued as she slipped into the boat.

After an exhilarating ride, he stopped the engine and joined her on the passenger seat.

"We do fishing?" he said as he dropped a line overboard. Then, after a pause, "I like kiss you", as he put his arm around her and tentatively kissed her lips.

She couldn't understand why, but she found herself responding. Maybe it was just because she had stepped out of her normal role for once. When he slipped her bikini top off and began to caress her breasts gently, the contrast with Mike's rough attentions in between affairs added to her pleasure. But suddenly he pushed her down and crushed her beneath him, urgently thrusting himself into her. She screamed and struggled but soon realised that she couldn't repel him, so lay back apathetically, looking up at the sky. A cloud temporarily obscuring the sun seemed to emphasise her plight.

So this is what rape is like, she thought desperately. *But really it's not much different to the way Mike treats me. I'm just a sacrifice to male lust.*

After his climax, he rolled off her, restarted the engine and, without speaking, took her back.

"Was good, yes? You not tell?" he said as she climbed out of the boat. Still deeply shocked, she wordlessly returned to the beach.

The sea that she never entered, for fear of marring the doll that she had become, now seemed strangely inviting. She walked into the gentle surf. The warmth of the water lapped around her legs and, as it rose, washed away the man's residue and eased her pain. She dived and swam underwater with her expensively styled hair streaming behind her.

The sea loves me and supports me. It wants me, she thought, gathering strength as she headed further out. She swam and swam until fatigue overtook her and she willingly succumbed to the waves.

A week later, a package containing the red file was delivered to the editor at the *Daily News*. Two days after that, the newspaper carried a report of Gemma's death:

Tycoon's wife drowns

Gemma Braidward (34), the wife of prominent corporate financier Mike Braidward (49), was found dead in the sea off Rhodes on the 24ᵗʰ July. There has been speculation about the cause of her death. Braidward couldn't be contacted, but his PA, Trish Mason, gave us this comment:

"Mike is too upset to talk at the moment. He knows of no reason why Gemma should have taken her own life. He asks that his privacy is honoured at this difficult time."

A month later, the *Daily News* carried the first of a sequence of expensive adverts for Braidward Corporate Finance.

Blind Fortune

GARRY LOOKED INTO THE MIRROR WITH PANIC. Returning from a relaxed Eurail holiday with his mates, he suddenly realised as he approached London that he had completely forgotten his interview at Bristol University.

The trip had been arranged on the spur of the moment for the Easter break. They had rationalised this indulgence to themselves by saying that they needed to take it easy so they would be fresh for the final assault on their A Levels in the summer. Now, back in London, Garry had no time to return home. He had to continue straight on to Bristol. A detailed examination of his image in the station toilet was far from reassuring. His jeans, torn and dirty, fell baggily over well-used trainers. He had a T-shirt on which bore the message, *Those who can, do...*; partly concealed by a lumberjack shirt which had lost most of its buttons. He sported almost two weeks of beard growth, which at last seemed to be going some way to meeting his wishes for it to look thick and manly. Finally, his hair was evidence of a lack of hairdressing skill amongst his friends, as it alternated between bare patches and protruding clumps.

Up to that point, Garry had enjoyed a charmed life. As an example, after he had lost his wallet with his passport and money in it, two days later he was approached by a stranger who returned it to him, saying that he had recognised him by his passport photo. There were numerous other instances of undeserved good fortune when disaster refused to strike – although sorely tempted by Garry's carefree attitude to life.

He gave himself his first wash for several days, and scraped his hands through his hair and beard. He tried stretching out the creases in his clothes – crumpled by many nights sleeping on trains – but they didn't look much improved. He peered into the mirror again. "You've done it this time," he told his pathetic reflection ruefully. "Your luck's run out. But better go. They won't give you a place, but at least you won't be recorded as a no-show. You never know who talks to who in the academic world."

So he took the train to Bristol. Sitting mutely, without hope or expectation, he racked his brains for a plausible explanation for his state. Injury? Kidnap? A sudden call to a dying grandparent? Nothing seemed like a story he could carry off.

At the university, Garry made his way sheepishly to the office of Professor Brewster, who was to interview him. He introduced himself to the professor's secretary, but before he could make any apology for his bedraggled appearance, she addressed him in a confidential tone.

"I have to warn you before you go in. It won't be obvious, but you should be aware that the professor is totally blind."

The Seller of Words

AMANDA AND CHRISTOPHER WERE QUIETLY PLEASED WITH their house in St Albans. It was a somewhat rambling old house with some strange rooms, but it certainly had character. They were delighted when they discovered its secret past. Apparently, it was built on the site of a tanner's shop which had stood there in the 15th century. It was reputed to be where King Henry had hidden after the first battle of the Wars of the Roses.

One evening, their son was playing in the kitchen when he caught a fragment of conversation.

"I think it was the Seller of Words, Amanda."

The boy was immediately intrigued. "What's a Seller of Words, Dad?"

"I didn't realise you were still up, Daniel. No time for questions. Go up to bed at once."

Once in bed, Daniel couldn't stop puzzling over the question. Perhaps it was a bookseller. They sold words. No. That didn't seem likely.

Then he remembered his dad getting very angry one morning. He had just opened an envelope, and shouted, "Bloody lawyer. This agreement is just four pages long. Maybe 1,500 words. He's sent a bill for three thousand pounds. That's two quid a word. Ridiculous." That sounded more likely, but his dad hadn't been shouting just before he came to bed, so it probably wasn't a lawyer.

Then – inspiration. Maybe Daniel had the wrong meaning. Perhaps it was the Cellar of Words, with a C. It might even be their cellar.

Daniel waited until his parents were safely in bed. Then, taking his torch, he crept down the stairs. At the back of the kitchen was a door, rarely used, leading to the cellar. He pulled it open. It creaked very loudly. He stopped to listen, but no sound came from upstairs, so he continued into the dark space below. His face brushed through cobwebs and he heard the scurry of disturbed mice, but bit his lip and crept downwards.

At the bottom of the steps, he stood and directed the beam of his touch around. An old gramophone. Lots of rusty tools. Kept-for-no-reason boxes abounded – but no words.

Then Daniel noticed some loose bricks. He carefully took them out and saw that they were part of an old gap in the wall. After more fumbling, he managed to remove enough for a small body to get through. He couldn't see much with his torch, so he wriggled through.

Now he could see what was beyond the wall. It seemed to have been a small room with a place to lie down.

"I wonder who stayed in here?" he whispered. Then, as he swept his torch from side to side, he saw some faint writing on one wall. It said:

I, King Henry, will pursue those traitorous Lancastrians. They, like Northumberland, will all be slain.

"So this is it," Daniel whispered to himself. "This is the Cellar of Words."

Editorial note: St Albans was the first battle of the Wars of the Roses, which Henry of the House of York won. Despite this, he was abandoned by his entourage in a tanner's house. He was suffering from one of his bouts of mental ill health and had been wounded in the neck. There is no available explanation for this strange behaviour towards a victor. Henry did, however, recover and eventually won the war.

Camouflage

SERGEY LAY IN THE THICK SNOW JUST SOUTH OF THE River Don. He, like all in his infantry brigade, was totally clad in white. They had crawled forward under darkness and were waiting for the order to mount a surprise attack on the German 6th Army.

Although he was well equipped, he nonetheless felt numb with cold. He thought of his wife in rural Novy Gorky, who must be preparing for the New Year celebrations. The image of his homely cottage seemed like a dream. Plucked from the village he had hardly ever left, after just two years, the fresh-faced country lad had metamorphosed into a callous killing automaton. They had been given the order to fight at whatever cost, and retreat would be punishable by death. In a curious way, this was a relief. It removed the fantasy of giving up – of the possibility of another revolution like the one which had ended the soldiers' involvement in the First World War.

With difficulty, Sergey pulled out his temporary rations from under the all-enveloping white camouflage. Although it was spartan fare, he felt lucky compared to the starving wretches they had overrun a few days before. They had easily slaughtered the Romanians, left with few resources to guard the left flank of the German retreat. Just two years ago Sergey would have been filled with pity for men like him, frozen and starving and far from their homes, but now, coarsened by the horror he had experienced, he killed without compunction.

Now they were in position for the big push. They had been told that they had to be in Stalingrad by New Year 1943. There was an eerie quiet. With no bombardment to soften up the German defences, they were to storm the enemy in a surprise attack.

In the German trenches, Wilhelm was dozing on guard duty. He hadn't eaten for two days, and was so cold that the pain of it had ceased. Looking out over the frozen wastes, he was astonished to see a host of white-clad figures rise up from the snow and charge towards them with fixed bayonets. He shrieked with panic, "*Achtung! Achtung! Angriffe! Angriffe!*", but before they could organise their defence the Russians were upon them.

Just before a bayonet ended Wilhelm's misery, he managed to shoot one of the Russians, who fell face forward into the snow.

In the aftermath of the short but bloody assault, a Russian officer walked along the line. He came across a young soldier lying face down. Gently turning the body over, he found the boy's papers. He saw that the victim was Red Army trooper Sergey Vetrov. The boy's face was twisted into an expression of murderous fury. On the chest of the corpse, a red stain had seeped through the white fabric to form the crescent shape of Stalingrad city.

A Dress to Die For

WITH A SIGH OF RELIEF, MAURICE SPENCER EMERGED from the Ministry of Defence. He disliked his role, and particularly his title. "Assistant Secretary," he muttered to himself. "Sounds like a filing clerk."

Increasingly he felt there was a huge gap in his life that he couldn't put a name to. Nonetheless, he strode down Whitehall, swinging his tightly rolled umbrella, imagining himself a traditional servant of the nation in a black jacket and pinstriped trousers sporting a bowler hat.

Biddy, his wife, picked him up as usual at East Grinstead Station.

"Don't forget it's my bridge evening," she reminded him. "I've eaten, but your dinner's warming in the oven."

Sitting at his lonely meal, Maurice again felt the sense of missed opportunity. After he'd eaten, he wandered about aimlessly. Eventually, he came into their bedroom and saw an angora cardigan lying on the bed. On a whim, he put the garment on. He liked the feel of the woolly fabric on his neck, and thought it rather suited him as he looked in the mirror. He found his excitement at this strange act incomprehensible, but that evening he was more at peace with himself than he could remember.

The following week he tried on one of his wife's blouses under the cardigan, and then, on an impulse, changed his trousers for a skirt. As he looked in the mirror, he once more had that feeling of ease.

After this, Maurice could hardly wait for Biddy's Tuesday night bridge evenings. He started his own collection of clothes – giving every shop the same excuse. "Present for my wife, you know." Each week he became his woman of choice. His favourite was 'Assistant Secretary'. High heels, short skirt, see-through blouse and a blonde wig. He began to video himself so he could relive the Tuesday excitement all week.

Six months later, an envelope was delivered to his desk, marked, *Strictly Confidential.* It contained many explicit photographs. A brief note said, *We hacked your iPad camera. Pay £1,000 into the account below and you will hear no more about it.*

In a panic, he paid the money, but the demands kept coming until he could pay no more. The next letter threatened to send the photos to his wife.

On the following Tuesday, Biddy was dropped off after bridge as usual.

Strange, she thought; *Maurice has left the car running.*

Opening the garage door, she saw, to her horror, her husband lying dead in the passenger seat, killed by exhaust gas. On his chest was a note, which she read as she drew back from the fumes.

In despair, she shouted. "You stupid, dear man. I knew all about it. When I looked on your iPad for Lottie's wedding photos I found your little videos. I didn't mind at all. I could see it made you happy, and we could have had such fun together."

Instructions for Cleaners

IT HAPPENED ON THE WEDNESDAY BEFORE CHRISTMAS. As she left to play tennis, Gill said, "Don't forget to give them the list." The list she was referring to was a scrap of paper headed, 'Instructions for Cleaners.' I often found myself struggling to convey some briefly described tasks to Tracy and Sharon, but we usually managed to work out what was required. I had a good relationship with our cleaners but not a particularly intimate one. The latter comment might seem unusual but it has a bearing on my story.

Normally, they incorporate the listed tasks very efficiently in a well-rehearsed routine which ends with them exiting the back door having mopped the floor of the utility room. That Wednesday was different, however. As they were going down the stairs, Tracy called out, "I almost forgot, I've left a couple of presents in the kitchen for you both. Happy Christmas."

This was an unexpected gesture so, naturally, I looked to see what the presents were. There were some mince pies and a box of chocolates. Beside them was a package loosely wrapped in festive paper. On removing the paper I saw that it was a packet of brief underpants.

"Well, that's certainly an unusual present," I thought. But not wanting to seem ungrateful I shouted down the stairs, "Thanks very much for the present. Don't know how you knew they were just what I needed, but don't expect me to model them for you next time you come."

There was silence below. *Oh dear,* I thought; *I should curb my facetious streak. Now I've upset them. Maybe they're thinking I'm a weirdo who really wants to be asked to parade around in his underwear.*

Later, I picked Gill up from the tennis club. On the way back I said, "Tracy gave us some Christmas presents. Some nice mince pies and chocolates, but rather an odd present for me – some underpants."

"Well, that is unusual. I suppose Tracy noticed your pants on the washing line. I'm always telling you to replace them."

When we arrived home and came into the kitchen, Gill checked I had transmitted her instructions correctly and then said, in a mystified tone, "Why did you throw the Christmas paper for Alex's present in the recycling?"

"I only threw away the paper Tracy had used for these," I said, showing her the underpants.

Gill burst out laughing. "You idiot. Those are the underpants I bought Alex for Christmas. I left them here ready to wrap up."

After Christmas, when our cleaners next came, Gill met them downstairs. I could hear them talking and giggling. I was sure they were talking about me.

When they came upstairs, Tracy and Sharon were both grinning broadly. "Come on, then," Tracy said. "Get your kit off!"

An Intriguing Call

It was a wrong number that started it.

As usual, Eric and Diana had been watching *News at Ten*. They had what observers called a 'solid marriage'. Diana, the daughter of a friend of Eric's father, had been recommended as a suitable match. Because of their similar backgrounds, and parental urging, they had drifted into a companionable marriage.

After the programme finished, Diana yawned and said, "I'm off to bed, dear. I'm rather tired after the preparations for the school play."

Eric knew that bed only meant sleep. Once the children had arrived, Diana had lost interest in lovemaking. Deep down, Eric was a passionate man, but, despite his frustration, he was a dutiful husband and father.

"I'll be up later, love," he replied as he picked up a book.

Immersed in the novel, he read for many hours. When the phone rang he started violently, but ignored the call. Later, noticing that a message had been left, his curiosity got the better of him. A woman's voice.

"Jeremy, you must answer me," she began. "You can't ignore me like this. I am desperate to sort things out. I need your love. You used to be so full of lust and it made me respond with such passion. Surely, you still want me? I know it is late, but come round tonight."

"Some blokes have all the luck," Eric said to himself as he crept up the stairs.

Lying beside Diana, he thought sleepily about the passionate caller. The phone rang again. Eric hurried down to answer it. The same woman. This time, he interrupted, telling her that he was not Jeremy. Surprisingly, he quickly became a substitute for the reluctant lover. They talked for a long time before the call ended.

Soon afterwards, the phone rang again. Eric knew it would be her.

"Please, please come to my house. You are obviously a passionate man and we would be so good together."

Eric had no idea how he arrived, but the next thing he was aware of was standing in front of a house in a formal garden. He rang the doorbell and the woman's voice commanded him to enter and come up. At the top of the stairs, he entered a bedroom. It was suffused with delicate light and the air was scented with a strange perfume. Turning, he saw a four-poster bed, upon which she lay, dressed in delicate silk lingerie.

"Come to me," she whispered.

Again, as if with no effort, he found himself in a naked embrace. With her lovely body curled around him, he responded with a surge of long-suppressed desire.

"What the hell do you think you are doing? Get off me! I don't know what has come over you. You are just a beast!" Diana shrieked as she thrust him from her.

Eric, now fully awake, realised with huge disappointment where he was.

As he lay there, thinking of the relationship which had only been a dream, the telephone downstairs rang again…

What Goes Around

"KNOW ANYTHING ABOUT THIS, HARRY?" I SAID, pointing out a report in the local paper:

> *Local man found dead in the Docks area. He had been killed with a shotgun. The police are seeking information from anyone who was in the vicinity on Saturday night. No weapon was found at the scene.*

Harry sat back in a corner of The Black Horse. He was all on edge, and took a large gulp of his beer. "I feel guilty about all sorts of things, but not about topping Charlie. He had it coming to him all right."

"You did what?! Those bastards'll want revenge for sure, and now you've made me an accessory!"

We had known each other since we were kids. After we dropped out of school, we'd drifted into petty crime. This just about kept us. Stealing cars and a bit of burglary, mostly. I was pretty sure Harry didn't feel guilty about any of that. It was just his way of speaking. He exaggerated everything. His jobs were all "mega"; his women always "lovely bits of stuff" who were "right up for it", with lurid details to follow.

"How would they know it was me? I made sure I had an alibi. Shorty'll say I was with him at the dogs. I even got a ticket." Harry's phone rang. "Hang on a minute.

"Yeah? Who's that? Nothing to do with me. Wasn't even in town Saturday. Who told you that?"

As he listened to the caller, Harry's face turned a yellowish shade of white.

"There's no way it was me. He's lying. Fuck off."

That moment of defiance put some colour back into his cheeks, but I could see he was scared.

"They've made Shorty admit I wasn't with him. They must have kicked it out of him. He's usually absolutely solid."

"You're a bloody fool. We've spent years under the radar but you had to have a go at what you called 'the big time'. That ice-cream van you used to deal drugs was a stupid way of invading their territory. I'm not surprised they set Charlie on you. He's their hitman."

"He threatened to top me if I didn't get out of their manor. I told him to fuck off and he said I was a dead man walking. So I nicked a shotgun from a farmer and got in first. Good bleeding riddance."

"Maybe, but now the rest of them are after you, and you've dropped me in it. I'm going to scarper."

I was dead worried, so I kept well out the way for a couple of weeks. But when I went to see me mum, the local paper had just been delivered. In it, I saw:

Local man found dead in the Docks area. He had been killed with a shotgun. The police are seeking information from anyone who was in the vicinity on Tuesday night. No weapon was found at the scene.

Waltzing Through Time

SARAH SIGHED WITH RELIEF AS SHE FINALLY ARRIVED at the antique shop in Horncastle. There she had located a Davenport writing desk which she was interested in buying. Not wanting to cut short the pleasure of browsing, she delayed asking the proprietor to show her the piece she had come to see. She slowly shuffled through the lines of antiques, opening a drawer here and sitting on a chair there – nothing made Sarah happier than imagining a life centuries before.

She turned the handle of a Victorian music box. It burst into life and suddenly Sarah was seized with panic. The reek of cigarette smoke seemed to surround her. She could feel a heavy hand dragging her, screaming, into a darkened room. Doubling up with a spasm of dread, she was almost physically sick.

"What is it? Are you ill? Do you need a doctor?" the alarmed proprietor said as he hurried towards Sarah through the rows of antiques.

"It's that music. Please, please turn it off!"

He turned to the music box, where a model skater was rocking to the 'Skaters' Waltz', and stopped it immediately.

By now the proprietor's wife had joined them. "Come with me, dear. What you need is a warm blanket and a nice cup of tea."

So she was taken into a cosy back room and fussed over by this sympathetic woman. After Sarah had drunk her tea and relaxed a little, the woman introduced herself as Hermione and gently asked what the problem was.

Haltingly, Sarah started to tell her about the music box. "My father had a cigarette box which played that exact tune whenever he took out a cigarette."

"Well, that seems nice, but obviously there is something more to this."

"Yes, Hermione. He was a brutal man who often hit our mother, and he shouted at us children and hit us too."

"How dreadful. But surely the music box was a nice thing to listen to?"

"No. It wasn't. Dad was often absent – mostly down the pub – so all was peaceful until we heard that tune. Then we knew he was back in the house and there would be trouble."

"It must have been terrible. I can see now why you hated it."

Hermione's gentle encouragement had led Sarah to relive events in her childhood which she had long suppressed. It felt good to speak about them at last. Now that she was reliving the experience, Sarah was tempted to tell this kind stranger something she had never revealed to anyone.

"Yes, I did hate all of that, but there was much worse. One night my mum went with my sister to her school play. I was fifteen, so had been left at home to do my homework. Dad came home and opened his cigarette box. That music started. Then, without stopping to light a cigarette, he grabbed me and dragged me into the back room…"

Sarah broke down and, through wretched sobs, all she could say was, "…and all the time I could hear that awful tune."

A Lifeline

"YOU THINK IT WILL NEVER HAPPEN TO YOU," MUTTERED Graham. He pulled the blanket more tightly around his shoulders as he crouched in the doorway he inhabited at night.

Graham had suffered a broken night's sleep, not only because of the cold, but also the foul smell of the companion who had joined him. He declined the offer of a cider/meths cocktail, but wondered how long it might be before such a drink was more of a benefit than a threat. He looked down at his Jermyn Street suit, now crumpled beyond all credibility for any job interview. Recent emails, read on his phone, had given him no vestige of hope. Now he couldn't even afford to top up his pay-as-you-go SIM card.

Once again he recalled the path to this degradation. His ascent to the board of his company had been rapid. His movement had always been upwards, and he suffered no setbacks to warn him of a possible decline in his fortunes. He remembered himself at the summit of his career – admired by his colleagues for his success within the booming mining business. That man now seemed like another person.

What an idiot, he thought. *How stupid to part from Janet and submit to the flattering admiration of Tracy – a trophy wife to complete your self-regarding image.*

The years with Tracy now seemed like a blur of consumption: the country mansion and town flat, the ridiculous motor yacht moored in an expensive marina in

Majorca, her designer clothes, their foreign holidays and expensive dining. He reproached himself for agreeing to such debt-fuelled excesses in exchange for fewer and fewer opportunities to satisfy his lust.

Then the bust. Almost overnight, the seemingly insatiable Chinese demand for metals came to a grinding halt. Graham lost his job and couldn't find another in the mayhem of his industry. Tracy just as quickly fell out of love with him and sued for divorce. After the manic music stopped, he found himself eking out an existence in a miserable bedsit. Even that had been unsustainable, as the little money he had been left with drained away.

Now, in the drab reality of early morning, Graham packed his few belongings into a soiled backpack and wandered down to the Embankment. His thoughts, now frequent, of seeking oblivion in the waters below, were interrupted by a familiar voice.

"Good gracious, Graham. I didn't expect to find you here."

"Oh, hello, Terry. Sorry to appear like this. I'm somewhat down on my luck."

"Well, look, old boy. I'm in a bit of a hurry but I will certainly see what I can sort out for you."

The brief surge of hope soon vanished as Graham realised the rapidly disappearing Terry had no way of contacting him. With black despair, he stared again at the swirling river...

"Most of us have a story to tell. One main story that led to you being here." The group leader looked around at the odd assortment of participants in the meeting. They had all been brought into the hostel for the homeless, and had come to value a bed and a shower, an address and the use of a telephone. The workshop was designed to help them move on from mere existence. "We believe it helps to tell that story, and, hopefully, some idea of how you see your future."

Graham had sat quietly through previous sessions. The stories, some of which had optimistic endings, had stirred in him a belief that he might emerge from thinking he had used up all his luck. He raised his hand and said simply, "This is mine."

"Thank you, Graham. We'd love to share your story."

"Well. When I came here I had no hope. All possible ways out of a desperate life on the streets seemed to have disappeared. It's not until it happens to you that you realise how hard it is to rise from the gutter."

"You're dead right there, mate," said a young man. "I came to London with a job offer in my pocket. But I spent most of my money on a deposit for a flat. When I contacted the company I was going to work for, they said they were sorry but they couldn't take me on after all. Business had turned down. Then I found out that the supposed landlord didn't own the flat, so I lost my deposit. A few weeks in bed and breakfasts, desperately looking for work, and I was skint. No option but sleeping rough."

"Thank you, Kevin. Back to you, Graham."

"I was a fool. I thought I had got it made with a very well-paid job. Then I made the mistake of leaving my family for a young woman who was very attractive, but avaricious. After I was sacked from my job, a bitter divorce followed. I lost my house and almost everything else as the debts I had built up to fulfil her ridiculous demands wiped me out. I was suddenly destitute and on the streets. I tried to get a management job, but no chance. No address and a suit that rapidly began to show my wretched existence."

"What brought you here, then?"

"The final straw was the day an old friend passed me and said he might be able to help. As he walked away, I remembered my phone was useless – so I had no way of communicating with him. I was standing on the bank of the Thames, ready to end it all, when one of the volunteers from this centre started talking to me. She persuaded me to come here. It's given me a lifeline. I was able to clean up and get Jobseeker's Allowance, with which I can just about survive and pay for a phone."

"Well, thank you, Graham. We'll end today's session on that optimistic note and look forward to hearing later how this proceeds for you."

Graham continued his search for employment, but not in what he now thought of as the rat race. He was looking for a role in which he could feel he was contributing more directly to society. He wanted to aim for happiness rather than boosting his ego. Alongside his job search, he was volunteering at the centre, where he found great satisfaction in helping other desperate people.

One day, while he was out on duty, he noticed a young woman begging. Moving towards her, he almost stumbled into someone who was also about to speak to the unfortunate girl.

"Good gracious. You look just like… Surely it can't be you, Graham?" she said.

"Yes, it is indeed me," replied Graham, realising he was speaking to his first wife, Janet. He hadn't seen her since his exit with his gold-digging girlfriend. "People rarely look how you expect them to, even when you've seen the pictures," he added, surprising himself with the joking reference to the lurid press coverage of his downfall.

"But you seem so different, and I'm surprised to see from your badge that we work for the same organisation."

After they had cooperated in dealing with the desperate girl, intrigued by the change she saw in Graham, Janet said, "Perhaps we should meet for a coffee. I expect you would like to hear how the children are, and I would be interested in how you came to be doing this."

They agreed to meet the next day. Graham walked away, thinking about this turn in his new life.

"Maybe we could..." he said to himself, but dared not continue the train of thought.

They are Just Like Us

"IT WAS LOVE AT FIRST SIGHT," SAID HENRY AS HE stroked Heidi's head fondly. Not an unusual scene, except that Heidi is a chimpanzee.

"Bit of a strange girlfriend," I replied, trying not to show any sign that I thought my old friend was behaving oddly.

"I can see that it seems strange. Heidi was pensioned off at the end of a research project. As I always wanted to carry out personal research into chimpanzee intelligence, she seemed the perfect subject. Wait till I show you what she can do."

At the end of a brilliant career, Henry was now emeritus professor of social anthropology at Oxford University. We had kept in touch since becoming close friends as undergraduates in the '60s. As we had both retired to Sussex, we had started meeting more often. Unfortunately, my previously madcap friend now displayed a rather humourless intensity.

Certainly, Heidi was clever. She was adept at using tools of all sorts and had a sign-language vocabulary of scores of words. Henry claimed she could construct simple sentences, and laughed loudly when she signed two words and pointed at me.

"What did she say?" I asked, mystified.

"She said you are 'large man'. You must admit you've put on a bit over the years." He then insisted I played a number-pairing game against her, which I lost badly. Henry told me not to be upset as chimpanzees have a much better memory for patterns than humans.

His continual boasting about his charge was getting on my nerves. I also harboured resentment for Henry's success in academia. My career had been successful, but didn't have the cachet of a professorship. I found myself looking for a way to poke fun at their triumphant partnership.

"Try her with the monkey-with-a-nut-in-a-bottle trick."

"She'll have no problem with that," Henry replied as he put one of her favourite sweets into a wide necked bottle and handed it to her. Heidi put her hand in the bottle, grasped the sweet and then realised she couldn't extricate her closed fist. Eventually, she gave up and withdrew her hand. Henry showed her how tipping the bottle was the obvious solution, but Heidi repeatedly fell into the trap. He got very angry, and she was also extremely frustrated. In the end, he said I should return the next day. He was sure she would have mastered it by then.

This little tableau cheered me up no end, and the next morning I went back, hoping that the paragon had failed again. As I entered his garden, I heard a heavy thud, as if the chimp had fallen from her favourite perch onto the hard floor.

I rushed through the door of his laboratory, and, to my horror, saw Henry lying on the floor amongst broken glass with blood seeping from a wound in his head. Heidi sat calmly eating a sweet, with the jagged neck of the bottle forming a macabre bracelet.